# Love Minus One & Other Stories

# Norma Harrs

HOUNSLOW

Love Minus One & Other Stories

Hounslow Press
A member of the Dundurn Group

Publishers: Kirk Howard & Anthony Hawke
Editor: Liedewy Hawke
Printer: Webcom

Front Cover Painting: FITZGERALD, Lionel Lemoine  Canadian 1890-1956
*At Silver Heights*, 1931
oil on canvas board
35.8 x 40.2 cm
ART GALLERY OF ONTARIO, TORONTO
Purchase, 1981
Photo: Larry Ostrom, Art Gallery of Ontario

Canadian Cataloguing in Publication Data

Harrs, Norma, 1936-
    Love minus one & other stories

ISBN 0-88882-173-5

I. Title.

PS8565.A77L6 1994      C813' .54      C94-931400-5
PR9199.3.H37L6 1994

Publication was assisted by the Canada Council, the Ontario Arts Council, the Book Publishing Industry Development Program of the Department of Canadian Heritage and the Ontario Publishing Centre of the Ministry of Culture, Tourism and Recreation.

Care has been taken to trace the ownership of copyright material used in this book. The author and the publisher welcome any information enabling them to rectify any references or credit in subsequent editions.

Printed and bound in Canada

Hounslow Press
2181 Queen Street East
Suite 301
Toronto, Canada
M4E 1E5

Hounslow Press
73 Lime Walk
Headington, Oxford
England
OX3 7AD

Hounslow Press
1823 Maryland Avenue
P.O. Box 1000
Niagara Falls, N.Y.
U.S.A. 14302-1000

# Contents

# ACKNOWLEDGEMENTS

Some of these stories have been previously published. "The Curate" appeared in the *Antigonish Review* in 1988; "Pauline" in the spring 1989 issue of *A Room of One's Own*; "Frangipani" in the *Toronto Star* in 1991. "The Girl in Black" was published in 1992 in the *Pittsburgh Quarterly*; "The Way to a Man's Heart" in the *Toronto Star*, also in 1992. "Saturday Lady" appeared in *Kairos* in 1994.

*For*
*Annie & Bob*

# THE CURATE

"Very sweet" was how she described him in her letter and very sweet was exactly what he was. He was attending the World Council of Churches gathering in Toronto and would have a couple of days to see the city. Would I mind? Yes, I minded. I always minded. Caroline collected stray dogs everywhere she went and set up impossible networks and expected all her friends to rally and extend house, home and warmth to the chosen.

Always, these "strays" when questioned, really only knew Caroline slightly, but wasn't she fantastic and wasn't she kind? Yes, I thought, far too kind with everyone else's time and patience.

He told me he would stand with a newspaper under his arm at the corner of Gerrard and University, and, of course, he would have his suitcase. As it happened, he needed neither suitcase nor newspaper to afford recognition. He couldn't have been anything else but English with his dappled pink and white complexion, his slightly too long hair and his Harris tweed sports coat. He stood out like a sore thumb. I noticed he wore no dog collar, but he was unmistakably a clergyman; he was the archetype for all that breed depicted so gently in novels about British rural life. He was clean and scrubbed with that "just arrived in the universe" look that begged to be corrupted. I doubted if there was any such thing as *bad* in his world, and if he discovered a hint, I could imagine he would turn a cold shoulder. It would be actually rather fun to bring him home and wait for him to realize that my husband, John, was away on a business trip and there were just the two of us in the house.

He climbed into the car awkwardly, banging his head on the door frame as he did so.

"It's frightfully good of you." The voice was British public schoolboy with wool trade intonations. It was those intonations that made him seem more human.

I smiled, determined not to utter the usual niceties about being happy to have him. I was curious to see if he had another expression than the one of sheer honesty and openness. A flicker passed over his face at my silence, but his equanimity returned fast enough and he smiled. Not for a moment would he allow it to cross his mind that I might be genuinely put out.

"Terrific weather," he forged on enthusiastically.

"Yes."

When I pointed out various landmarks on the way home, he stared rather disinterestedly at them and turned back to gaze at me. No doubt he'd come to this country with no expectations and, having spent four days bunkered in the Convention Hotel, nothing had happened to change his idea that basically it was a new, but dreadfully dull, city.

"You're not really looking," I accused.

"Yes! Yes!" He hastened to assure me. "Actually I'm more interested in people." I noticed he seemed terribly pleased with himself as he made the pronouncement as though he expected some commendation: three red stars, a ribbon for his humanitarianism perhaps.

"And do you find out about them by staring?"

Now he looked genuinely embarrassed.

"Was I staring?"

"Yes," I smiled, "Do you find the North American species so different?"

"I really wasn't thinking of a species when I looked at you."

"No? What were you thinking then?"

I knew the truth would not out; he would find something inoffensive, yet flattering, to say.

"I suppose I was admiring the quality of terrific self-confidence. I expect that comes with being a performer?"

I already had him terribly off balance and I felt a cruel but profound satisfaction in creating his discomfort. Perhaps he would go back to Caroline with tales of my awfulness and her "strays" would cross Toronto off their itinerary.

Actually it wasn't that he'd come at a bad time, he hadn't. I was more or less resting, having finished a series of recitals that had taken me across the country and into the States, but I would have preferred the time to recoup my energy by doing absolutely nothing.

In a way I was slightly amused at having a clergyman in my power. I had this terribly prejudiced view of the clergy, perhaps gleaned from British literature ranging all the way from Austen to Trollope. I saw them as a parasitic little band who managed to arrive at their parishioners' houses at teatime or lunchtime. I was sure all clergymen had fantastically low grocery bills and quite high standards when it came to choosing the right house for a good meal. I perhaps wrongly condemned that profession as being a marvellous sinecure for the basically lazy. I probably did them a grave injustice. Still, his easy acceptance of hospitality from someone he didn't know, except through Caroline, had helped to reinforce those views.

He talked about his Conference most of the way home, but not so much the ideas that might have come out of it as about the contacts he had made for possible trips in the future. No doubt contacts for free room and board, I thought cynically.

He was impressed with our house. He wandered from room to room with his hands clasped behind his back. I could visualize him deferentially cruising British drawing rooms waiting for sherry to be served.

I prepared a light lunch which he attacked ravenously. I hadn't seen anyone scrape off a plate like that since I'd helped out one winter at the Salvation Army. I knew the topic of his Conference had been world hunger, but was it possible that guilt had made the delegates eat lightly?

He talked rather a lot about himself. He'd studied law but never practised, deciding at the last moment that he really had a calling for the church. He told me he was thirty which made him five years younger than me. I felt like Methuselah by comparison. I envied his attitude to everything and his freshness; it reminded me of how I'd been at eighteen.

It seemed virtually impossible to puncture him. He had the kind of unabashed enthusiasm that kept him waving and ducking at whatever shot came in his direction. I hadn't intended liking him, but it would have been impossible not to.

While I put away the dishes he wandered into the living room and I heard him playing the piano. He seemed to be a fair pianist although he was playing so softly it was almost impossible to make any proper judgement.

He looked up brightly when I came in from the kitchen.

"Jolly nice piano!"

"Thank you."

"Would you sing something?" he asked eagerly.

I shook my head. "I seldom perform on request." I realized how stuffy it sounded and immediately regretted the decision.

"Only for money?"

I smiled. "No, but today I'm on holiday."

"Since I am on holiday, and I'm a rank amateur, maybe I'll tinkle a little if I may?"

"By all means."

He knew an amazing amount of opera repetoire, and I found myself singing along. I joined him at the piano and finished one of the pieces I'd started humming in the kitchen.

When I'd finished he looked up at me in delight.

"You're absolutely splendid!" It was a suitably ambiguous statement most likely referring to my voice, but his eyes nevertheless took in all aspects of my face the way they had been doing since he'd first climbed into the car.

I noticed he'd taken off his jacket and rolled up the sleeves of his shirt as though he was settling in for the afternoon. I had the feeling he thought that we were going to start chummily getting to know one another and that was something else that required too much energy. I could lock myself in my room and leave him to his own devices, but he had an expectant look on his face that made me feel vaguely guilty.

I outlined all the possible alternatives for the afternoon, hoping he would get the hint and offer to go off on his own. When I decided that he would probably enjoy a trip to Toronto Island, and some bicycle riding, he seemed to automatically assume that I was including myself in the adventure. It was actually a perfect time to go to the Island, mid-week, very few tourists and even less children, so the idea wasn't entirely unappealing. Philip's enthusiasm for our expedition grew even more when I packed a small hamper with some goodies for an afternoon picnic.

He found everything about the boat ride across to the Island delightful. He managed to pretend not seeing a large red setter which had come on board with its master, lift its leg and pee down one of the iron railings. It would definitely not be part of his memories of the day.

"Imagine, so peaceful and yet so close to the city," he repeated over and over again as we walked towards the bike rental. It was an extraordinarily beautiful day. The quality of light in October was always superb. Cold air meeting warm usually managed to produce a slight haze on the landscape. The trees were in full blaze of colour and the Toronto skyline rose rather smoky and phallic, seemingly imbedded in the bush of golds and reds in our immediate foreground.

"It's so marvellous! What a super place to live," Philip enthused.

We collected the bikes and tied my hamper and blanket onto the back of my bike. We selected the beach as our picnic spot, but decided to see everything we could first. It was like having an enthusiastic teenager in tow. His cheeks had turned a marvellous pink from the exertions of riding and we had to keep stopping every so often for him to stare and marvel. We settled finally on the beach we'd selected and spread the blanket. It was totally deserted. He wanted to eat almost immediately. I wasn't in the least hungry, but he managed to eat for both of us, washing it down with tea from the flask I'd brought along. He lay back finally and stared up at the blue sky and circling gulls.

"Millions of them!" he said, his eyes following the movement of the birds. "Yes, too many."

"If you sort of narrow your eyes it's lovely, like seeing snowflakes suspended." He squinted upward.

"When you live here, there isn't much charm in seeing snowflakes." Why, I wondered, was I always deflating? At first I'd felt some joy in doing it; now, I felt pricks of conscience.

I lay back and closed my eyes, trying to relax and just enjoy the moment. When I finally opened them again, he was hunched sideways leaning on one elbow, staring at me.

"Have you had a very hard life?" he asked suddenly.

"Hard?" I laughed. "Not at all."

"I'm glad of that." The sun was almost exactly above his head so that when I stared up at him there was a sort of glow around him. He looked like one of those beatific haloed heads in icon pictures: golden curls, clear blue eyes, and the look of total innocence. I closed my eyes again, shutting out the goodness.

"I'm sorry you're so unhappy," he said quietly.

I sat up abruptly. "I am not unhappy. I don't know what gave you that idea."

"The first time I saw you I knew you were unhappy."

I was amused rather than angry at his assessment. Little twerp, I thought, practising his amateur psychology on me. He needed to be humbled.

"I was tired," I said levelly. "I had an exhausting couple of weeks on tour and I was enjoying my peace and quiet and Caroline sends me another of her waifs."

If I'd expected the admission to hurt him, I was disappointed. He was grinning.

"It's nice you're having such a good time then," he said cheerfully.

I burst out laughing. "Yes, I am having a good time."

"That's better. You hardly ever laugh."

"You've known me all of two minutes. I think you know precisely nothing about me."

"I know a lot about you. I told you I'm interested in people." I could sense he was warming to his subject.

"You have all the things you want in life. Your career is going well, but there's no one really there for you, is there?"

I smiled, but I was more than a little irritated. "Perhaps Caroline didn't mention it, but I am happily married."

"She did say you were married."

"Well, I'm sorry to spoil your theory, but "happily" is the right term."

I knew I could have been truly angry with him, screamed any kind of invective, but he wouldn't have flinched; he was one of those infuriatingly forgiving souls, a quality that makes ordinary mortals feel tiny and mean.

He took my hand and when I tried to pull it away he only tightened his grip. I couldn't think of one thing I'd done or said to encourage the gesture, and so awkward was I with it that I lashed out again.

"Haven't you ever thought of going somewhere where people really need you — where you'd dirty your hands, Bangladesh, or somewhere like that?"

"It's extraordinary but I find people need me everywhere."

"Or extraordinarily smug," I retaliated.

"You might call it that."

He squeezed my hand, then let it go. He lifted a handful of sand and contemplated it with narrowed eyes. I felt the prick of conscience once more. I stood up and straightened my skirt. "I'm sorry, I'm an absolute bitch."

He released the sand. "I don't have to stay overnight, you know. I'll get my suitcase and find somewhere else."

I folded the rug, tying it into a small bundle, and attached it to the back of the bicycle. "And leave me filled with remorse at the way I've treated you?"

He grinned, immediately cheerful again.

"No, I suppose I couldn't do that."

We returned the bike, but couldn't find the young man who had rented them to us. I propped them against the wall of the shed.

"Are they all right, just leaving them like that?"

"I expect so. I don't think anybody pinches things here."

"Is that a fact? I wish it was like that in Britain. You have to padlock everything."

"Oh, we're not exactly sinless; there's a lot of stealing going on in the city, but sometimes the honour system does work. I think perhaps it works here on the Island."

"Like a commune?" he asked.

"Not quite. Not quite so intrusive, just gentle caretaking."

"God would approve," he said, linking his arm with mine.

"I doubt God has much to do with it."

"I would have thought God has a hand in everything."

I speeded up my step ever so slightly; I had no intention of hearing a sermon. He had to do a slight hop step to keep apace.

"How do you feel about God?"

I turned and looked at him. "Is this some kind of quiz that I might fail?"

"No, I just wondered."

"I seldom think about him." I could see the ferry making its way slowly towards the Island and quickened my step again.

"I was quite religious when I was young, but I think it was more a kind of superstition than any real fervour. I gave up superstition quite early on. I don't really believe in worship of any kind."

"What about your audiences who think you're marvellous? Isn't that a kind of worship?"

"I don't much approve of that either."

"Would you be where you are now without that?"

"Are you telling me God wouldn't exist without the worshippers?"

"No, of course he would."

"What then?"

I smiled. "Well, then we're agreed on that." I pulled his arm. "Come on or we'll miss the ferry!"

There was a lovely soft pink light in the sky as the boat made its way slowly towards the mainland. The buildings were silver stalagmites now caught in the evening sun. Then, as it began to sink lower in the sky, it was as though a furnace smelter door was opening, yet there was no meltdown, just a quiet transition where everything turned to burnished copper.

"It's breathtaking," Philip said softly.

"Yes, it is."

There was no real reason to go home. The office workers had already disappeared to theirs, but the streets were still alive with the people who lived in the downtown core.

"Can we walk a little?" Phil asked. At the same time he took my hand. The action seemed so spontaneous and natural I didn't have the heart to take my hand away, but he might have sensed my discomfort for he let go of his own volition almost immediately.

"I might compromise you, mightn't I?" he said boyishly.

"Nothing so dramatic," I smiled.

"But it's true."

"If you like."

"I'm glad you've stopped being sarcastic; it doesn't suit you." He put a hand on my back as we stopped at the traffic light. He was one of those "touchers," a surefire enthusiast for his fellow "handshakers" in church on Sundays. However, I didn't mind any more. In fact, now that his hand was gone from mine I missed the contact.

I noticed people looked at him as they passed. He was so obviously a foreigner and, as he walked with a pleased grin on his face all the time, it was hard to ignore him.

We passed some of the strip joints on Yonge Street and he peered at the photographs on the windows outside.

"It's like Soho!" he said grinning, but with no hint of disapproval.

"Have you ever been in one?" I queried.

"No, never."

"Do you want to see what they're like?"

"Could we?"

I hadn't expected such enthusiasm. I was sorry now I'd made the offer. God knows what it would be like, and I would end up being embarrassed as though I was sitting watching the sex act with my son. But he had already gone up to the doorman.

"When's the next show?" he asked.

"Five minutes."

That in itself was bad news. If it had been a longer wait, it would have been easier to walk on and forget about the idea.

He was already buying two tickets though, showing no hint of embarrassment.

It was terribly dark inside, so dark we stumbled until our eyes adjusted to the sudden deprivation of light. The place smelt of stale beer. It was impossible to make out any kind of decor. I suspected there were lots of acoustic tiles and much black paint masquerading as style.

There were hardly any customers, just a couple of lone men scattered at random around the tables. A long ramp ran down between the tables.

I was more and more regretting the impulse that had brought us in, but he was excited like a teenager. A waitress wearing a red satin bunny outfit came to our table. She looked incredibly bored.

"What's it doing out there?" she asked, referring to the weather. I could see from Philip's baffled face that he hadn't a clue what she was talking about.

"It's nice," I replied, almost sorry not to be able to report to her that it was raining or snowing.

She shrugged, "You never know in here."

"I imagine not," I sympathized.

"What'll you have?" she asked.

"A martini, please."

"An' you?" she asked Philip. She looked as though she didn't approve of him being there and I couldn't blame her. He quite definitely wasn't the type she would be accustomed to seeing, either as a regular or even a tourist.

"A glass of wine if that's possible?" He turned to me. "Do they serve it by the glass?"

I nodded.

"If not, a ginger beer would be fine."

She screwed up her nose, she obviously didn't know what ginger beer was. "We have rosé."

"Fine, that's fine."

She disappeared and I noticed that he was staring at her legs as she moved away from the table.

"You're not frightened of being excommunicated?" I asked.

He laughed. "No, our bishop's been to a strip show. He used it of course for a sermon. If he can go, I reckon I can." He pronounced "reckon" with a North American twang which sounded terribly out of place.

"And you'll do the same?" I asked.

"No, of course not."

"You don't disapprove?"

"Only if they're being exploited. I suppose then I'd disapprove. I'm told they don't see it that way."

"I'm sure they don't. If they have nice bodies, they've decided they have something good to show the world. It's just the same as having a voice."

"Is it? I'm not sure I quite agree with that. I mean they just don't stand there, they're deliberately provocative."

"You sound as though you've seen it before," I teased.

"I've seen films."

"It's all in the eye of the beholder, isn't it?"

There was a very peculiar drum roll and music began to play. Spotlights in a ghastly green shade lit up the stage and ramp, and a girl in purple feathers and lots of gauze appeared, her arms waving like windmills caught in crosswinds.

Somebody in the background was thumping on a drum almost violently, as though in a vain attempt to give her some rhythm. It made no difference; she was an excruciatingly bad dancer and her body, once unveiled, was little better. She had breasts like mismatched turnips with long medicine stopper teats. I wondered how she could sleep at night with such appendages. There were clumps of flesh on her thighs with moon crater indentations, but she wafted her tulle around them a lot so that we could catch only glimpses of those more ample parts.

It was all very pedestrian and awful, until she began doing something with a bread roll that in the hands of a good dancer might have been suggestive but in her incapable hands was plain vulgar.

I was scared to look at Philip.

"So much for your theory about the right to show off a nice body," he whispered. "Who's exploiting whom?"

"Have you had enough?" I asked.

He nodded, but I noticed he sat on making no attempt to move. We stayed until it was all over.

"I wonder who gets the bread roll?" he said with a grin.

"They should make her eat it herself as punishment," I said.

He took my hand again as we came out into the street. I told myself that it was such a natural gesture it wasn't worth worrying about, a sort of "I am your protector," clerical impulse.

"What now?" he asked cheerfully. "That is unless you've got something better to do?"

"Plenty!" I laughed. "I've already told you, you're a damnable nuisance."

He threaded his arm though mine. "I'm hungry."

I wasn't surprised after seeing the amount he'd managed to tuck away since we'd first met. It was obviously important to keep the energy fuelled.

I took him to a Japanese restaurant in the basement of a men's boutique. He'd never had Japanese food before. I guessed he was very much a roast-beef-and-potato man. I took a perverse delight in forcing him to try something different.

He was enchanted that he had to take off his shoes and even more thrilled that we had to sit cross-legged at the low tables.

"It's wonderful," his eyes gleamed with genuine delight.

"It's mostly raw fish," I told him, watching his expression. A flicker of disgust crossed his face.

"But you like it?" he asked.

"I love it."

"Good! Then I shall too."

I wondered what it would be like to wake up every morning for the rest of one's life to face such insufferable optimism. I knew that for most of the day I'd been caught up by his enthusiasm, but I told myself that it would be tedious to put up with it for more than a day at a time.

They brought us sushi and he smelt it and prodded it before putting it into his mouth. He fumbled with the chopsticks, dropping the sushi many times before it found his mouth. They had brought hot saki and he was downing that too as though it were tea. He had drunk several cups of it before I thought to warn him that it could be quite lethal.

There was a slight recklessness about him now that worried me.

"I've had a wonderful day," he said between mouthfuls of rice. "I shan't forget it."

"I've had a lovely time too." I could say it in honesty, for although there were irritating moments, I'd found myself for the entire time alternating between wanting to bash him and hug him. It was an altogether frustrating mix of emotions that I had trouble coping with.

"You're a lovely person." He set down his chopsticks and groped for my hand. "And no matter how hard you try to make me think you're terrible, I think you're quite wonderful."

I told myself it was the saki taking its toll on me now and that alone was causing my insides to feel coated in thick velvet. I allowed him to play with my fingers. He ran his forefinger up and down between each one. He might have been delving into the private parts of my body, no less was the sensation of erotic enjoyment. I could interrupt, lean forward, remind him again that I was happily married, but to do so would make more of the moment than I should allow; this was a friendship gesture, I rationalized.

"You're not married?" I asked looking down at our linked hands.

"No."

"No girlfriend?"

"Nobody special."

"I can't think why." I looked up into his face.

"I was sure you didn't like me," he said eagerly. "In fact, that you hated me."

"I'm not sure I do like you," I confessed. "But there are certain moments when I think you're more than all right." It was out before I could prevent it. His entire face lit up. "I presume this will all be material for your next sermon?" I said, determined suddenly to break the mood.

"What next sermon?"

"Perhaps for the bishop, something about the Seventh Commandment."

"Why do you do that?" he said darkly.

"What?"

"Keep spoiling things."

I stood up from the table. "I think we'd better go, don't you?" But my legs were shaky underneath me. Instead of worrying about his consumption of saki I should have worried about my own, for after all, I was the one who had to drive home. Luckily we had quite a long walk to the car, so there was time to sober up in the night air. I was confused too about whether my "high" was induced by the saki or his company.

"What would you have been doing if I weren't here?" he asked on the way home.

I shrugged, "Practising ... resting, who knows."

"I'm truly sorry about this."

"There's nothing to be sorry for. I'm glad you're here." And it was suddenly true, all the things I'd been hating about him weren't there any more.

We drove most of the way in silence and I was glad of that. When we were almost there he said contemplatively, "I thought it would be crass and awful in North America."

"And it's not?"

"No, I love it."

"I haven't heard you say a negative thing all day. I would have been surprised if you hadn't liked it."

"I like life rather a lot, I suppose."

"I'd noticed."

I pulled into the driveway and the garage door opened automatically, and then we were inside the garage sitting side by side in the car in that illuminated space. He got out quickly, banging his door on the lawn mower in his haste to come around to my door and open it for me. I wasn't used to such chivalry and was already halfway out of the car. So tight was the space that we collided, and up close I could smell the rather sweet smell of his body, like a baby's body. I was filled with instant remorse for every single put-down of the day.

And suddenly there, in amongst the smell of gasoline and weed killer, we were kissing and it was the loveliest thing imaginable. The sweetness of his breath and the body smell overpowered the inappropriateness of our surroundings. He was kissing my neck, my ear, nudging in behind my hairline and God knows where it would have ended if he hadn't bumped a rake that was hanging on the wall, and it fell, clattering to the ground. I managed to push him away and slam the car door shut, but at the same time my skirt got caught so that when I came to move away there was a great ripping sound. He opened the door and released the skirt. There was a huge tear in the hem.

I went quickly through the side door into the house. I could hear him behind me.

"Perhaps I'd better go to a hotel," he said meekly, his eyes downcast.

"Oh, don't be ridiculous."

"I feel dreadful."

And indeed he did look rather awful.

There's nothing to feel dreadful for, is there?"

I could see by the droop of his shoulders I'd hurt his feelings again. I was furious with myself, furious for registering every change of mood, furious that I'd thought it would be fun to corrupt him in the first place.

"Please just go to bed!" I dropped my handbag on the dining-room table and turned to the kitchen. I knew he stood there for a while and then I heard his footsteps on the stairs.

God knows what was going through his head. I was pretty sure he was suffering, but then he wasn't alone.

I noticed that the lights were flashing on the telephone answering machine. I pressed the rewind button and heard John's voice.

"Just phoning to say Hi! I'll call again first thing in the morning." Never mind that it sounded a million miles away; it was exactly what I needed, his voice friendly and caring. I needed reminders. I'd prided myself that in all our years together I'd never once cheated. There had been moments on tour when ardent fellow singers had tried to interest me in going to bed with them, and there had been the odd temptation, but nothing that was ever a real test until now.

I went slowly upstairs to the bedroom after turning out all the downstairs lights. I slammed my door, making far more noise than I ever would normally.

The bedroom seemed incredibly lonely. I'd left the window wide open that morning, and a slightly chill night breeze had started up and was wafting the curtains, creating a tunnel effect which circulated cold air even more efficiently around the room.

I heard him on the landing outside and the sound of the bathroom door shut. I undressed slowly, inspecting the ripped skirt. It looked quite beyond repair. I hung it in the cupboard where it was destined to face me every day for the next year, a testimony to momentary madness.

It was cold in bed, the sheets particularly hostile to my body tonight. How I missed John's warmth, even his complaints about my cold feet. I wished fervently that he was there. I heard Philip's steps going past my door and then the sound of his door closing.

I tried reading for a while but couldn't concentrate. I could only remember the shattered look on his face and feel a great burden of shame that I'd deliberately dallied with him. I got out of bed and, getting my robe, I went out onto the landing. I could see there was still light underneath his door. I tapped.

"Come in!"

I opened the door. He was lying with his hands behind his head. Perhaps he was composing a letter to the bishop in his head, admitting his transgressions. He struck me as the kind of person who would have a heavy heart about holding guilt to himself for any length of time. I didn't want to be part of any story told to the bishop.

"Look, about tonight. I don't want you to think that you're in any way responsible. No guilt! It was entirely my doing."

"Was it?"

"Yes, entirely. So go to sleep! I accept full responsibility."

"You look lovely," he observed softly.

"You're impossible!" I slammed the door and went huffily, yet secretly warmed, to my room. For a while I stood against the open window, masochistically receiving the cold air against my chest, enjoying the discomfort. It was an incredibly bright night, the moon wasn't yet quite full, but it promised perfection.

I turned out the light and climbed into bed. The entire room was illuminated with an eerie blue-white light. I wasn't sure how long I lay there or whether or not I'd actually fallen asleep, but suddenly, when I opened my eyes, he was standing there at the end of the bed. He was wearing those ridiculous English pyjamas, striped things that made him look like Oliver Twist. He calmly turned back the comforter and climbed in beside me.

Hours later it was unclear who was guilty of corruption. With pyjamas long since shed, he lay like a beautiful sleeping martyr on top of the counterpane, his head peacefully on one side. What could he possibly say to his bishop now?

Four weeks later I had a delivery from Britain, a handsome box of lavender toilet soap and a brief thank-you note. The message was clear. I was only surprised that the soap wasn't carbolic to wash away the stain. For my own peace of mind, I gave him the benefit of the doubt and decided he had done the honourable thing by ignoring the whole episode. The last thing he would want would be to break up a happy marriage.

I had trouble forgetting him. Also, I had some trouble forgetting how totally unselfconscious had been his lovemaking. My body had been eased so expertly from its shell of guilt and explored without any hint of repression, that at moments I had wondered about him, only to rationalize that it had been so good because of deep feeling on both sides. The lavender soap and the precise, correct little thank-you note perhaps even confirmed how deep that feeling had been.

I tried to put him out of my mind, but often, especially on the road, I couldn't stop thinking of him when I should have been missing John. When I was at home, on those nights when the moon was almost full, the memories came back. I smelled again the baby smell and could imagine the marvellous, sweet, innocent taste of his mouth. Then I would get out of bed and touch the skirt with its ripped hem hanging in the closet and remind myself that it had happened. His lack of any real contact was because of his finer sensibilities, and that only heightened my longing for him.

❋

Eighteen months later, when I went to London to give a recital, I arranged to have lunch with Caroline at her Club in Kensington. It was an elegant Georgian mansion with black railings and window boxes and a doorman with white gloves.

We sat in one of those very proper English oak dining rooms on green silk Sheraton chairs in front of an immaculately laid luncheon table, sipping sherry out of Waterford glass, and only the cut and cloth of our surroundings, the air of imperturbable respectability, had kept me from blurting out the only question I had in my mind. What had happened to Philip? I had tried to contact him at the address he'd given me only to be told he'd left and there was no forwarding address. But we were halfway through our sole amandine before I could summon up enough courage to ask.

"And Philip? What do you hear of Philip?"

Caroline took a great gulp of white wine and gave a little giggle.

"Oh yes, of course, Philip, you did meet Philip, the naughty boy."

"Yes, I met Philip."

She set her glass down and looked at me curiously. "I suppose I should have warned you, but I was never sure whether he would really get in touch with you." She poked at her fish with her fork. "Do you find this fish fresh? I'm not sure it is. Mine tastes of cardboard boxes. God, I hate frozen fish."

My mouth felt totally dry at that moment. In my agitation I knocked my napkin ring onto the floor where it rolled under the table beside us. I made no move to retrieve it; I was mesmerized by Caroline who was still delivering a diatribe about the quality of the food. I was in agony for her to go on about Philip but couldn't show any real interest or she would suspect.

"And Philip, you were saying?" I finally managed.

"Well, he's been banished to the Hebrides or some other God forsaken spot. He seduced a vicar's wife in Pimlico. Can you imagine? I mean awfully stupid really. We all knew he had a taste for "taken" flesh as it were, but the vicar's wife? I ask you."

I felt my mouth go loose.

She leant over and touched my hand. "He didn't try to seduce you too, did he?"

"I barely saw him," I lied. "He stayed for a couple of days, but he went his own way."

It was time to retrieve the ring from under the neighbouring table, just to remove myself from Caroline's knowing eyes. I groped amid the diners' feet and grasped the silver ring. When I straightened up I saw Caroline observing me with interest. I knew the blush that suffused my face probably told her everything she wanted to know, but she had sensibly decided that if I was going to lie, she would play along.

"Good girl!" she managed unconvincingly.

"He's an absolute sweetie, you know. Frightfully good in so many ways, but he has this terrible weakness. I mean we used to put gorgeous young virgins in his path, but he never took a second look." She giggled. "I used to think he was so pure. I must confess I had a little fling with him myself. He's absolutely wonderful in bed. Too bad in a way you didn't give yourself a little treat." She stared at me again; her eyes were innocent and as large as saucers.

"I think you would have liked it." She threw her knife and fork down amid the wreckage of fish carcass and sighed deeply as she beckoned to the waiter.

"But then John is everything to you, isn't he?" She leant back and looked at me with raised sceptical eyebrows, "Marvellous, that kind of fidelity."

# LUELLA, LUELLA, WHERE ARE YOU?

Ralph kept on having the same dream over and over again. He saw himself watching Margot from behind a pillar in the basement of the old Grain Exchange Building where the Manitoba Players' Guild had their rehearsals. Always the same dream: it was stifling hot, he could see her get restless, tug the blouse away from under her arms to try and stop sweat stains, then touching her nose with a finger, testing for dampness; then she excused herself and picking up an oversized key to the washroom, she would disappear along the corridor.

He always followed her in the dream, although how they got to the tenth floor wasn't part of the dream. She would turn when she heard him and come towards him with her arms opened out, and then just when they were about to touch, a huge hole opened in the floor underneath her feet and she went plunging down screaming and screaming. He always woke up in a cold sweat.

He prayed one day the dream would be different. He went to bed each night planning a better ending to the dream. He imagined what she would look like in bed or waking up in the morning beside him, but all his images were spoiled by what he knew of the women in his own family, and all the good bits would disappear and he was back in the kitchen where his sisters Willie and Bena were fighting for time before the only decent mirror in the house; Bena rolling her long hair into a sausage curl and pinning it tight against her neck; Willie working with her curling tongs, coaxing her coarse hair into kinks and then trying to comb it backwards so that she looked like she'd been dragged through a hedge. The hairs, black and coarse like horse's hair, falling onto the washed dishes on the draining board. His mother screaming at them, not because of the hairs, but because nobody was helping her get the breakfast ready. And all the time the kitchen filling with the smell of frying onions and bacon so that all day the smell was on his clothes.

That was what Ralph liked about living in Winnipeg. The only breakfast smells in the kitchen of the house on Chestnut Street were of burnt toast, his own burnt toast. He always forgot that Loretta Clarke's toaster didn't pop up anymore.

He enjoyed padding around her kitchen in his stocking soles, trying not to make any noise that would wake up Loretta. She had insisted he drop the "Mrs" as soon as he had made out the cheque for two months' rent. He wasn't allowed to cook in his basement room, only boil a kettle for coffee or tea. He had to prepare his own breakfast because she didn't rise before noon, so it was blissfully peaceful in the house, so different to home where everyone screamed at everyone else.

*"Jesus, Bena, don't hang your stained panties in the john!"* Even though his mother's plea was supposed to be for her men's sensibilities, she always yelled her commands loud and clear.

The bathroom he shared with Loretta had no personality of its own. He had come to the conclusion that women over seventy had no odour at all. There was only ever the faint smell of the Dettol she swished around the lavatory bowl every night. On the shelf above the sink, amid piles of mysterious burnt-out matches, there was a bottle of some kind of frosty pink liquid that was labelled "calamine lotion," a bottle of iodine, the label stained orange, and a tiny pair of rusted nail scissors, otherwise nothing that distinctly belonged to her. Over the towel rail there was a yellow towel with a worn satin appliqué that said "His." He never touched it on any occasion. There were no signs of underwear or hairs in the wash basin, nothing to show that she actually washed there or powdered or even combed her hair.

In exchange for cheap accommodation with Loretta, he had to shovel the snow from the walkway whenever it snowed. He was also expected to watch television with her from time to time, although she never put it into so many words.

He hadn't totally made up his mind what he thought about Winnipeg. It was as if he was waiting for the lens to focus before he decided. It still shocked him that he could walk the length and breadth of Portage Avenue and not see a single solitary face he knew. Large cities were supposed to close one in, comfortably enfold, but Winnipeg opened out, disappearing into infinity. The

buildings could be flicked down with a fingernail. They had no more substance than cut-outs in a children's storybook: single dimensional and cardboard.

He felt his own body floated somehow in his new environment.
Occasionally he had the sensation that, instead of walking normally, his arms
and legs flailed like an astronaut's struggling with a loss of gravity. It was why
he always carried his knapsack with the strap firmly across his chest; the comfortable press of the strap made him feel more secure. Whenever he had to
take it off, he felt oddly scared and short of breath, like a solitary tree waiting
for a thunderstorm.

His job at the newspaper depot was all right. It paid just enough money
for him to manage. All he had to do was make sure that the routes under his
jurisdiction were serviced, and if any of the boys were sick he had to find a
replacement.

It was the nights at the Manitoba Players' Guild that made everything
worthwhile. He had to thank Art Carnody, his district manager, for both the
job and the introduction to the theatre group where they wanted him to be
their unofficial photographer.

Art, like himself, hailed from Minnedosa, not that he had ever been particularly friendly with him there, but he had been his only contact when he
had first arrived in Winnipeg.

Ralph got paid nothing for taking photos of the actors, but Art promised
that they would all be only too eager to pay him when the show was over and
they wanted to remember their moment of glory.

Aside from being official prompter for the production, Art had one line in
the play. He had to rush into a brothel in Scene Three unbuttoning his pants
and calling out, "Luella, Luella, where are you?" Even though Ralph knew
nothing at all about theatre, he knew the casting was crazy. Art's voice was too
plummy and his lisp all wrong for the single desperate line. Art had taken the
part because nobody else in the group had wanted such a small part.

Art took it all very seriously. He was always taking up the director's time
to ask where the emphasis should be and whether he should be yelling
"Luella" before he actually came on stage, or start it after he was on stage.

What made the rehearsals all worthwhile for Ralph was Margot, Margot
Raymonde. When she pronounced the "Raymonde," she made it sound all
French. When someone new came into the group, Ralph liked to be near her
and hear her give her name. He also liked the way she offered her hand: the
palm always parallel to the ground as if she expected it to be kissed, not shak-
en. It had thrown him the first time he met her and he had held onto the
hand far too long, until she'd finally withdrawn it and held it slightly out from
her body. Either she planned to wash it right away or else the handshake had
meant something. He preferred to think the latter.

She was playing the lead in the production. From constantly watching and listening to her, Ralph knew her lines almost as well as she knew them herself. Plucking up courage one night he finally told her, "You sure fall into natural poses." She smiled distantly and said, "I'm not photogenic," but you could see she liked the attention. He marvelled at the variety of ways that she could sit and always look graceful and modest: a hand draped carelessly, an arm up and a hand behind her head, her eyes dreamy and faraway.

Eric Cowan, the director, always treated her as though she were special. She didn't do things the way anyone else did. She was always "walking through" lines as she called it, getting the feel. Anyone else who tried walking through got hell from Eric, but Margot was allowed to "feel" as much as she liked.

There was an old biddy in the play, Isobel Bradley, who seemed to hate Margot. She had big buck teeth and pronounced consonants carefully, like she was English. Ralph thought she talked as though her tongue was always curled, spitting lots of *s*'s in all directions. She fancied herself too. Ralph had always heard the expression "looked down her nose" but had never actually seen anyone who could do it so well. She claimed she had trained in pantomime in England, but Ralph could only imagine her playing the horse. She was always off in a corner complaining to Eric about how she never knew what to expect from Margot.

They had told Ralph he didn't have to go to all rehearsals, but he wouldn't have dreamed of not turning up. Each night he chronicled new wonders in Margot. He often thought about actually following her when she made her nightly treks to the washroom, but he could never summon up enough nerve.

He turned up each night of rehearsal with his army-surplus knapsack well stuffed with newspapers to make it look important. When anyone spoke to him it was usually to tease him about what was in the knapsack. Art said it made him look like someone "passing through," carrying all his worldly possessions with him — someone who might sleep on park benches.

Although Ralph had spent all his savings on his camera equipment, it was still only mediocre by professional standards. His family were always full of scorn about his fooling around taking photographs.

"*Whadya want to go and take all them farm machines for?*" his mother frequently complained, "*... an' grain elevators. Landsakes I never seen nothin' as plain as a grain elevator.*"

She didn't understand about elevators at sunset and elevators at dawn. It was no good showing her the results. He had once, and she said, "*Looks like a grain elevator to me,*" and handed it over to his father who grunted and threw it down on the table with barely a look.

"*Make a heck uv a lot more sense to take the girls' picshures than them goin' all the ways up to Winnipeg to have themselves took at the Bay.*"

Mostly Ralph took photos of Margot at the rehearsals. He felt he could maybe understand something more about her if he had her on film. He hated the nights when there were no rehearsals, no Margot. He mostly stayed home then. The only person he knew in Winnipeg apart from Art, and the other actors, was Loretta. When he was home he usually felt obliged to watch the "idiot" box with her. She sat in her upholstered wing chair with her thick legs stuck out like barber's poles and resting on a hassock. She was constantly knitting enormous multicoloured socks for herself. "They keep the old circulation going," she informed Ralph repeatedly.

Usually at ten in the evening, just before the news, and whenever there was a commercial break, she would heave her broad beam out of the chair and disappear into the kitchen to make hot chocolate for him. There was always a plate of digestive biscuits covered with thin slices of processed cheese. The edges of the cheese were already a deep pumpkin shade and brittle because she left the plate prepared and uncovered on the shelf. Once he had gone into the kitchen and Manchu, her cat, was up on the shelf licking at them. After that he had totally lost his appetite for her little snacks.

Ralph couldn't stand Manchu. He was the kind of cat that rubbed against your legs looking for attention and then when he had it, would try to bite your hand.

To avoid those nights of television watching, Ralph mostly pretended he was working in the laundry room which she allowed him to use as a dark room. But then, next morning, she always wanted to see what he had done, so he was forced to get out all his old photographs and pass them off for ones freshly developed.

He still hadn't developed any of the photographs of Margot and the others. He preferred, for the present, to keep her in his head, but it was infuriating that he could only ever conjure up bits of her face in his mind's eye. He could never put the whole face together, just parts: the city-pale face, the nose a bit too long and with too much upward curve, and the pale-lashed, blinkered eyes, speckled green and brown, changing colours with her moods, and then the parts would slide away and he forced himself to concentrate, to try to capture them all at once and move them into the right order. Only in his dreams did she come together, but never did she seem to move into his arms.

There were a lot more rehearsals now. As the opening drew nearer, nobody was allowed to look at the script, nor even have the benefit of Art's prompts. Surprisingly, it was the old biddy Isobel who screwed up her lines the most. She'd learned every sentence with her moves, and if anyone else took a wrong step she was suddenly all panicky; her big mouth would fall open and her eyes glaze over. Ralph got a photograph of her that way.

"My dear Isobel, move, speak, say something, anything at all, darling!" Eric bleated. She stayed silent and Ralph took another photograph, hoping he had captured her snooty face all broken up and bewildered.

When words didn't come to Margot, she invented new ones; sometimes they sounded pretty stupid, but at least she didn't stand around with her mouth open.

"What is she saying?" Isobel would demand.

"The play must go on, Isobel," Eric reminded her.

"What play? Some soap opera she's writing in her head?"

Eric turned to Margot. "She is right, sweet one. The playwright wouldn't like it."

Margot closed her eyes and her chest heaved. Ralph saw she was actually crying.

"Ten minutes!" Eric announced. Ralph would like to have taken a shot of her that way, but his instincts told him it wasn't the right thing to do at that moment. They all went out to the corridor, everyone in awe of Margot's breakdown.

Tess Black, the stage manager, knew the reason for the tears but kept quiet, smugly proud to be Margot's only ear. Tess was seventeen and stagestruck. She thought Margot was wonderful and hung around her as much as possible.

"Is she ill?" Ralph managed to corner Tess.

Tess shook her head. "Worried. She thinks she isn't really in the part yet. Isn't that ridiculous? She's absolutely wonderful."

Isobel overheard. "She's right. She hasn't got it, the lines anyhow."

"Acting is more than lines. She worries, which is more than anyone else does," Tess was hot in her defence.

Art made a faint gesture with one shoulder. "I don't sleep nights with my one line".

They all stared at him. A giggle came from somewhere. Ralph knew that most of the cast thought Art was a joke, but he wasn't sure whether or not *he* was part of that joke.

Margot passed them in the corridor, her face turned away. Tess touched her arm and Margot shrugged it off, reluctant to stop.

"Prima donna!" Isobel muttered, loud enough for Margot to hear.

"Shut up!" Tess commanded in her stage-manager tone.

"There will be a blue moon in the sky before I stand for a seventeen-year old snot telling me to shut up." Isobel's nostrils whitened and Ralph could see her pink tongue, like the rolled ham his mother did for parties.

"Oh, come on!" Stu urged. "Let's get on with it!"

As it got closer to the night of the performance, Art got more and more jittery. He wondered whether he should invite his family to come up from Minnedosa. He kept telling Ralph over and over again that he would fall apart knowing they were in the audience.

Ralph knew the Carnodys quite well and he knew they wouldn't be much affected one way or the other either by Art or the play. Old man Carnody was only ever interested in his pigs and playing bingo. Anyway, Ralph was puzzled why Art was so worried about what Eric always referred to as "a running line." Even if Art closed his eyes and dashed on stage saying it — that would be it, it would be over. But it was growing in importance in Art's mind. He obviously practised his make-up at home too and came in to work with traces of it still showing around the edges of his jawline. He kept his eyeliner on for most of the day and the rest of the district managers tittered and laughed about him when he wasn't around. They would mince and prance in ghastly caricature of Art's walk and ask each other if their lipstick was smudged.

The cast and crew were all expected to sell at least ten tickets for the play. Ralph sold one for opening night to Loretta and then realized that it meant he would have to take her.

Loretta didn't know what Manchu would think about her going out for an evening. It obviously hadn't happened for so long that she was thrown into a turmoil. She even removed her red and white football socks for the occasion and put on a pair of stockings that were firmly secured with thick rubber bands. Her best dress was a mauve crepe that had washed up, so that when she sat down rolls of flesh spilled from between knicker top and the elastic bands on her stockings. She had a balaclava helmet for going out at night and a piece of mangy fur that she called her "silver fox" which she wrapped around her neck so that she looked as if she were being eaten by some hairy beast. She kept calling Ralph her "excort," mispronouncing it coyly.

"How does my excort think I look?" Her mouth was an clumsy gash of purple.

She had never been to a play before and she was highly excited, not sure what to expect. When it started she kept complaining she couldn't hear, until someone in front of her turned around and said, "Lady, neither can we. If you would shut up, we might have a chance." She kept right on talking. "Why can't they all speak louder?" she asked petulantly.

After it was all over, she claimed that it had been one of the most exciting evenings of her life. She talked about all the cast members: the pale one you couldn't hear, Margot; the fairy, Art; the one who shouted, Isobel; the one with all the fungus on his face, Margot's leading man. "Why couldn't they have spoken up?" she repeated over and over again on the bus going home.

Ralph shut out her ramblings and tried to think what it was going to be like the following week when there would be nothing to look forward to, no Margot. He would be left with only her photos.

Saturday night, the last night, Art's family came down from Minnedosa. Art was a bundle of nerves. For some reason the entire cast were on edge. Not long after Isobel's entrance in the first act, she forgot her lines. She forgot them because Margot had moved to a spot on the stage where she normally never stood. Isobel seemed frozen to the stage, almost haughty in her terror, waiting for some kind of deliverance.

In the third act, just before Art's entry, Isobel froze again and skipped about two pages of the script, and suddenly Art's moment was gone, there was simply no place for him to enter. All the practising, all the make-up jobs, the worry about what to wear and poor Art had missed his moment of triumph.

Later, when it was over, old man Carnody came rampaging backstage yelling at Art about having wasted his time, while Art tried to explain what had happened.

At the party Art got very drunk. Everybody else had forgotten the disaster of the night and were remembering the good performances. Margot's face was flushed with success. Ralph, sitting close to her, heard some friend of Eric's telling her that she should head for Toronto where she would be a sensation. Across the room Art kept staring at her with glazed eyes.

"Stupid little man!" Margot said to her companion. "One line, what a fuss!"

Ralph, leaning against one of the big speakers must have been blocked from her view for he heard her say distinctly. "And that dreadful friend of his, Ralph. Always mooning around with that camera. There's definitely something odd about him. Gives me the creeps."

Ralph felt his skin going cold all over and it was like some hard hand eviscerating him, a cruel tug that produced pain that radiated from his stomach to his throat. He felt himself grow solid against his backrest, pressing against it to reassure himself of his form and substance.

He could sit on until others came over and she had forgotten what she'd said and was properly into the party atmosphere, or he could gather whatever thread of dignity was left to him and stand up, letting her know he'd heard. He opted for the former. He barely knew how long he sat on with his bottle of beer in his hand, his back ramrod stiff against the speaker box. Then when he did rise much later, he heard her voice.

"Not taking pictures then?"

He realized she was talking to him.

"There's nothing worth taking, is there?" he said and with that he set his empty beer bottle down and lifted his knapsack.

"That's you taken care of," he heard someone say to her. It was followed immediately by her familiar trill of laughter. He was glad it would be the last time he would hear that laugh.

The next night he developed all the photographs, fixing them up to dry on the lines he had strung across Loretta's sink. Margot hung all around him, her pale face peering down at him from every angle. He had at least a hundred photographs of her: profile, semi-profile, full face, face down, face upwards, but they all looked the same to him.

Nothing could animate the almost medieval blankness he found in her now. The Margot he thought he had glimpsed on all those nights of photographing, or the Margot from his dreams, was nowhere in the lot that hung around him now.

Finally he took down one of the grey plastic garbage bags that Loretta kept on the shelf and without a flicker of regret he dropped each photograph of Margot into the bag and, twisting the top, he fixed a tie around it and set it in the corner. Then he switched on the overhead light.

# SLIP-SLIDING

"What did I say just now about split infinitives?" Miss McCarthy tapped the desk with her ruler and directed the question at Patricia.

Patricia hadn't been listening since class began. She was sick of the correlative conjunctions and unrelated participles that McCarthy had been bleating about for the past week. The only thing in her head were thoughts of Sean McCardle and the fact that it was snowing outside and had been snowing since noon. There was a decent layer of the white stuff actually lying on the ground — a phenomenon for Belfast.

All the gang would gather in the field behind her house after school, all the crowd including Sean who was home from school on holidays.

"I don't know what's the matter with you girls, nobody is paying a jot of attention." McCarthy pressed her chalk, scraping it spitefully on the board.

"The infinitive is split only when an adverb or a phrase separates 'to' from the infinitive form of the verb ..." She engraved it on the board, digging the chalk further in, until Patricia's eardrums felt shattered.

The classroom smelt like an abattoir today mostly because of Brenda Eadie in the desk beside her, who obviously had the curse. At the beginning of term when she'd been feeling all silly and soft, Patricia, in a burst of pity, had sort of adopted Brenda.

There was a rawness and redness to Brenda that the others had all shunned. "Country bumpkin" might have been engraved on her forehead. Her hands were early-morning milking hands, chapped and rough from farm work.

Christian charity had made Patricia choose the seat beside her. Each day she bitterly regretted being so sappy, for once the seats were chosen, that was it for the rest of term.

Nobody would listen to her now if she wanted to change. Patricia wasn't a favourite with the teachers. Too often she'd been in trouble for not doing her homework, for talking too much in class, writing notes to her friends, generally causing trouble. The teachers would look on Brenda as her penance. So each day she had to suffer the life cycle of smells that came warm and fresh each morning from the Eadie farm in the Castlereagh hills.

If Brenda hadn't smelt so ripe, Patricia might have felt a twinge of jealousy, for all in all, it was an odour of adulthood. She still hadn't gotten her period and was pretty sure she was the last "holdout" in the class.

The other girls in class used their "handicap," or so they called it, to escape having to do gym twice a week. Patricia knew, for sure, no matter what, rain or shine, hell or high water, she would never miss a gym class. Aside from art, it was the only thing about school that she could stand.

Maybe that was why she was so slow to menstruate: on the one hand she longed to be "grown up," which to her mind meant breasts and bleeding; on the other hand, if it meant giving up gym once a month, she would stay a child forever.

As Patricia swung from parallel bars and hurdled over the wooden horse she sometimes imagined she was some kind of wild animal swinging from trees. The walls of the gymnasium disappeared and the mysteries of "split infinitives" became some adult joke.

She was the gym teacher's prize pupil, a little undisciplined, but willing to try anything. *"Now look at Patricia,"* Miss Arundel was fond of saying. *"She doesn't let a little monthly discomfort bother her one little bit."*

The others, in their knowledge, smirked knowingly. They waited for Patricia to admit the truth. Patricia swung from the rings and ignored them. If there had been no roof she would have sailed right through.

Until last week Patricia hadn't been the least bit interested in boys, but last week she'd met Sean McArdle for the first time and all that had changed.

Sean was a boarder at a Catholic boys' school. The McArdles were the only Catholic family on the street. Patricia knew them all from a distance and often heard her mother refer to them with more than a hint of cynicism as "that McArdle lot." That same "McCardle lot," she'd heard her best friend Molly's mother say with some scorn, "... could live off the smell of an oily rag."

There were eight brothers and one sister, and except for the girl, all were like peas in a pod, all dark, handsome and distinctly Catholic looking, although what it was that made them so, was impossible to say.

Sean was a friend of John Edwards, one of their group. He wasn't like the other boys they played touch football with in the field behind the house. That first day, he'd come wearing his blazer, looking terribly formal as though it was important to prove something to the "Prods."

Her first instinct had been to laugh at his curious stiffness, but his manner and clothes hadn't held him back one bit. When it came to the actual game, it had taken him only an instant to shed the blazer and plunge into the spirit of the play. But he still had a veneer of manners that was missing from the usual old gang who went to the ordinary grammar school.

You could tell he didn't meet many girls because he was a little awkward with them, almost too polite, but anything was a change to the usual crude stuff that came out of the mouths of the grammar school lot.

He smelt different too. She noticed it that first day. You were always supposed to pass the ball in touch football the minute you were tagged, but when he tagged Patricia she hung on pretending that he'd grabbed a handful of wind and he'd followed yelling and grabbing at her until he'd wrestled her to the ground. While everybody jumped and yelled that she'd cheated, he lay on top of her for more than a few seconds, his grey eyes peering down at her so closely that she was certain she could see her own reflection. His breath was extraordinarily sweet.

"Cheat!" he said grinning at her, but there was something almost threatening about his easy authority over her. Without knowing why, Patricia felt a bit frightened, but almost as quickly again he returned to his former awkwardness when the others gathered chanting and hooting, and then he was off her and standing up in a flash.

"Don't they know the rules?" he'd said in a sort of superior voice.

"I know the rules," Patricia jumped in defensively. "I wasn't tagged," she lied, brushing her skirt off in indignation. She couldn't bear to look in his direction. It was as though she could still feel the weight of his body over hers and something had changed. She didn't feel like playing anymore.

"Come on!" Molly tugged her arm.

"You go ahead."

"Don't be silly."

"I'm not being silly. I'll watch."

Molly shrugged and ran back to the others. Patricia hung around the periphery, knowing she had his attention. He wasn't properly in the game. It gave her an odd feeling of power. She felt peculiarly puffed up, important in a way she'd never felt before. When he had been on top of her for that instant she'd felt quite queer, all breathy and excited.

In bed that night she had a dreadful nightmare: the teddy bear she'd always slept with was crushing her to death, and when she woke up she was sweating and panting. In terror, she threw the poor stuffed animal across the room.

She got out of bed onto the cold floor and padded across the room to take off her pajama top and see where the wounds were. She stared in disbelief at her pale undamaged skin in the mirror. The dream had seemed so totally real she couldn't believe there wasn't a mark. She looked at the unsatisfactory suggestion of breasts and the bony shoulders that looked for all the world like someone had left a coat hanger inside.

Her mother always told her she had lovely shoulders but she could see nothing but knobs sticking out that made her look as if she were from Belsen. She felt ugly as sin. To make matters worse she found a fine hair sprouting beside one nipple. Had her stupid body not even made up its mind whether it was supposed to be a boy or girl? Not only was she half-woman, maybe she was half-animal too, and she'd be stuck midway forever.

She got back into bed again and lay staring at the abandoned bear lying in the corner of the room where she'd tossed him. She imagined his amber eyes glowing angrily at her in the half-light, but she felt no remorse. The dream was still too real and she still felt she had some internal damage.

The snow was still falling when school was finally over. The whole school seemed to empty out at once. Usually the girls straggled out lethargically. Today with an enormous "whoosh" they burst from the doors, slipping and sliding onto the steps and falling into the road, gone crazy with the novelty of the white stuff. There was screaming and yelling as girls stuffed snowballs down their friends' backs, slid on their bottoms down the snow-covered verges.

The vice-principal, Miss Prentice, came to the door once and clapped her hands ineffectually and then retreated. There was quite simply nothing to be done. Tomorrow all traces of the snow would probably be gone and things would be back to normal. Now, nothing short of a cannon volley, would stop the chaos.

The naked cherry blossom trees that lined the street like empty coat racks in winter were transformed by the snow. Molly danced under one, like an out-of-season May Queen. Patricia joined her, linking hands, and let the younger kids pelt them with snowballs.

They collapsed in laughter, stockinged knees pillowing into the cushion of snow, the flesh between their knickers and stockings ice-cold, but somehow wonderful. Patricia looked down to the place where she'd sat and the snow was bright pink. Molly stared too and then she began to giggle.

"Candy floss," she pointed.

It was minutes before it dawned on Patricia what was happening. She was menstruating. Surely it wasn't supposed to happen miles from home, like a sneak attack?

She was conscious of a sticky warmth between her legs. At the same time she was sure that the whole world knew what was happening. They would be able to track her home like a winter *Gretel* leaving tell-tale tracks in the snow. All she could do was pray that a thaw would come and melt away the stain.

It had finally happened, but why here for goodness sake? Patricia could understand now why the girls at school hadn't wanted to do gym class. Surely no pad, no protection could hide this mess.

The boys were waiting in ambush for them on the way home and pelted them with snow. Patricia felt none of the joy she'd felt only an hour earlier when she'd tumbled and rolled with the girls outside school. She was leaking blood for all the world to see. It was as though she was spurting from all the cavities of her body. She raced for home, away from Sean.

Suddenly he didn't seem good-looking anymore, he was just too different, he stood out like a sore thumb compared to the others.

Patricia didn't go to the field the next day, but the following day Sean was waiting for her at the bottom of the avenue where they both lived. His face went beet red as he tried to pretend he just happened to be there.

He kept pace with Patricia.

"Are you all right today?"

Patricia shrugged, "I'm fine."

"I just wondered. You didn't come back yesterday."

Patricia smiled and didn't say anything.

"Would you come to the dance up in the Malone Hall with me on Saturday night?" he blurted out.

"I can't dance," she said abruptly.

"That's all right, I can't either." The absurdity of his offer didn't seem to strike him.

"I could come and pick you up?" He looked so scared as he asked that Patricia felt sorry for him all of a sudden.

"If we can't dance, what would we do?" Patricia asked bluntly.

"We could talk."

"Hm!"

"You'll come?"

If she refused now, he would think it was because he was a Catholic, Patricia rationalized, so she said yes. He became almost jaunty beside her.

Now that she was committed, she just wished he would go away. When they were almost home, there was a sound of running feet behind them and one of his brothers came up beside them, making a long, suggestive whistling sound, and tugging on Sean's sleeve as he loped by. She could see Sean was furious, but he didn't say a word.

"Who was that?" Patricia asked, knowing perfectly well.

"Brian," he pronounced it like Breean, a very definite Catholic pronunciation and Patricia felt a peculiar squirrely feeling in the pit of her stomach.

"He's at the stupid age," he said with contempt.

"I suppose your parents won't like me asking you out?" he blurted out suddenly.

It was odd, but she hadn't thought about anything like that at all.

"They won't mind," Patricia said casually.

"Mine will," he said looking at her with a half grin, "... and now they'll know because Brian is a big 'yap'."

"And what will they say?"

He shrugged, "They won't say anything, but they'll not like it for sure."

It had never occurred to her that Catholics might not want to associate with Protestants either. The idea rather puzzled her and she wondered if he were lying. It wasn't something she thought they should talk about anyway; after all, they weren't about to be married. At the same time, it made too much of the Saturday-night date.

She hadn't lied when she'd said her mother and father wouldn't mind her going out with him. They barely paid any attention when she told them who had asked her out.

In a way it wasn't much fun being a *late* child, an *afterthought*. Sometimes she felt like a nuisance, an interruption in her parents' life. They had been settling down for old age and along she'd come, rudely bursting in on their well-earned peace and quiet.

Patricia often longed for a sign that they worried about her, but they seemed to face everything with a tired calm. Patricia knew for a fact that Molly's mother would have hit the roof if it had been Molly going out with Sean McCardle. She would have put her foot down for sure. It would be far more convenient to have strict parents. Sometimes she felt like her own parent, setting her own limits.

Waiting nervously for Saturday, Patricia tried to remember everything about his face that she possibly could, but it was as though she'd lost her memory; just fleeting bits and pieces of him came to mind. Then when she tried to piece him together, the picture in her mind was unrecognizable.

She imagined phoning him and telling him she felt sick, but then surely his mother would say, "What do you expect from those damned Prods?"

On Saturday Patricia changed clothes three or four times, uncertain of how she should look. She could see her mother and father were amused by it all and she could have killed them for their insensitivity. They were letting her down when she needed them most.

She had pains in her stomach all day with worry.

"No later than 10:00 p.m., remember!" Her father said when Sean came to pick her up. Patricia had fantasized some mad scene at the front door with her father being unreasonable, not the mild-mannered plea to be home at 10:00 p.m. What was even worse was her mother sitting in the background with the familiar soft smile on her face, mending a bedsheet. She despised them both at that moment.

Sean looked so respectable Patricia hated him all over again. They hardly exchanged a word as they walked down the road. She could tell he was as miserable as she was and wondered why he'd bothered coming at all.

On the bus he sat on the outside seat and paid the fares smartly. Patricia couldn't bear to look at him, but she was aware that he was staring at her, perhaps waiting for her to say something. She stayed stubbornly silent.

He had meant what he'd said about not dancing. She supposed she hadn't really believed him. Even though she hadn't tried it before, she imagined there wasn't anything to it. They would simply rise and float onto the floor like Marge and Gower Champion. What made matters even worse was that most people seemed to have come unpaired. There was a long line of boys on one side of the room and a line of girls on the other. Each time a new dance was announced, there was a massive stampede of boys to the girls' side.

Sitting, perched beside him on the chair, while passing dancers occasionally tromped over her feet, Patricia felt like one of the ugly sisters at the ball. She knew that nobody else would ask her to dance because it was an unspoken rule you didn't barge in on a "twosome."

Sean continuously tapped one foot nervously on the floor. Patricia noticed with contempt that even that wasn't in time to the music. She wished fervently, and often, as conversation started and died again, that she was at home reading a good book.

After what seemed like eons, when they turned the lights down low, he finally asked her for one of the really slow dances. She could have cried with relief. Anything was better than sitting there praying the whole evening could be over.

They did a kind of shuffle, which in the dimmed lights might just have passed for dancing. And somehow there, in the semi-dark, it was all right again. They were hanging on to each other grimly and there was a kind of comfort in the contact.

Patricia couldn't remember whether they talked about leaving or whether the idea struck them at the same time, but he collected her coat and they were mercifully outside in the cool night air and he had her hand in his. Somewhere around the back of the hall beside a large bush he suddenly kissed her.

Patricia remembered all the class discussions of types of kisses, French kisses, whatever. She didn't know what it was they were doing, but it didn't matter that it had no name. She'd been wrong about him being polite, he wasn't in the least polite, there was no "by your leave" or "please," but Patricia made no protest.

It was quite beautiful until she began to shake. It was one thing discussing types of kisses, but nobody had warned her about the effect. She felt her knees almost giving up, and she knew that she suddenly didn't want to go on, but not to was to hurt his feelings again.

It was odd how the kissing took away Sean's awkwardness. He seemed authoritative suddenly, the way her father was with her mother. Patricia felt as if he'd taken too many leaps, while she was taking only wobbling steps.

"I think I love you," he said when they were close to home and Patricia had to resist the urge to giggle nervously. She suddenly wanted to run for her life. She had an immediate vision of them married and living in a house like the one he lived in now with sixteen children running around. She knew all the Catholic jokes that made the rounds, and they didn't seem so funny anymore.

"Do you like me?" Sean asked, pressing an arm around her shoulders.

Patricia was confused by the question and stayed stubbornly silent. Her lack of response made no difference, his grip tightened around her waist.

"Will you be my girlfriend?" he asked at the front door. Mercifully, the door opened before she had time to answer, and her father stood there. Usually at this time of night he was dozing in the armchair with his glass of scotch at his side and nothing disturbed him until her mother shook him awake to go to bed. Patricia felt like hugging him.

Sean's face fell at the sight of her father.

"Hallo, luv, did you have a good time?"

Patricia nodded, "Yes, great!" She could afford to wax enthusiastic now she'd been reprieved.

"Thank you, young man, for bringing her home on time!" Her father held out his hand in a dismissive handshake, and Sean, with a forlorn look, took the proffered hand. He nodded towards her.

"Good night, Patricia!"

"Good night, Sean, and thank you." Patricia knew he would be gone back to school by tomorrow night, and by Monday things would be back to normal again.

The pile of mending beside her mother had grown since Patricia left. Taking off her glasses, she rubbed her eyes. Right now Patricia was grateful for her half-blindness, she wasn't sure she wanted to be checked over.

Feeling a moment of tenderness for her, Patricia bent and kissed her cheek. For the first time she was thankful that neither would ask any more questions. Perhaps, after all, she was much luckier than Molly.

"I could have done some of that for you," Patricia said, indicating the pile of sheets and socks.

"Hm!" Her mother smiled up at her with that skeptical look Patricia knew so well. "There'll always be more."

"Good night, then!"

"Night, dear! There's a hot water bottle in the bed for you."

"Thanks!"

Patricia climbed the stairs to bed. Her teddy bear was still lying in the corner where she'd flung him. Patricia picked him up and brushed him off, seeing for the first time how truly worn and shabby he really was. It was probably terribly unhygienic to sleep each night with this scruffy thing, but how dear he was even now. She hugged him tight to her chest and stood in front of the mirror looking at her reflection. The hair she'd curled so carefully had somehow come unstuck, tricked out of its shape by the usual Irish damp: some parts curled while others lay straggly around her face. For the world she couldn't see what anyone would find to like about her.

She sat down on the edge of the bed and kicked off her shoes, contemplating her feet and the bump on her heel that throbbed painfully from the uncomfortable shoes and the long walk home.

Patricia remembered again how nice it had felt when Sean had put his arms around her. It was odd really how she liked him best when he wasn't there. It didn't make any kind of sense.

She undressed slowly and climbed into bed and curled herself around the hot water bottle. *She was on the field behind the house again and Sean had just tackled her to the ground; again she was trapped, exactly as she had been that first day, staring up into his eyes, and he was raining kisses on every part of her face and neck, and it was wonderful because there were no words spoken.*

Her aching heel kept sending horrible pins and needles through her foot, interrupting her half-dreams, until finally the pain began to ease and she was able to concentrate on the images that drifted in and out of her mind.

Reaching for the teddy she put him beside her again. Laying her cheek against the long-flattened and worn fabric of its body, she ran her finger over the smooth marble that was the eye.

Her last thought as she drifted off was that it was so sad, and yet somehow right, that Sean would be gone back to school the next day.

# PURVEYOR OF LOVE

I've often wondered why no word has ever been devised for a husband who cheats on his wife. Perhaps, because they could find nothing quite as splendid as "cuckold." For onomatopoeia "cuckold" cannot be beaten.

What did it matter anyway? If there had been a word to describe what Edward had done to me I would have been reluctant to use it. I was as much to blame for what had happened to our marriage as he was. Five years ago, if someone had mentioned "erogenous zone," I would have categorized it as something geological, perhaps the earthquake belt around the earth. In that I wouldn't have been so terribly wrong, but the fact is I had no interest in sex as I knew it, and who can blame him for turning elsewhere. "Stop it!" I can hear the psychiatrist saying, "You are at it again, taking the blame when it properly belongs to him."

Unfortunately, I was always conscious of Edward's lovemaking. It was nothing we ever fell into blissfully. It was something as planned as a visit to the chiropractor, the only difference being that the chiropractor could usually find the right spot and Edward never could! Edward always asked for directions but was useless at following them.

But then why did I marry him? I fell in love with him. He was a sort of poor man's Woody Allen, always stumbling, always begging to be picked up, and I was there to pick him up. Marjorie, my best friend, has had me pegged from the start. She could tell me in a hundred and one detailed ways how I invited failure, needed failure. Was she right? I have no idea. Maybe that was why I thought somebody else taking control might be a good idea. And so I let her pick out my psychiatrist and I attended faithfully for six months, nodding in agreement as he pegged me too. How could it be that I was such an open book to the rest of the world and such an enigma to myself?

The psychiatrist, as well as Marjorie, had long ago decided that what I needed most was an orgasm, and to this end I had agreed to meet with a sexual surrogate. "Orgasm," what an odd word. It sounded like a giblet that had been overcooked in an oven. That is until it happened. Then I knew it was something bordering on perfection.

At first I talked to the surrogate over the phone — comfortable, matey chats. Around the fifth call I became certain that this elusive "orgasm" was something oral that would occur courtesy of Bell Telephone. That is until my surrogate came to me through the summer haze.

The summer had been a nightmare of high temperatures: a thick vortex of heat and humidity seemed to suck at the body, day and night. I had drifted from room to room in the house, searching for a cool spot. Like a mole trying to disappear into a hole, I'd longed for the corners to close around me, protect me from the stifling air. The drapes were kept closed all day and the windows until night time. The semi-gloom also hid the fact the house was a complete mess; papers piled up, bills littering the kitchen shelves, and over everything there was an inch of dust. I felt no guilt about the disorder, I had enough other problems without worrying about all that.

Until the moment he came to the door, I hadn't considered what I'd done as something I really needed to follow up on, unless I felt like it.

I kept the screen door closed protectively, and at first he was only a bulky silhouette against the blinding light I'd been avoiding all summer. Then, as my eyes became accustomed to the brightness, I saw him for the first time.

With the prototype of Freud in mind, I rejected the figure who stood before me now. This man could be a professional baseball player, an athlete of some sort, rather powerful and square-faced with the look of someone used to winning.

"Can I come in?" His fingertips eased the door open a notch.

"Oh, I'm sorry. I am rude." I pulled the door open with a clumsy tug so that it rattled on its hinges. The noise yet another reminder of the fragility of the door's setting and the need for some good maintenance work around the place.

"Marion?"

I nodded.

"Gary. Gary Anderson."

"Yes, I gathered that."

One of the new colognes that demand to be eaten not worn, something vaguely reminiscent of ripe apples and cinnamon wafted upward as he stood close to me, grasping my hand. His hand was slightly damp against my own. The pressure of the handshake was exactly right, self-assured but not too domineering. He still held on to my hand. He looked intently at me forcing eye contact, a less than subtle reminder of the hours of telephone intimacy already established: but during those talks I'd schooled myself for a Sigmund Freud clone, or at least someone hairy, who would in no way tempt me — not this person before me. *Why, oh why had I done this? A sex therapist ... After all it wasn't me who needed counselling, it had been Edward.*

"You're pretty, much prettier than I'd imagined." He released my hand.

*Had my voice on the phone not been pretty then?* Anxiety was altering my body temperature, turning it from hibernation coolness into something unpleasant and sweating.

I followed him closely down the hall and into the living room. I had been ready to lead, but he walked as though he knew the house — no faltering in his step. I wanted to cry halt, turn him around and start again at the front door where less would be assumed and where I might have a chance to gather myself and swear that I didn't need all this, that it had been someone else's idea of what I needed.

"Yes." He looked around appraisingly. "What I'd imagined."

I refused to feel ashamed of the disorder. It was my own effort to try and do a little groping for reality. I had to remind myself that I didn't care what he'd imagined or what he was thinking now.

"Would you like a coffee?"

"Yes, thanks!"

I had hoped he would stay where he was but he followed me into the kitchen. The kettle had already been boiling for quite a while and condensation was running down the front of the cupboards. I unplugged it and pulled out a cloth to dry off the moisture.

He scrutinized the kitchen. "I like it in here," he nodded his head slightly in approval. He perched himself on the high stool beside the refrigerator.

"I'm very conscious of vibrations, there are bad vibrations in the hall."

"Vibrations?"

How easy to confuse what he was talking about. I was experiencing my own turbulence. I turned away from him. I needed time to build the wall that would protect me from his professional expertise. I was already determined to be his one failure.

He smiled and I felt immediately irritated.

"Don't you ever get feelings about houses?"

I shook my head, uncertain if my lack of positive response indicated I was a total failure.

"What is a house after all but an extension of a person? You can tell a lot about a person by their house, their car, the way they drive, the way they walk, the way they hold themselves."

*God forbid I should live in a shack and drive a Lada or a Volkswagon!* I giggled nervously to myself and spilled some of the water as my hand shook on the kettle handle.

"Careful!" He stood up as though to come over and steady me. "I said something funny?"

I shook my head. "Cream and sugar?"

"Both, thanks!"

I held up the sugar spoon in query, and he indicated just one spoonful.

"So what can you tell about me?"

"I'd have to look in your cupboards first."

I felt myself flushing. He might as well have asked to look in my pants.

"The kitchen cupboards would do for starters."

I shrugged, trying to pretend it was a normal request.

He walked around slowly and only paused for any length of time at the cupboard with the spices. He even stopped and opened one of the bottles and examined the label.

"May I look in the fridge?"

*Oh God! The fridge, that keeper of petrified food.*

"Certainly."

*The first time I'd gone to the doctor as a teenager with breasts and pubic hair and had lain naked on the examination table I'd felt exactly like I did now.*

He opened the door and inspected everything carefully, even taking out a jar of homemade salad dressing that had grown a thick head of grey hair. I was conscious suddenly of the stale smell that came from the innards of the fridge. It might have been like that for months, but I was only noticing it now. I wished he would hurry up and close the door.

"So, what's the verdict?"

"Can we sit down?"

"Certainly."

"Let's start in the living room."

"I thought you didn't like the vibes back there?"

"Precisely why we should start there."

He followed me into the living room and waited until I'd chosen my seat. Then he moved to the window.

"Do you mind if we have some light?"

I noticed his shoes for the first time. They were old shoes, highly polished, but you could see quite distinctly where the leather was cracking across the uppers. It reminded me suddenly of my father. My father could never part with a favourite pair of shoes. He would literally wear them until they were totally cracked. It had nothing to do with impecuniousness, merely comfort.

He saw where my gaze was focused and stared down at his own feet.

He came and sat down, pulling the seat closer to mine. I leaned back a little in the chair for it seemed we were far too close, I could lean over and lay a hand on his arm. I'd never liked being too close to people I didn't know.

"My father wore shoes like that." A little trickle of sweat inched down my back. I longed to get up and run.

"That is he wore his shoes until they were definitely goners."

"Tell me about your father!" He leant forward now, his elbows resting on his knees, and peered up at me. He had incredibly light blue eyes, I noticed, and they seldom swerved away — it was quite unnerving. I had much preferred the long telephone conversations.

"My father's dead."

"You already told me that."

There was an endless silence. He leant back now, perhaps hoping for distance to draw me out, but I didn't speak. He looked around the room again as though content to wait and then he stood up slowly and walked over to the shelf where all the photographs were. He squinted closely at them and picked one up. He held it out.

"This was your mother?"

I nodded.

"When was this taken?"

"About a year before she died. I was twelve then."

"And this is your father?" He pointed to another photograph.

I stirred uncomfortably in my seat. "I thought we were going to talk about my cupboards?"

He looked at me quizzically. "You want to avoid talking about him. I wonder why."

I shrugged, "I just don't think he has anything to do with this, that's all."

It was the eyes again, penetrating, very straightforward, forcing my own into avoidance.

He came over and sat down beside me again.

"All right, the cupboards: the cupboards of a sensual woman, a woman who likes food. I've seldom met a woman in love with food who wasn't also a good lover."

*Bunk!* I wanted to yell out. *This lover has shrivelled the food, aged the salad dressing.*

He lifted my hand from my lap and held it so that it was almost impossible to draw it away, even though I tried.

"That makes you uncomfortable?"

"Yes! Yes, it does."

"... fresh spices, spices that are used frequently."

*Not true, the turmeric came with the house fifteen years ago, and the paprika is a fossilized red pillar from lack of use.*

"Never mind the fridge, you have no appetite now, you probably aren't even eating properly. When marriages break up it frequently happens." He turned my hand over and traced the lines in my palm.

"A long lifeline." He drew his nail exquisitely down the centre of my palm and it was like a fine string had been plucked that resonated through labyrinths of synapses and nerves, bringing them to instant life.

I pulled the hand sharply away and stood up, then walked to the window. He followed me but stood beside me staring down at the plants.

"They need water."

It was true and I hadn't noticed. The Christmas cactus had lost its normal splendid tautness; the usual fat plump fronds were slightly wizened. Its very marcescence so reflected my inner state that I could barely stand to look at the thing.

"I've always hated Christmas cactus!" I said vehemently.

"Why?"

Again, how ridiculous it seemed to waste such spleen over this sad-looking thing.

"I don't know. I suppose I've never much liked Christmas, all that false gaiety." I touched the ends of the plant. "When I see it blooming, I'm sure they're not real flowers but paper things that someone's stuck on, a sort of temporary decoration." I walked away from my position beside him. There was a kind of energy emanating from him that frightened me.

"You keep moving away," he observed from his place at the window.

"And I shouldn't do that?"

"You're running away."

I put my hand up on the marble mantle, temporarily enjoying the coolness against my sweating palm.

"That first Christmas after she died. It was awful. We had a tree, presents, my father cooked a turkey, but it was horrible, dry, no dressing. He didn't know how to do that. I felt so sorry for him ..."

"He loved your mother a lot?"

I looked at him in surprise as he asked the question.

"No! No, it wasn't that. He just seemed so helpless."

"He didn't love your mother?"

"No, I don't think he did. Not that they ever fought, but they weren't affectionate."

"And he was with you?"

"Yes."

I sat down on the sofa, glad now that I couldn't see Gary's face, just his outline silhouetted against the window. Memories of that Christmas night were filtering into my consciousness. There was something I needed to recall, perhaps something that would be ultimately important.

Gary was a silhouette no longer. He was right beside me now, actually on his knees before me and had put his head onto my lap, deliberately vulnerable, waiting defencelessly either for my violence or tenderness.

Then I was conscious of the hand underneath my skirt caressing my thigh, the bare flesh.

"Remember," his voice was as soothing as his hand which without any effort was finding its home. I felt myself trembling uncontrollably and then as always the sweating started, but his voice was helping, repeating ever so quietly a trance-like incantation. Once I thought I heard him say, "I am not your father," but that too was hazy and dreamlike. I was losing all sense of time and place, but there was no stopping, no interruption — I was in a lovely space that invited no intruders. His voice and my body in rhythm, alone in long corridors of perfect understanding. And then a marvellous, quiet awakening.

"Very good! That was terrific. One step at a time." His hand caressed my back. "How do you feel?"

"Wonderful!" I almost tottered as I stood up, the musculature of my body was letting me down. He stood up beside me and put his arms around me. "It's all right! Next time will be better."

We talked quietly, his arm still around me and I knew that this man could delve deeply for all the things I'd kept closed for so long inside me. All the misgivings I'd had about what I was doing were gone. After all, every other bodily need was catered to by doctor, dentist, minister, grocer; why should the most important part of me be neglected for so long, uncared for?

I felt remarkably peaceful after he'd gone. I tried to remember what I had actually told him and couldn't. Nor did it matter anymore. I watered the parched plants. I even spoke soothingly to them pretending they could hear. Then I realized that I was actually hungry, hungry for the first time since Edward and I had broken up. That in itself was a small miracle.

I had a whole half-day of bliss. Later that evening I had the phone call.

"Hello, Marion Lavin?"

"Yes."

"Gary Anderson here. I believe you've been waiting to hear from me? Dr. Williams contacted me about you quite a while ago. I'm sorry there's been such a delay, but I've been away for five weeks.

"Hello, Mrs. Lavin, are you there?"

"Yes."

"We could start your therapy any time. I think it would be a good idea to meet first though, see if we can establish any rapport. Dr. Williams did make it clear to you that there must be mutual consent, didn't he?"

"Yes!"

"I think it a good idea if we perhaps meet at his office first. Would that be all right with you?

"Mrs. Lavin? Dr. Williams's office to start off with, would that be suitable? Are you there, Mrs. Lavin?

"Mrs. Lavin!

"Hello! Hello! Are you still there, Marion?"

*My therapy has begun. Dr. Williams, how could you do this to me?*

"Marion?" The voice was gentler now but still so far removed from the one I had been talking to for weeks.

Or had I been talking to anyone? Had the whole episode been part of the missed summer? Had I been hallucinating?

"Mr. Anderson ..."

"Gary, please ..."

"Mr. Anderson, I've been talking to someone on the phone for weeks who claimed to be you. He visited me today ..."

Just as simple as that and it was over. A week of talks with the police, even an artist drawing a composite picture. I rather enjoyed that. What I didn't enjoy were the kinds of questions asked. Why had I not been suspicious? Did I not find it strange that he didn't want me to meet with him first in Dr. Williams's office? Of course I hadn't; the anonymity of a disembodied voice on the phone had been exactly what I'd been looking for at the time. Something I could hang up on, stop whenever I wanted, control entirely. In fact, when I think about it now, there were things that didn't seem quite right when he had first phoned. He had made odd little grammatical errors. But then it was hardly necessary for good lovers to have perfect syntax. Even that day when he came to the house, the very disparity of my vision with the reality had made me pause and wonder, but it hadn't really mattered. He'd known far more about me than anyone before or since.

And the real Gary Anderson? Well, there was no rapport, nor was there any with the others brought in over the next six months. I finally signed off with Dr. Williams and now I spend most of my time getting on with life, but always looking for that face in the crowd.

"Pervert"! "Creep"! "Molester"! I would shout if I saw him. But then again, could I? Could I malign the first man ever to give me an orgasm? An *orgasm*.

He never did phone back. I suppose he knew when the real Gary Anderson was coming back from his holiday. I always thought it highly commendable that he didn't press for more that day. After all he must have known it was his last day. I was grateful for that and yet wistful.

If he ever is caught, how will he defend himself in court? I can hear him now. *"It was something I always wanted to get into, Judge. I didn't have the qualifications."* What were the qualifications for that kind of job anyway? I suspected the real Gary Anderson had some kind of university certificate, but he had no ability to read minds like my Gary Anderson. My Gary Anderson should be listed in the yellow pages under "Purveyor of Orgasms," or if you want to be moralistic about it — "Purveyor of Love"!

# GIRL IN BLACK

He was wearing an impeccable pin-striped suit in the newspaper photograph:

*Cramer Industries is pleased to announce
the appointment of Maurice Grodin to its
Board of Directors.*

No need of course to list his achievements, the entire country knew those. One eyebrow was slightly raised in that "I am bored" expression. The same expression he had worn at Vivienne's funeral.

It would have been no surprise to Vivienne that her father continued on his path onward and upward. Her death had not altered that, not even the way she had died. It definitely had shocked him that she had been found in a sleazy apartment block in an untidy room: altogether a messy death. I'd caught just a glimpse of his face that day she'd died and he'd been ashen grey. Whether out of sympathy for Vivienne or because of the stain on his own integrity who knows, but there had been, at least for a moment, profound shock. But Maurice Grodin had the power to arrange for almost anything to be kept secret and he had succeeded well in keeping her death a mystery.

He would stand in his Club accepting condolences. I imagined that most of that lot had known personal tragedy; they had learned not to pass judgement. While they might have perfect control over their corporate lives, they were much less fortunate privately.

I despised men like Maurice Grodin. The public was more generous. They would say, *"Poor chap! His daughter had a queer death, you know."* The queer death would remain just that to everyone, except to me.

From the first moment I saw Vivienne Grodin I knew I had to paint her. She reminded me of a raven-haired version of Augustus John's *Marquesa Casati*. She had the same fragile, haunted look.

I watched her from my window that first day as she unfolded from the carapace of her shiny black Porsche: an exotic butterfly emerging from a chrysalis, crackling against the somber, November grey city gloom. I couldn't imagine anyone like this actually living in our building with its creaking stair-cases and sagging floors. I decided she must be visiting, but then I kept seeing the car coming and going and realized that she was one of us. In fact, living in the apartment above me. I would see her get out of the car, then hear her on the stairs coming past my apartment and then the sound of her footsteps on the floor above. Almost all the clothes she wore were shiny, vivid reds, purples, royal blues, all in silk, satin or vinyl. But no matter how dramatically she framed herself, it was the body and face that were interesting.

I was startled by her appearance close up, at the unmistakable unhappi-ness reflected in her eyes. They were dark brown eyes, almost black, and her skin was a green-white tofu colour. Nothing could hide the fact that under-neath all the clothes she was bone thin. But neither that, nor the extreme con-trasts of her face, the deathly pallor, the wound scarlet lips, the heavy mascara, could alter the perception of her extreme beauty.

It became a kind of fascination for me to watch her come and go. She was a vivid slash on the landscape, an assault on the senses. So that even after she had climbed into the Porsche and roared off, a kind of fluorescent light seemed to linger where she had been. I knew it was purely imagined, or some trick my retina played, but whatever, she was still with me each day long after the disappearance of the car.

Almost every day a new man would come home with her; often I would see him leaving in the morning. The same one seldom came twice. That too seemed almost fitting.

I was determined to meet her, but the weeks went by and the days short-ened even more and no opportunity presented itself. I resented the diminish-ing light of December, not only for my painting, but because I was missing her comings and goings except as footsteps on the stairs and the occasional sound of laughter that resonated briefly and hauntingly outside in the dim hallway. She somehow represented a life that I didn't know and could only guess at, and I was greedy for her aura.

I wasn't sleeping well anymore. I seemed to balance on the edge of con-sciousness at all times, like an animal in hibernation waiting for the first sign of spring.

It was close to Christmas when one night in my semi-comatose state, I heard the screaming. At first the sound seemed to emanate from my own body, a long, thin, painful outcry that didn't force me to leap from bed but rather to open my eyes slowly, place my hand on my throat to track the reverberation, until I realized that the sound wasn't from my body but came from somewhere above where I could hear scuffling noises and the unmistakable protest that furniture makes when it is being moved violently across the floor, and then another scream.

Scrambling into my pants and not bothering about a shirt, I climbed the stairs to her apartment, two at a time. Nobody else appeared on the landing, but that wasn't unusual. I seldom saw the other residents of the building. They had built themselves successful bunkers of privacy.

I pounded on her door. "Open up or I'll call the police!" I yelled attempting to stifle my nervousness and uncertainty by this peremptory command. There was silence for a minute or two and then the door opened. The man stood there defiant in his nakedness, perhaps intending to shock. He was sweating heavily.

"What the fuck do you want?"

She appeared behind him, "It's all right, he's leaving." She had her hand clutched to the side of her face.

"Who's this asshole?" the man asked over his shoulder.

She shook her head. I stood my ground. I might have retreated if I hadn't heard a door open behind me on the landing opposite and knew that I might possibly have some support.

"Are you in trouble?" I asked.

"It's all right. He's leaving." She took a step back as though afraid that he might turn on her.

The man eyed me, then the couple who had stepped onto the landing to give further support. He looked at Vivienne and then back at me and shrugged.

"O.K! O.K! If that's what you want?"

"It's what I want," Vivienne said in a flat voice.

Without any ceremony he pushed past her and disappeared into the bedroom. She was standing with a black satin wrapper pulled tight around her, clutched with one hand, her other still up at her cheek.

"I'm sorry about all the noise," she apologized.

"Gerard Michaud, your neighbour from below." I held out my hand. It seemed an inappropriate time to be exchanging names or handshakes, or even small talk, but that's what we did until he re-appeared abruptly out of the bedroom swinging his jacket over his shoulder.

"Bitch!" he flung at her as he swept past. On the landing I heard him spit at the curious neighbour.

"Show's over!"

The couple retreated. I turned to look at them and offer a nod of silent thanks for their moral support. They closed the door reluctantly.

"Thanks again!" she held the door tight against her side, half prop, half barrier towards any idea that I might have about prolonging the meeting.

"He forced his way in ..." she said finally. "He's my ex."

I wasn't giving full attention to what she was saying. I was absorbed by the structure of her face, feeling the shape forming under my paint brush, stretching white and grey across the canvas of my imagination.

"Anyway, thank you. If there's ever anything I can do for you." It was the kind of thing people offered, and didn't expect to have to deliver.

"There is as a matter of fact. Could I ask a favour?"

She looked surprised.

"I would like to paint you."

"You're an artist?"

"Yes."

"What do you see in me?"

The question was merely rhetorical. For how would I have answered any real query? What I wanted was too elusive to name.

She was an unpredictable sitter. Some days when she said she would come she didn't show up. On those days I didn't work, even though the impact of her body was emblazoned on my sensory memory. I knew I could have closed my eyes and allowed the brush to move over the canvas and find complete truth. I wouldn't so much be painting her, as an idea: deprivation in its most intense form; not deprivation of food or money, but deprivation of love. I had the naive belief that when this painting was finished it would change the world. I felt renewed, imbued with superhuman strength when I did work, forgetting all about the botheration of diminishing light, about friends, about eating. I took my telephone off the hook and didn't answer the buzzer when it rang.

The canvas fed me, providing its own special light. Strangely, in my preoccupation with the act of creation, I for the most part forgot about my obsession with the real Vivienne and whatever pain she might be suffering.

I never let her look at the painting, I was scared of what she would see. But then again she hardly ever asked, just as she barely asked about my life, my relationships, or my family.

For a period over Christmas I didn't see her. I was close to finishing the portrait, but I felt singularly depleted, run down. Then I began to worry about
her. I decided to go and knock on her door. There was no answer. I knocked
harder and then I heard signs of stirring from inside.

She came to the door and opened it a crack. She was looking dreadful.

"Are you all right?"

She nodded, "I've been a bit sick." She opened the door wider. "What day
is it?"

"Thursday."

"Thursday?" She sounded surprised.

"Look! Perhaps I can get a doctor," I offered.

"No!" She turned and walked away from me. I followed her inside. The
apartment was sparsely furnished: there were two heavily carved huge oak
chairs of no great antiquity I suspected, perhaps theatre props, or stock from
one of those plush steak franchises that come and go in and out of bankrupt-
cy. There was a divan bed covered in black velvet, speckled with lint and dust.

By the window a rather expensive-looking round mahogany table was littered with books and magazines, not to mention half a dozen coffee mugs and
a collection of ashtrays with stubbed-out cigarettes. The apartment was airless
and stifling hot, the atmosphere perfumed with her own particular brand of
heavy sweetness that barely masked the stale cigarette smoke, and an odd
smell that reminded me of goat cheese.

She wore the black satin robe that I knew so well. It was so tightly lashed
around her that it seemed literally to be holding her together, following the
lines of her body like a second skin. Only when she turned in the light could I
see again how really sick she looked: like an ailing actress with too much kohl
around her eyes, a stark extra from some Brecht play. The intense pain in
those eyes made me flinch. Her entire body was shaking now, almost convuls-
ing.

"Could you do something for me?" she could barely get it out. She didn't
wait for an answer but went into the bedroom and came back with a purple
crocodile handbag. Her fingers fumbled at the clasp and the purse slipped
from her grasp onto the floor. Dropping to her knees, she grabbed it in desperation, and I could see the tears coming from her eyes.

She emptied its contents onto the floor. Then opening her wallet, she
pulled out a wad of money.

"Go to Rory's on Queen Street! You know it?" She looked up at me desperately.

"I think so."

"Ask for Jamie. They'll know who he is." She thrust several fifty-dollar
bills into my hand. "Give him this and he'll give you something in return."

"Look, why don't I call your family?"

"No!" She snapped immediately. "I have no family." She put her hand out and tried to snatch the bill out of my hand. "Forget it! I should have known you didn't want to be bothered."

I pulled my hand away from her so that she couldn't reach the money.

"It's not that I don't want to help ... It's ..."

"Forget it!" She put her hands over her ears and began to rock back and forth on the carpet. "I don't need the lecture."

I stood up, "Are you sure he'll be there?"

"He's always there."

She got to her feet. I was certain her entire body would dissolve in convulsive spasms. One arm grasped her other arm. The long ligatures in her neck were stretched cords, holding desperately to some final control of the jawline. "I'll give him a call and tell him you're coming."

I wasn't naive — I understood what I was about to do. Nor was I squeamish or even scared, but a voice inside me shrieked that it was a lousy idea. I should call someone, a doctor, an ambulance, any number of other things, but I was terrified of losing her. Not that it had anything to do with the finishing of the painting, it hadn't. But to reform her would nullify what I had painted, would turn it into a lie. In retrospect, of course, I know I was a little mad; in fact, I've been a little mad since the first minute I set eyes on her.

I did as she asked and bought some groceries for her too. I was pretty sure her fridge would be bare.

She practically fell on me when I got back and disappeared greedily with the package. I busied myself putting the groceries away and chucked out whatever remnants of decaying food I found on her shelves. There was indeed a plate of goat cheese with an angora wrap of fungus sitting on the counter top. The smell in the kitchen was intense and rather awful. I forced a window open, almost breaking an arm in the process, and put my face close to the merciful February coolness, allowing it to sting my face and purge the stench of the apartment from my nostrils.

Unpacking the bread I'd bought, I made her a sandwich with some meat and poured milk into a glass. She was gone for some time and I could hear the sound of the shower going.

She finally appeared, the black robe gone and in its place a bright-yellow track suit. She had her head wrapped up in a towel. The shaking had all but disappeared, only a tiny tremor in the hand betrayed her previous suffering.

"What's this?"

"I bought you a few groceries."

She smiled. "You'd make a good wife, Gerard."

I noticed there was no sign of shame, no remorse. She didn't expect anything of herself and she didn't care what others thought of her either.

I decided to jump in with both feet.

"You know what you're doing to yourself?" I hated the sound of my own voice. I tried to master a non-recriminatory tone, but it was there.

"I told you, no lectures!" She stood up abruptly and stood staring sightlessly out of the window.

"There's no one out there who gives a shit anyway. Right?"

She turned and stared at me, a half smile on her lips. I knew in that instant she recognized that in a sense I was using her too.

"That's O.K., it's mutual. There's no one out there I give a shit about either!" The drug had now obviously taken its full effect and she was operating once again on all motors.

"No father or mother?"

"You mean Grodin Enterprises?" She gave a contemptuous snort. "My father killed my mother with indifference years ago, I'm just a living reminder." She placed a palm flat against the windowpane and studied her spread fingers.

"You see, the trick is to get the money to me fast enough, then there doesn't have to be any contact. His secretary always handles that. It's so terribly efficient. The rest of the world knows just how generous he is to his only daughter."

She turned and her eyes had the familiar blank look. There was barely any passion even in her anger. To have argued with her assessment of the relationship with her father would have been useless. I was perfectly sure that every word she spoke was true anyway.

She came to the table and sat down again. Lifting the sandwich, she stared at it for a moment or two with distaste. She made no effort to take a bite.

She set the sandwich down untouched. "I suppose I still love him." A wry smile appeared on her lips. "A lot of use that is." She flicked at the bread with a fingernail.

"Anyway, there's always lots of money. Whatever I want ... when I want ... tons of money."

"Why do you live here?"

"Here?" She looked around. "Why not, what's wrong with here?"

"If you've lots of money, why did you choose these apartments?"

I realized that she really didn't understand my question. She might simply have run out of gas one day and found herself in front of the apartment. She wouldn't have noticed the taps that constantly dripped, the ancient bathtub, the doll-sized kitchen sink, the inadequate cupboards, the cockroaches.

Then I knew suddenly that, with or without the cocaine, she had no desire to mesh with what she saw around her, and I knew too, at that moment, that there was nothing to be done for her. She would deteriorate with drugs long before the benefits of any kind of therapy could take effect. She would go from degradation to degradation.

She came once or twice more to sit for the portrait, but I knew that I didn't need her there. I had reached the point where I could paint with or without her, so vividly did I know what I wanted on that canvas. She was vaguely puzzled that I wasn't more demanding of her, but she was so frequently lost in her own world I had a feeling that time had no meaning for her anymore.

Then she stopped coming altogether and, like before, I didn't see her for several days. I knew I should check on her but I was working feverishly now trying to block everything else out. Then one evening I heard the tapping on the floor. I ignored it at first until it became more persistent, and then I decided to go up and check.

The door was open. The room was a disaster, a trail of clothes littered the divan. On the mahogany table there was an aluminum-foil dish half full of stale Chinese food, around it a scattering of little packages: plum sauce, soya sauce, all of them unopened. A bunch of very dead flowers, still wrapped in clear plastic, lay beside the food.

I found her in the bedroom. I thought for one amazed moment that my canvas lay face up on the floor. Her body paralleled almost exactly the figure I had painted. The black robe lay open, displaying her limbs stark white against the black. Her lips were swollen and cracked and her eyes gazed sightlessly into space. At first I thought she was dead, but I lifted her onto the bed and realized that she still had a pulse. I got some water from the kitchen. It came ochre and rusty from the tap as it always did when it hadn't been run for several days.

Propping her up, I fed her the water.

"Please Gerard! ... Please give me some stuff!"

Right then and there of course I could have called the hospital or her father, but I decided against it. Under her instructions I gave her what she asked for. I knew perfectly well she was done for and I was only hastening things for her, but it didn't stop me. They put animals down when they're suffering, I rationalized. What difference a human being. But of course this was all nonsense; I was only helping her do what she had done a hundred times before.

There was no miraculous recovery the way there had been the last time. I left her lying on the bed, a dreadful stillness over her, and I went back downstairs and finished the painting. Then I slept a long, deep sleep, completely dreamless.

Waking next morning was horrifying; when the realization of what I had done, or failed to do came, it jolted me back to life. Barely taking time to dress I flung myself out of the apartment, taking the stairs two at a time. Her door was unlocked as I'd left it and she was lying exactly as I'd left her the night before. Her face frozen now into a total and final stillness. I had never seen anyone dead before, heard only the platitudes about how lovely people looked in death. There was nothing in her face to indicate that there had been any last-minute reprieve from sadness, she had lived unhappy and died unhappy.

I knew that painting would make my name, but I couldn't part with it, nor could I show it to anyone. It seemed I fought a terrifying battle between life and death that year after she had gone. I was obsessed with the painting, I couldn't stop looking at it and thinking about what I'd done. I had in effect played God. I had made a decision that only God should make about another human soul and there was no use rationalizing it away by saying that someone else would have given her the last, fatal "fix." There had been no one else there.

I finally stored the portrait away in my locker room in the apartment and buried myself in new work. My paintings were selling at a respectable rate, and then I was approached by one of the better galleries to put on an exhibition the following year. Attention from them was a kind of passport in the art world. I knew this but I was strangely unmoved by the knowledge. I knew too that if they saw the painting of Vivienne it would become the focal point of the exhibition. I kept it tucked away and worked frantically, hoping to produce so much work that it wouldn't be necessary to bring out the painting. I would somehow exonerate what I had done by producing work that was even better. And though my style had matured and my technique improved enormously, nothing I managed to finish had one-tenth the power of that single painting.

Elspeth Franz from the gallery came and looked and enthused over what she saw and I realized her flattery wasn't feigned, but in the end I knew I had to produce Vivienne.

She said nothing for at least five minutes after I showed it to her. She stared at it, her eyes wide, as I knew a million eyes would stare at it from now on, and suddenly I wanted to rush and cover it, to protect Vivienne. After all, what did it matter what message I thought I could transmit. What mattered was that it was Vivienne exposed to raw bone.

"This is a most extraordinary work, Gerard," she said, and I knew there was no protection for Vivienne any longer. I had picked her bones.

"You must have been very much in love with her."

When she said that, I felt icy cold. I wanted to protest, make a thousand denials.

"The painting isn't for sale." Until I had actually said it I hadn't realized I had no intention of letting the painting go anywhere.

"You mean someone has already bought it?"

"It's just not for sale."

"But we must exhibit it."

"If you think it's really necessary.

"It's essential." I could see the gleam in her eye and I was already sorry I had agreed.

❄

I folded the newspaper away with the announcement about Maurice Grodin. I promised myself that Vivienne at least would remain anonymous. She would be ineffectually titled *Girl in Black, Study in Black,* something totally innocuous, and when people asked, I would say, "Just someone I knew."

When it came time for the opening of my show I knew I couldn't go. Elspeth Franz was annoyed with me, but not so annoyed that she made any great commotion. I suspected that an elusive artist might help sell the paintings more than one who hovered, and I was probably right.

She phoned me the following morning, ecstatic about the show. The newspapers were going to do an article and wanted to know all about the *Girl in Black.* She bubbled on; not the least of her enthusiasm was of course caused by the fact that ten of the paintings had been sold. A very good start to any exhibition. She had "hold" on several others and was already talking about the next show.

"The best news of all, the Art Gallery is interested in having the *Girl in Black* for its permanent collection."

"No! It's not for sale."

"Listen, Gerard, I know what you said, but I also have the feeling that it's you who won't give up the painting. It's suicide not to accept an offer like this. It's the beginning for you. It's what most artists would die for ... a most incredible opportunity."

"No!"

There was silence at the other end of the line.

"Is there any use in my coming over?"

"None whatsoever."

I couldn't have foreseen the outcome of my decision, I told myself a hundred times in the weeks to come, but it was little comfort. Word got around very quickly, perhaps spread by Elspeth, that I had turned down the Gallery's offer. Overnight I was hot property, and yet all I could feel was incredible distaste for the entire farce.

The show was over and the *Girl in Black* was now in my apartment. It seemed pointless to stow it away in my locker, it would be like trying to contain the spirit of a restless ghost. Now I perceived different things in the portrait, things I'd never seen before. There were nights when I woke up sure that I heard that light tapping on the floor above. I would sit up in bed, and often the light from the window would shine on the portrait, and where Vivienne's eyes were there were only hollows, and I would start to shake. I had the feeling she was actually there in the room with me and wanted something from me, something I was unable to give.

Weeks later, when I felt that I was headed for some kind of breakdown, I finally phoned Elspeth at the Gallery.

"I've changed my mind, Elspeth. I'm going to let the portrait go."

"Smart move," she said quickly with pleasure in her voice.

I wanted to vehemently protest at her form of expression because it implied that what I'd done had somehow been planned. I felt quite ill, sure that this was how the others would see it too, but I was too weak at this point to truly care.

Once the portrait had gone to the Gallery, things changed perceptibly. For a while I felt tremendously depressed, but at least the waking up in the night had stopped, and then strangely my strength began to return, little by little. My body for the first time in a year felt uninhabited. Like a slow moving cloud the remorse began to dissipate. I felt I was coming back to life again after a long illness, but I wasn't completely better for it was a long time before I could bring myself to go to the Gallery and see where the portrait had been hung. I had to steel myself when that day finally arrived; all the old trepidation and dread returned full force.

The Gallery had given her a marvellous space, a kind of angled corner that was perfect for light and maximum effect. A group of schoolchildren with their teacher were noisily making the rounds, and just as I made my way to Vivienne, two of the rowdier ones arrived there also.

"Heh! Look at this neat one!" the girl yelled to the group behind her and more of them moved to stare at the portrait.

"Phew!" somebody whistled, letting out an intake of air. "She looks so sad."

"I like this one best," someone else behind her commented.

"So do I," someone else said.

The teacher arrived and stood behind the group contemplating the painting.

"You kinda want to know more about her," said a girl with spiked hair.

I didn't wait to hear any more. Like a blind man I made for the front door, through the maze of curves and turns that could have had me forever running in circles.

A kind of thumping pulse somewhere in my ear seemed to mask another sound like a voice calling. Barely conscious of the curious looks from the passive, meandering crowd in the Gallery, I broke into a slight trot until I was suddenly there, by the front door.

The full force of daylight made me momentarily shade my eyes; the din of traffic drowned out the other sounds from inside my head. I could feel the breath finally freeing itself from my body, issuing not from its usual high spot in my chest, but coming from somewhere deep in my lungs.

# DRESSAGE

The marzipan fruit sits in a rather horrible miniature orange basket waiting on my desk. There isn't a note, but I know it's from Geraldine McEwan who teaches history to the Grade Sevens and Eights. I suppose the present is for work well done, papers quickly typed and copied, but it might just as well be for anything.

I've come to expect gifts from Geraldine, come to dread them in fact, because although there's never a note, there's always Geraldine at the end of the day. Heavy with musky perfume she will sidle into my office to be grateful about something, some small task performed no more for her than for the other teachers; sitting across the desk from me as though there was something she was waiting for, or something she had to relate.

The marzipan banana looks like a fancy eraser and feels like an emery board. It might as well be either, for I hate the over-sweet gritty density of marzipan. It's interesting that Geraldine has managed to select for a gift the one thing I can't eat.

I'm perfectly sure that Geraldine has been told my story by Sybil. Some days I imagine everyone at Berenger knows my story.

I hated Berenger when I was a pupil fifteen years ago. I hate it even more now that I'm beholden to it and to Sybil. I hated the pettiness of the teachers and the narrowness of their vision. It seems to have changed only marginally. It was then, and still is, a school for rich girls. There are only a few scholarship girls; they were looked on as charity cases then, and still are, the only difference being that now, people cloak their prejudice better.

In fact I was the school's only proper charity case. I was the daughter of the school cook and to be doubly pitied because I had epilepsy.

It was never a secret why Sybil let me enrol: she enjoyed having a visible example of her *largesse* around, it made her a better person. I remember more than once coming to on the floor of a classroom with Sybil bending over me, having performed the ritual technique for making sure I didn't swallow my tongue. After these bouts Sybil seemed to glow with pride, enlarged somehow by her own charity and goodness. I was useful in many ways to Sybil. Besides giving her a humanitarian reputation, I more than paid my keep by cleaning out the stables and grooming the horses.

The Berenger estate and horses had been left to the City in the 1890s along with a sizable amount of money to run the establishment as a girls' school. The horses were to be used for training the girls to ride.

Old Hibbert Berenger's only daughter had been mad about horses, but she had died young of some wasting disease that had never been named.

When my mother first became cook, the school was still a boarding school. Rising costs had forced the City to turn it into a day school in 1965.

I'd been born at Berenger and we'd moved to the gatehouse when I'd turned five. The only part of my childhood with truly happy memories is the part that included riding. There was nothing in the world I loved as much as horses and in particular one horse, Brutus. It was only with him that I felt there were certain truths.

I was very good at riding, and in keeping with the school policy that there should always be someone representing them at horse shows and jumping competitions, I was their star performer.

My epilepsy had been a severe handicap in my everyday life; for some reason it had never been a problem when I was around horses. I'd represented the school with some distinction and many of the trophies in the library had been won by me.

Most of my schoolmates in those days, as well as the teachers, had known how to deal with my fits, but as it became increasingly clear that they seldom happened when I was around horses, I was often forgiven for spending far too much time in the stables.

Nowadays medication almost totally controls the condition, but it's still something that many employers don't want to deal with. The Human Rights Commission is supposed to be there to look after things like that, but I knew in my heart that most employers could easily find some reason why I wouldn't fit into their firm. That was one of my reasons for staying on at Berenger. The other was that Sybil had always made me feel I owed her something. Whether or not it was my entire life, I'd never decided, but Sybil had a way of making it plain that I was somehow necessary to her.

I take lunch with Sybil every day, both of us closed off from the staff room by a heavy carved oak door that decisively isolates us from the noise at recess and the eddies of girls milling around the corridors, sorting themselves into classrooms like so many selectively trapped fish.

It feels as though I have been taking lunch with Sybil forever, but I suppose it's true that anything not enjoyed takes on an eternal quality. I bring my sandwiches to Sybil's office and she brings her orange, her yogurt and figs. At the end of lunch she attacks the orange with her small, sharp, even teeth, the juice squirting onto her upper lip and colouring the light line of moustache that frames her mouth. There's barely a sound, just the hand pumping the orange and her mouth closed on the pitted skin. She closes her eyes periodically while she performs the ritual, and it's impossible for her to disguise a certain amount of ecstasy. Leaning back replete, she pushes back her swivel chair and settles her short legs on the desk so that she's reclining at a perilous angle from the floor and waits for my daily report.

I think of Sybil as a girl-guide leader-type. She's brisk and compact in form, tending to be pear-shaped and heavy in the leg, a fact that she keeps well hidden beneath the British academic gown she wears all day long.

I've seldom heard her raise her voice. She has no need to. There is an air of authority about her, so that when she goes to a classroom she commands total attention from the youngsters. There's also a subtle air of righteousness surrounding her. The moral code is carried square upon her shoulders but never elucidated in so many words.

When Sybil appears in the corridors, the silence rolls and catches into an absolute wave of stillness and fear. It's palpable and astonishing to witness. I understand why it happens because I have been afraid of Sybil since the first day I met her.

My function more than anything else is as a sort of liaison between Sybil, the staffroom and the classrooms — an "informer." On bad days I think of myself as a criminal variety of "stoolie." The secretarial details are inconsequential — the typing of exam papers, the taking of phone calls from irate parents, the bookkeeping all get done. The "informer" part of my job rates the highest: it is the *pay-off* for Sybil's charity.

Sybil gives a little "humph" of contentment as she watches the clumps of girls beginning to gather in the playing field outside the window. Her eyes skitter occasionally towards me and I know she's waiting. Sybil is discreet. She knows how to hold her silence until the room fills with expectation and unspoken thoughts.

Today, I talk about Geraldine's gift of marzipan. I'm sure I manage to keep things neutral but Sybil turns to look at me, a slightly opaque quality in her eye, so that she might be listening intently or thinking about something else altogether.

I change the subject, I talk about the staff, I talk about the girls, I talk about the parents, aware all the time that like a specimen pressed between glass, my true essence is emerging and being examined minutely. I amaze Sybil, I amaze myself with the clarity and merciless quality of that talk. I have diverted all my annoyance about Geraldine, turned it in different directions — lashed out. There is no charity in me and my mouth is sour by the time I'm done.

On an occasional day, Sybil will talk instead, mostly about her weekend adventures with a "chum." I smile at the absurdity of a fifty-year-old spinster having a "chum." It's a very foreign term to me and makes the telling even more innocent and girlish, in sharp contrast to my own monologues which seem rife with gossip and a kind of pettiness which I despise in other people.

There was a suitor in Sybil's life once. He came to the school a few years previously on a visit from England. He was an Oxford don she'd known for some years. He was unremarkable in looks: rather solid and respectable in appearance, more like a seller of mutual funds. He wore an impeccable grey pinstripe suit and navy tie.

He'd proposed to her, she admitted, and she'd toyed with the idea of accepting. The proposal had been restated in written form some months later. She kept the letter in the top right-hand drawer of her desk and had actually shown it to me once. It had seemed civil, very down-to-earth, not a trace of a romantic thought, but more a kind of "arrangement"-type proposal, where it sounded as though she might be quite useful filling a gap left vacant by a wife who had made an untimely exit from life. The sentiments seemed no less utilitarian than Sybil's own consideration of their possible "arrangement," for she talked about nothing else but what it would be like to live in England again and nothing whatsoever about what it would be like to share his bed.

I'd seen the letter often as I'd been sent to Sybil's drawer for one thing or another. Why she kept it I'd no idea. Perhaps as a reminder of what her fate might have been. A chocolate had melted on one corner and there was a coffee stain where a drip had leaked into the drawer.

Sybil doesn't pry into my life, but then I suppose she doesn't have to because she has known from the beginning all about the basic facts: my father's alcoholism, my loneliness since my mother's death, and the fact that there are days when I feel utterly useless.

There's no more competitive riding, that's a privilege of the rich. I accept that and don't brood anymore. The fact is I still have the horses and at night I can even still ride. That's a pleasure that nobody has taken away.

I know none of it touches her. To her, I am still a failure who must be rescued. She assumes, like all academics, that secretarial work for the female sex is some kind of waiting station for the right man to come along. When, in reality, for me at least, it's a waiting station for an idea that might spark me back to life again.

I have always found people difficult to understand. With horses everything is symmetry. There's nothing more wonderful than dressage: the feeling of control, the tremor of the horse beneath you, not knowing whether it is his tension or yours, knowing it doesn't matter, for you are one, in perfect harmony of purpose. Together you own the world. There is nothing to compare with that.

Because of the low rent of the gate lodge, because of my father, because of the horses, the job suits me as well as any would. I could almost be happy if it weren't for the lunches, if it weren't for having to witness Sybil at work dealing with the world around her.

Geraldine's pity I'll ignore, for I suppose that's what brings her to my office over and over again. It won't overwhelm me because I know that at least I'm better at my job than Geraldine is at hers.

She's a dreadful teacher, always flushed pink and flustered. Although she's probably only in her late thirties, she appears to be suffering from premature change of life — beads of perspiration seem to have made their permanent home on her top lip. She wears hopelessly feminine blouses, often with pierrot frills at the neck, all of which manage to add to her air of not quite being able to cope. It isn't uncommon to pass her classroom and see some of the youngsters standing on their chairs or throwing paper darts at one another.

Sybil seems to ignore Geraldine's inability to teach, which is surprising because she is a stickler for quality in everything. When I mention the noise from Geraldine's classroom, Sybil changes the subject. When I make gentle fun of the gifts she brings me, Sybil frowns and wants to inspect the lunch register and make sure that everything is up-to-date.

Then there are the days when I have to witness Sybil's handling of the girls. I know from personal experience what this feels like and have had it reconfirmed by the pupils who lie around from time to time on the couch in my office, waiting for aspirins to kill their aches and pains. They validate what I remember about those awful interviews with her in the past.

Now I'm commanded to bring my notebook and take a seat for her performances. For what purpose I'm not sure, but I do as I'm told and take my seat, wondering whether I should use the pad and, like some movie continuity girl, write down each move.

Sybil stands solemnly in front of her desk, framed by the enormous, imposing portrait of Harriet Elizabeth Bennet, the previous principal. I know her only by reputation, but she is now depicted for posterity in depressing Rembrandt brown tones and hangs on the wall behind Sybil's desk.

In what seems like a parody of H.E.B., as she has long been known by Berenger's alumni, she stands hands clasped in front of her and lips grim, waiting for the knock on the door. The transgressor comes in timidly and Sybil gazes at her with a sad expression, keeping her eyes fixed on her for what seems like an eternity. The girl will brave the look for perhaps five seconds and then drop her eyes. Sybil continues to stare, not moving a muscle and looking for all the world as though she has just lost her last remaining relative. The girl will eventually look up, to confirm, if for no other reason, that Sybil is still looking sad. The girl then bites her lips, and silently the beginning of a tear oozes out of the corner of her eye. Sybil shakes her head ever so slightly and, with an infinitesimally small gasp and a quiver of the bottom lip, she shakes her head and then moves one hand out in a tiny helpless gesture, only to be instantly immobilized again by the enormity of the child's crime. The youngster's tears come fast and furious now and only then does Sybil talk.

*"How you have disappointed me. I relied on you above all the other girls in the class and you have let me down."* The lines have changed very little over the years.

Floods of tears now; and then, with a visible effort, Sybil pulls herself together and wipes away her own imaginary tears. Pulling a handkerchief from beneath her gown, she gives it to the crying youngster. It is a hanky stained with the tears of a thousand children.

When the door finally closes on the unhappy child, she is nothing short of triumphant. I've been witness to her power again, just as I'm witness every day as I talk and talk and she continues to suck her orange, to the fact that like the orange I am dehydrating slowly, being literally wrung out. I only know that H.E.B.'s mythical rages and violent hand-canings must have been infinitely more bearable than Sybil's form of despotism.

By the beginning of June all thoughts are focused on exams; we are busy, so busy in fact that I can avoid some of the dreaded lunches with Sybil. Geraldine seems to have retreated, the presents are fewer now. I find myself softening towards her. Where once I could imagine myself joining in the collective action, leaping on chairs with her Eighth Grade class, I now pity her.

The grounds around the school are growing quite lush from the alternating downpours of rain and brilliant sunshine. The lilacs, late this year, are bushy and heavy with bloom and smell; the stones have the heavy scent of cemeteries in spring; the musky smell drifts through open windows and forces thoughts far away from the smell of chalk and erasers, to the stables where everything makes sense, where everything is simple, peaceful, and above all mutual.

Tonight the children straggle off down the long driveway past my little lodge, unaware and uncaring about whatever private tragedy plays out inside that little house. My father won't notice them, never does, as he sleeps away the day in his alcoholic stupor. The children's energy seems depleted by the unseasonable warmth of the day; nevertheless, they still manage to lazily shout, and banter with one another. The sound of their young, high-pitched voices drifts harmlessly in my window.

Later, after they have long gone, the silence is magic. As though suddenly delivered from a plague of gnats, the ears take time to readjust to relative peace. With the heat in the school turned off, even the beasts that reside inside the radiators have withdrawn and gone into hibernation. The very walls seem to exude a perfume of aged oak not unlike the smell of a sun-warmed church. The only sound is the tip-tapping of my fingers on the word processor. My eyes squint before I realize that it's getting really late and the light has faded fast and that the heat of the day has collectively piled up and rolled through my window, so that my blouse sticks to my body.

Collecting the exam papers, I stack them neatly. Sybil's letters I gather up. Usually she comes to sign them at the end of the day, but this time she has forgotten. I open my door and make a foray out into the dimness of the corridor, enjoying the momentary coolness of the passageway that has escaped the afternoon sun and has stayed at morning temperature. I plunge on towards Sybil's office, ignoring her closed door, positive that she has gone. I tap lightly but then immediately plough in, the letters in one hand, flicking on the light with the other, realizing before anything else that the air is heavy and warm just as it has been in my office — but there is something else, the sweet, heavy smell of Geraldine. There is a quick scuffling sound and a gasp of surprise. Rising from Sybil's knee is Geraldine. Her pierrot blouse unbuttoned to well below her breast, her flossy blonde hair gone madly punk, her face crimson.

I advance eyes downcast and drop the letters on Sybil's desk and turn, aware that Geraldine's voice is fluttering on, explaining.

"I'm sorry, I thought you'd gone." I mumble.

"We were going over some papers," Sybil, barely in command, explains.

Back in my office I sit in the darkness, hearing the wailing of distant fire-engines, and the muted hum of the world going on outside the walls of Berenger.

So much is explained now, of course: her overlooking Geraldine's problem with discipline; the "chum" who never did have a name; Geraldine's predilection for sitting in my office, close to her lover; the gifts, nothing to do with feeling sorry for me, but more to do with buying goodwill.

There is a knock on the door. It's the caretaker, George.

"Sorry to disturb you. I thought I saw you in the corridor. Working late? Or are you not feeling well?"

"I'm feeling fine."

I am actually feeling fine. The longing to be elsewhere is less oppressive. I could sit on indefinitely behind the large oak desk, admiring the neat pile of work just completed.

"Yes. It's the first hot one," George says, hating the darkened room and longing for familiar ground, yet not daring to turn on the light. George can always be relied upon to talk weather. Tonight I am content to let him talk. I know he is perplexed by my stillness. George is used to being hustled on and has geared himself to withstand signs of impatience.

"Hot weather does funny things to people," he says sagely, obviously unwilling to move until he has certified that I'm not about to do something strange.

"A neighbour last year sat out on the balcony next door without a stitch on. Couldn't have that, of course. They took her away eventually."

"Away?"

"To the loony bin. She was an odd one anyway."

He turns back to the door, "I'll let you get on with it then."

Later, I walk slowly down the corridor towards the assembly hall. Switching the lights on, I stand at the door feeling very, very tiny. I'm not used to being in that particular room without swarms of children. Every move I make echoes queerly in the emptiness. I'd never counted the portraits on the wall, but I knew there had been ten previous principals up to, and not including, Sybil.

I stop at the first one, Ellen Germaine McCleod, 1893-1914. There is no question Ellen Germaine would have been a severe disciplinarian. She has a thin mouth, and one senses that the portrait painter has been kind and painted out any blemishes or warts and probably the more definite wrinkles that could only further incriminate her type.

I move down the line slowly, aware, as I've never been before, of the depth of the lives behind the oil and canvas, and somehow, like the carved oak that only seems to convey its essence on a day like this, the very pores in my body are expanding to take in things seen and unseen, voices heard and unheard: the clip of a thousand feet tramping in to roll call, yet not one tread the same. Just as the faces on the wall hide a million nuances, so does the collective march to the ritual of assembly and prayers disguise a few odd and rebellious hearts, out of syncopation with the world around them.

I think lazily and with less dread than usual about going back to the gatehouse and the nightly ritual search for father's hidden whisky bottles.

The image of George's neighbour sitting on her porch stark naked comes to my mind, only it isn't his neighbour anymore but a vision of Sybil. Just as quickly the mind-picture of her breaks up in hundreds of tiny glistening shards. As a child I remember getting a gift once of a kaleidoscope, where with a simple twist of the wrist what seemed like an immutable pattern could, in a flash, be altered. How I'd been fascinated by the eternity of dramatic permutations that only a tiny motion could produce — the randomness of that movement of the wrist and the resulting extraordinary pattern.

# MORIARITY AND THE AUNTS

"He's a wee puke," Billy announced after Moriarity, the new curate from St. Clement's, had left on Thursday night.

"He's only around here because of her doing her routine on him," Billy jabbed a finger towards Peggy. Peg stuck her tongue out at him and went on filing her nails.

Mother gathered up the tea things with a sigh. "I wish to God he'd phone before he comes, then we could tell him we're out."

"How can you tell him yer out when yer in?" Billy scoffed.

"You know what I mean." She heaved the tray up and stood at the door, waiting for one of us to open it for her. Nobody moved. Moriarity had that effect on all of us. A kind of rigor mortis set in after he'd left each week.

"Are youse all lame?" Mother demanded from her position at the door.

Too bad Moriarity was such a puny thing for starters or you could have been cruel to him right away. He was all knobbly wrists that stuck out from a wee, shrunken black suit with worn lapels and missing buttons. His nose looked as though it had been rubbed in sandpaper and he had a voice that oozed out of him in damp coils.

It was a bit of a novelty at first having a Belfast curate with a thick Dublin accent, but there was nothing musical about his tones; instead, he sounded like a record that had stuck.

"What a droner," Meggie Dinsmore said that first Sunday outside the church.

"There's more life in a rotten egg," her husband Fred added.

You could see by the gleam in Mother's eye that Moriarity was going to be rescued from stuff like this. When he came out to offer his limp hand to the regulars at the service, she invited him around for tea.

Ten weeks later, as though that invitation had been "writ in stone," Moriarity was still coming. Only the visits weren't limited to Sundays. He'd turn up other nights, always when you least expected him, and there he'd be on the doorstep with some wee useless knick-knack wrapped in a bit of recycled paper. He would give the present to Mother before the teapot appeared, and Mother would unwrap it like she expected to find an emerald from the Taj Mahal.

Adam Moriarity didn't improve on closer inspection. His hands were pale and his nails were long and dun coloured, the kind of nails you might expect to see on a corpse. He had the horrible shrinking demeanour of someone who demanded to be punished or, at least, insulted.

It didn't take any genius to work out why he came. First of all it had been a rescue mission directed at Father who never went to church, but when he turned up, Father would suddenly remember an appointment with the garden shears and the hedge.

Moriarity then turned his attention to Peggy, also a frequent absentee from church. She mistook his attention for something sexual and simpered like an eejit as though Warren Beatty was working on her.

I never could understand Peggy. It didn't matter whether it was the milkman or some hunk, she was a "gonner" for any attention at all.

Mother, in her own way, was as bad as Peggy. With anyone from the church she acted as though she were on probation for heaven! Her not so mild swearing, normal in her everyday conversation, turned into surprising, but harmless enough, "drats" and "darns" and "good griefs." It was a mother no longer recognizable, one gone genteel overnight.

A family "gab" over the problem of Moriarity was long overdue, but finally it was the aunts arriving one night while he was there that solved our problem. Moriarity was disturbed to find Father missing yet again, but little did he know that the aunts were about to provide him with far better rehabilitation material.

Sybil and Bernice were related on Dad's side of the family, the one Mother always referred to as "the drunken bunch." Sybil had left her husband years before, taking her cheque book and shared bank account with her. Bernice's long suffering husband, Ernie, had died in a car accident around the time that Sybil had run away. Now the two of them were like Mutt and Jeff, inseparable.

They never arrived quietly when they came to call. They were always "well oiled," my mother's euphemism for drunk, and there was a great deal of hilarity as they exploded into our otherwise quiet household.

When the doorbell rang that evening, Mother excused herself and went out to the hall. I tailed along, hoping it would be some emergency that would take us all away from the house, and Moriarity.

"Dear God! It's them." Mother raised her eyes heavenward and pounded her forehead. No good dimming lights, playing dead. The sound of the aunts' giggles carried through the partition. Having seen our shadows, they were already rapping on the smoked glass demanding entry.

They tumbled into the hallway like two exotic wilted birds, with creased dresses and high heels that could have stabbed a fallen body to death in one trample.

"Jesus, what kept you?" Sybil complained.

"Hello, darling!" Bernice enfolded me in her arms. She smelt of stale perfume and gin, an oddly sweet combination.

"Ssh!" Mother cautioned. "The curate's here."

Bernice giggled and opened the drawing-room door and was in before Mother could turn her in another direction. Moriarity looked relieved at the interruption. His conversation with Peggy had obviously been flagging.

After the flurry of introductions, everyone arranged themselves around the room. Sybil stuck a Balkan Sobranie into an enormously long ebony-and-gold cigarette holder and, staring at the tip with crossed eyes, lit it. She blew out a cloud of smoke and challenged Moriarity with a look from across the room.

Tight and tense, Mother stood poised at the door.

"Mor-ee-ar-i-tee! Don't you sound more like a wee Fenian than a Protestant," Sybil said playfully.

"No! No!" He cleared his throat noisily and gave emphasis to the second no. "Deceptive, deceptive, but always a Protestant."

"Sure there's no need to apologize, it happens to the best," Sybil said mischievously.

"A wee drop of lemonade, Sybil?" Mother asked from her stance by the door.

"Lemonade? For God's sake! A gin ...What's happened to the gin?"

Mother winced perceptibly. Of course the lemonade would have been gin, but Sybil had no intention of playing games.

"Right! Right! I wouldn't have thought of that." Mother's voice was faint and insincere.

"The same for you, Bernice?"

"Make it a double!" Bernice seemed to be further gone than Sybil. She never wore her glasses when she'd been drinking and she had terrible trouble focusing her eyes. Right now she was squinting at Moriarity.

"Reverend Moriarity ..." Mother paused at the door. "Could I maybe get you a wee sherry?"

"That would go down nicely, Mrs. Montgomery."

"Sure you'll be gettin' on horseback and ridin' straight to hell next," Sybil said giggling.

"Even Reverend Ferguson takes a wee drop from time to time," Moriarity said piously.

"I'll bet he does." Sybil blew out another cloud of smoke. Smoking was always something I'd thought Sybil did purely for effect. She seemed far more interested in the exhalation than the inhalation as she watched the coils of smoke rise to the ceiling. Bernice, on the other hand, sucked on her cigarette as though it was her lifeblood.

"Now what were we all talking about?" Sybil asked once Mother had returned with everyone's drink.

"Before you girls arrived, I was just telling Reverend Moriarity about how we had some clergy in our family," Mother said.

It was a foolish opening to give Sybil.

"Good old Basil Porter ..." she said with fervour. "... God, wasn't he the one. They hanged him after the Battle of Ballynahinch for supporting the Republicans. Now that's what I call guts."

Despite what she might think about Moriarity, Mother was mortified to be let down in this way.

"Now Sybil, you know that's just a rumour."

"Rumour be damned! Isn't it in the records?"

Bernice had started to laugh, but it wasn't quite clear what she was laughing at. She had already downed most of the double gin and seemed to be in her own little world.

"Now how do you feel about the good old Republican cause?" Sybil directed at Moriarity.

"Ah, to be sure, there's been wrongs on both sides," Moriarity said nervously, almost draining his glass of sherry. "I tend to be liberal myself seein' as how my father was a Cat'olic," he pronounced carefully, making sure that none of us could possibly miss this admission. "Lapsed mind, but Cat'olic none the less." The news of our family renegade seemed to have given him courage to seek common ground with the family. Everyone stared at him.

"Aren't you the little devil?" Sybil teased, and Moriarity blushed scarlet.

"I think it's nice to have two views of things," Peggy said grumpily, peeved that she was no longer the centre of attention. Moriarity shot her a grateful look.

Bernice rose unsteadily from her seat.

"Is there something wrong, Bernice?" Mother asked nervously as Bernice swayed dangerously.

"My glasses ... left my glasses in the car." Bernice tottered past Sybil, going over on an ankle and almost coming a cropper into Moriarity's lap. From the back view she looked all pressed flat as if she'd been lying on a bed somewhere. The back of her head displayed a distinctive bald patch.

At one of the family christenings Bernice had left the party to be sick. For want of a better receptacle, she'd vomitted into her handbag and come back with the bag slung over her arm. Mother didn't want a repeat performance.

While Bernice was gone, the conversation was strained. Mother's hands were knotted tight in her lap as though waiting for the worst to happen. She wasn't to be disappointed. The front door slammed and Bernice came crashing through the drawing-room door.

"Jesus, it's on fire." She pointed an arm backward.

Sybil fixed her with a glazed stare. "What?"

"The bloody car's on fire. You and your cigarette holder. I told you that you'd dropped a cigarette onto the floor," Bernice accused Sybil.

The entire gathering moved to the front door to verify Bernice's claim and sure enough smoke was curling out from under the doors and through the open window. Mother disappeared towards the telephone.

"Did you get the gin?" Sybil clutched Bernice's arm.

"No! How could I ?"

"So you're just going to let it burn up?" Sybil was already down the walkway at an unstable trot, heels catching in the paving stones, arms waving in an attempt to balance herself.

Moriarity took off after Sybil. "Mrs. Osborne, you'd better stay away ... I heard tell of cars blowing up."

Sybil paid no attention but flung open the back door, and battling with the swirls of smoke, plunged herself in to rescue the night's supply of gin. Mother, coming back from her phone call, rushed off down the path after Sybil. Moriarity made a feeble attempt to restrain her.

"Stay away from the car, Mrs. Montgomery. It'll surely explode!"

Mother shook him off, her real feelings about him finally showing. She glared at him as though he was some kind of bug that had dropped onto her arm and that she might squash at any moment.

Sybil reappeared from the car, the gin bottle held triumphantly aloft. Minutes later a screaming fire brigade arrived.

Little clusters of curious neighbours had now collected in the gathering dusk of the evening. I could only guess at Mother's mortification. Mother hustled Sybil onto the front step again.

Later as we watched their less dramatic and very practical dousing of the fire, Sybil broke free from Mother's grasp. She waved the gin bottle at the firemen.

"You were brilliant, men!" she said beaming. "How about a wee drop for all your hard work?"

Mother hustled us into the house. Moriarity for the first time had some colour in his face, he looked positively flushed from the excitement.

"I don't know what you must think, Reverend ..." Mother said apologetically. "Won't you sit down again?"

The excitement made him throw all caution to the winds. He held out his glass immediately when Mother offered him another sherry.

Sybil returned shortly without the firemen but with the gin.

"Mrs. Osborne, you must allow me to drive you home in me modest little rattletrap of a car," Moriarity offered Sybil enthusiastically.

"Isn't that kind of you, Father." Sybil's sudden transference of Moriarity to the Catholic church seemed to go unnoticed.

"Now that I'm not driving I think we could top the drinks up," Sybil said, ignoring the rescued bottled of gin and holding out her glass for some of Mother's.

Moriarity seemed to have forgotten about his preoccupation with our immediate family. Perhaps sensing a rescue mission, he was almost animated; his entire face had turned pink to match his nose. He was actually quite handsome.

It was obvious that he'd never in his entire life met a pair like Sybil and Bernice. Used to reverence, their sheer disregard for "the cloth" was distinctly appealing. They were totally outside the realm of his experience.

You might say Moriarity had fallen in love again, but it was a love that promised redemption, nothing sexual, and that was infinitely more seductive. Rescue of my father must have paled in comparison to the "promise" of Sybil and Bernice.

Eventually we saw the three of them off down the path, Moriarity in the middle, Sybil hooked on one side and Bernice on the other — the three of them stumbling ever so slightly amid a lot of giggling and laughter.

Mother slumped onto the sofa when the front door finally closed and surveyed the disarray of the living room through the fog of stale smoke.

"Bloody little hypocrite!" Mother said, holding the sherry bottle up to the light. "He just about finished the sherry!"

# SLEEPWALKERS

The black onyx clock on the living-room mantlepiece occupies Lily's full attention. The clock hasn't worked ever since Lily has been at the Beckers, but it still sits centre stage on the mantle.

Frau Doctor Becker has some obsession about that clock. So too has Lily. It somehow seems to represent her own life since she has been in North America — a life which has come to a halt. Without proper landed-immigrant papers and little hope of ever getting them, her life belongs to the Beckers.

Lily focuses on the clock with its static hands, dusting its poor face. Once, when she found dust between its tiny pillars, Frau Becker had lectured Lily endlessly about how young girls no longer had any work ethic; her anger had seemed out of all proportion to the crime.

There are numerous lectures at Number 31: a lengthy sermon on how to properly iron and fold Herr Becker's white shirts; another on proper toilet-bowl sanitizing; one on the correct amount of furniture polish for certain pieces of furniture.

Frau Doctor Becker has arthritis and is a semi-invalid; otherwise, as she tells Lily frequently, she would prefer to do it all herself. The unspoken thought being that it would then be done properly.

Number 31 is a large detached red-brick house on a corner lot — a house with five bedrooms, hardwood oak floors, walnut panelling, each room filled with dark furniture, the floors carpeted with Indian rugs. The walls are weighed down with paintings, dark oils, for Frau Doctor's taste in art runs to turbulent seascapes, sailors foundering in storms, and shipwrecks.

The house is in an East European neighbourhood. Coffee shops dominate the street, their windows filled with homemade truffles, strudel, and almond tortes, rich with butter fat.

On good days, when Frau Becker's joints don't ache too much, she meets a friend in one of these shops. Over cappuccino and Black Forest torte, they sit stiffly, looking remarkably alike, their skirts barely covering their fat knees: two well-polished chestnuts, all plump and shiny, their hennaed hair in 1960s style pompadours, their shoes tight on salt-swollen feet, delicately forking strudel between their shiny red lips, their minds already at work on how to justify second helpings.

Frau Doctor is a different person with Herr Doctor. She is often cold and cutting with him. He doesn't seem to notice or care. He is very self-contained and private: a slim man with a pale face and very red lips, who is always polite with Frau Doctor, even when she is at her worst. There is usually an upward turn to his red mouth, not quite a smile, more like scorn, which maddens Frau Doctor even more. No doubt he hears some other dialogue in his head when she is lecturing. Only occasionally do they argue, and then it is all carried on in hissed and tense whispers that seem to leave them both exhausted and penetrate the walls more disturbingly than any shouting.

There are moments when Lily feels warmth for Frau Doctor. Sometimes she tries to tell Lily how she might brighten herself up. Lily has no illusions about her own looks. She long ago gave up trying to make anything of herself. She can do nothing with her hair which is straight and fine. A boyish crop is her answer to the dilemma. Her body has never had any definition, only the missing penis identifies her as a woman. She knows without having to be told that nothing is going to make her attractive.

Sometimes Lily reads books about love since she's not seen much of it in operation around her. Amazed, she reads about the hero's or heroine's emotions. Sex, to Lily, is something furtive that has to be endured but definitely never enjoyed.

Lily moves from the fireplace to dust the old, rectangular grand piano which needs a different duster and a different type of polish. She picks up one of the photographs in a silver frame and peers at it more closely. Frau Becker had once been beautiful. Herr Doctor, beside her in the photograph, is both handsome and interesting-looking. The way they gaze at one another in the photograph is touching and charming.

"We were very much in love then," Frau Becker says suddenly. She has come up quietly behind Lily. Lily catches a whiff of her breath and thinks of fetid cheese.

"See how he looks at me as though he could eat me up. How impetuous he vas, but of course I couldn't allow it. Nowadays, there is no magic, is there?" She looks at Lily as though for confirmation. "They all have it right away now. They don't know what they miss, poor things."

Frau Becker looks down at the photo again. "The first night we knew we were in love, it was like the whole world had changed. The very air was heavy. I could feel my whole body from tip to toe, like I vas so powerful, so full of energy, like a magnet," and for an instant she is swollen and alive with memory. Her normally dull eyes shine. The harshness has gone out of her tone. "It was magic. The very best time of my life. I didn't want it ever to stop."

Feeling odd, as though she is eavesdropping on a private conversation, Lily coughs and Frau Becker is back to the present, brisk and sharp as ever.

"This frame is looking like gold instead of silver. You'd better get the polish." The moment is gone as swiftly as it has come.

Frau Becker seems most like a real human being when she is feeling low: when her knees hurt and she has to be helped up and down stairs, or the time when she slipped on the front step and broke her ankle. Crooked and sad-looking, all bluster gone, she'd been in too much pain to even care about the pearls that had burst from her neck and scattered around her. Her neighbour, a young woman with four small daughters, helped Lily lift her. The little girls chased the rolling pearls, picking them up as adeptly as avid little sparrows pecking for crumbs.

Frau Doctor acknowledges the woman now, but mostly with stilted greeting. "It is dangerous to know your neighbours too well," she tells Lily. Why it is so she doesn't say.

The neighbour, Mary Harvey, doesn't seem dangerous at all. There is something glowing and alive about Mary and the disorder of the yard around her house, so different from the neatness of the Beckers' manicured lawns and trimmed hedges.

Mary is heavy with child now.

"She should get herself fixed," Frau Becker had said, peering through the lace curtains at the sight of Mary negotiating the front steps of her house with a stroller and several bags of groceries. She makes the pronouncement as though Mary is some kind of dumb animal.

"Disgusting to keep breeding in times like this."

"She likes children," Lily offered, feeling somehow she had to defend Mary.

"A lack of discipline, that's all!" Frau Becker pronounced with venom. "Just look at her struggling every day, back and forth to the grocery store to feed them all. He should have it cut off," she pronounced with ugly emphasis.

✳

Some two months later, on one of those August days when the air is thick and warm in the house from morning 'til night, husband and wife meet over the breakfast table. It is something that rarely happens because Frau Becker usually has her breakfast in bed, but she had spent an uncomfortable night on the sofa in the living room where it is marginally cooler. She is mussed and bothered-looking now, her colour high from a night of struggling to stay cool.

Herr Doctor, far from his usual cool self, rustles the newspapers as though trying to create a breeze to lighten the air. Earlier, in the kitchen, Lily had heard the angry hiss of their voices as they squabbled about something.

Lily pours freshly squeezed orange juice into their glasses. She often feels the heat in her little attic room, but last night had been the worst yet. She had struggled like a drowning person for a breath of cool air. Nothing, not even the huge shady elm outside the front window, had prevented the heat from penetrating every crack in the house. Despite this, Frau Becker refuses to open the windows.

Whatever it is husband and wife had been squabbling about is still heavy in the air between them. Lily passes the scones which she has warmed in the microwave to Frau Becker.

"Mary Harvey came home from hospital yesterday," Lily offers as some sort of leavening to the atmosphere.

"Another girl!" Herr Doctor said from behind his newspaper. "He gave her another girl, poor fool."

Frau Becker plasters the butter thick on her scone, and it crumbles under the pressure. "What right do you have to criticize. It's more than you could ever do." She doesn't look at him as she speaks; her thick fingers try to restructure the broken scone.

Wild-eyed and shocked, he lowers his paper and stares across at his wife in disbelief. She still avoids his eyes, knowing she has gone too far. Herr Doctor's hand crushes down on the newspaper, crumpling it without a thought — something he would never have done in normal circumstances, obsessed as he is with tidiness, always demanding the newspaper be kept in perfect order.

There's a look on his face Lily's never seen before. A tiny facial muscle flickers beside his mouth. He rises heavily, and before Lily's and Frau Becker's eyes, his hand moves out deliberately and he pulls the tablecloth, so that it comes clean away from the table, the dishes crashing and smashing in all directions, the orange-juice jug tipping and spilling its content over the polished mahogany table. The scones fly in three different directions. The butter dish skids and jumps off the table until it lies upside down on the Indian rug, its runny content spreading an oily stain.

"Damn you!" He moves quickly and is out the door and down the front steps, his jacket still in his hand. Lily bends quickly and with embarrassment tries to scoop the melting butter back into the dish.

There's a great gulp above her, and a sort of glugging noise as though Frau Becker is choking, and then a wild sob. Lily sits back on her hunkers and stares at the sight of the distraught and dishevelled Frau Becker. Her usually neat coiffed hair is all askew from her restless night; her large flowered wrapper gapes across her chest. As her upper body collapses, a wealth of pale flesh folds out. Her forehead touches the mahogany tabletop, and her tears spill on its well-polished surface, no thought given to the dangers of wetting its perfect finish.

Lily, her fingers covered with grease from the butter, stares helplessly at the mess. Rising slowly, butterdish in hand, she makes a move towards Frau Becker and then realizes she can do nothing with the butterdish in her hands. She puts it quickly on the silver tray on the sideboard, and picking up a napkin, wipes her fingers free of grease.

Going to Frau Becker, she puts a comforting hand on her shoulder. It's as though she has delivered an electric shock to the woman. She looks up wildly.

"You know nothing. How could you know vat it's been like, living for forty years like this, a virgin. How could you know what it is to burn up?"

A great feeling of nausea sweeps over Lily. If only she could start the morning afresh. Forgetting entirely about Mary Harvey.

"He loved me so much before we were married. He couldn't keep his hands off me then. Only, it wasn't allowed. Men didn't respect women who let them have their way. He was so hungry for me and it was so vonderful. Then we got married and nothing. Nothing! Nothing! Year and years of nothing! Wondering all the time what was wrong. Do I smell? Am I in some way revolting to him?" She hangs her head for a moment and then looks up at Lily again.

"Well, what do you think? I am revolting, that's it, isn't it?" Standing up, she grasps Lily's hand and digs her fingernails into the palm so that Lily emits a little gasp of pain. "That's it, isn't it?"

Lily shakes her head. A look of horror suddenly sweeps over Frau Becker's face.

"So vat are you standing there gawking for? Get back to work!" she screams. "Get back to work and leave me alone!" Lily backs off, terrified by the vehemence of the woman and alarmed that she might strike her.

Trembling, Lily turns and runs, pushing through the swing-door into the kitchen and stands for a moment leaning against the door, her entire body shaking as though she has been physically assaulted. She feels like throwing up.

Herr Doctor stays away for three days, and Frau Becker keeps to the house, silent and seemingly semi-paralysed. When he comes back, neither of them speak. He merely nods and goes towards the stairs as though it is just another day and nothing has happened in between.

For the first time since she's been in the house, Lily turns the key in the lock of her bedroom door that night. She lies awake most of the night, half expecting to hear the familiar "shushing" sound his slippers make on the landing.

It is a week before Lily hears the handle on her door turn. She holds her breath and huddles under the blankets. Then there is the lightest of raps but no other sound. Finally, she hears the shuffle of his slippers and knows that he's gone away.

She tells herself that there is no need to feel guilt. It isn't as if what Herr Doctor sometimes does to her in her tiny bedroom is in any way connected with a real interest or a real passion. It is merely as though he has missed his way to his study, which is beside Lily's small bedroom. His body, thin and hairless, as it presses against hers, might be a child's body, functioning in some kind of dream mode. To cry out, or to protest, has never seemed the right thing to do. And not by a glance or look next day is there ever a hint that anything untoward has occurred.

# LOVE MINUS ONE

The furniture had been re-upholstered and the grand piano refinished, the scratches and gouges French-polished into oblivion, but nothing, neither wallpaper nor paint, could disguise a pervasive dry rot that Julie always associated with the house.

The heating radiators, so familiar in many of the prairie houses, sent out cranks and groans, as though some prisoner were trapped inside and crying for rescue.

It was the first time that Julie had come back to visit. She had seen Liz and David twice since she'd left town, but on her own territory, and there it had been all right. This time, Bob had to do business in town, and she had come ahead of him.

Odd how the strange vibes in the house affected her. The familiar sensation of helplessness was already invading nerves and synapses, robbing her of will as powerfully as some awful degenerative disease of her central nervous system might have done.

The guest-room had been redone in a trendy apple green wallpaper, and all the marvellous oak had been painted over with a sort of dark turquoise shellac that should have cried out in protest against the other shade but was peculiarly in keeping with the rest of the house. The smell of the paint was still pervasive. Trying to pry the windows open, she burnt her hand against the roasting-hot shanks of the radiator. She winced and clutched her burnt hand. The room felt stifling hot.

Liz had turned down the bed already and a single-stemmed peach-coloured rose lay in the centre of the pillow. It was a typically thoughtful touch, one of the many that Liz would be sure to orchestrate for the following couple of days.

Julie sat on the edge of the bed and contemplated the perfection of the rose. Moving her hand to lift it, her finger caught on a thorn. She dropped it quickly, and just as swiftly a tiny spot of blood from her finger dotted the duvet, only to fade instantly into the surrounding pattern of pink rosebuds. More carefully she moved the rose to the night table. There was a bud vase there, obviously waiting to host the single-stemmed rose.

She lay back on the duvet. Liz had always had an obsession with roses. The very first time she and Bob had been invited to the house, there had been a profusion of magnificent apricot-coloured roses sitting on the piano. She had been mesmerized by them and by Liz's largesse which seemed almost overwhelming. The drinks she poured for them had been far too generous and far too crippling. After two drinks she'd felt totally light-headed.

In those days, all those years ago, she had believed that like the whales, humans were meant to mate for life. For each individual there was a counterpart, and naively she felt that in Bob, she had found hers. Even then, that night, with her hand in David's, and those strange green eyes of his intensely focused on her, she tended to put the odd fluttering of emotions down to the liberal potion poured by Liz, but there were other signs of disequilibrium which she chose to ignore.

Later, as though in justification, she had thought a lot about what had really happened between them at that first meeting, and in harsher moments had classified it as a mere recognition between victims.

He came in late, meandering into the living room perhaps forgetting where he was going or why he was there at all. He didn't seem to belong in the room; his body movements signalled that displacement to an almost alarming degree.

He was tall and dark-haired, his skin terribly white in contrast, the eyes unmistakably blue; in fact, the bluest eyes Julie had ever seen in a human being. He reminded her almost instantly of a Siamese cat. He seemed to carry with him that same air of indifference to time and place. Except, she still remembered his handshake, the peculiar, comforting fit of their hands.

Liz had been trying to coax the fire to light when they arrived and had abandoned the grate and smoking newspapers for David's arrival and attention. They had listened at length to stories about David's prowess as an athlete. Under Liz's instructions, or commands, because that's what they soon became, his entire body faltered, was suddenly bereft of feline grace. As though to give lie to her claims, he was clumsy, almost oafish in his attempts to force some life into the fire. The urge to remove Liz and, by doing so, restore his body grace became an overwhelming one at some point, but as always it was countered by Liz's extraordinary gift to make one feel completely precious and wanted.

Later when she knew them both better, Julie began to change her mind about David's response to Liz's forcefulness. That first night she had been horrified at Liz's disclosures about how she went about capturing David. Perhaps after all she was no different from many people who once they spot what they want, go single-mindedly after their victims. Certainly, David smiled all through the telling. Either he had heard it before, or he'd been the willing victim.

Watching Liz, Julie decided she reminded her of a raven. She was small, dark and smooth, sleek, and the possessor of an intensity that was almost frightening. She seemed totally unconscious of her startling good looks. She talked in hyperbole, but this was fascinating after meeting so many people who didn't seem to have opinions or, when they did, voiced them with so little passion.

There was a wonderful lack of formality in her hospitality. Nothing seemed preset or planned. The house was just as randomly careless. The furnishings an odd mixture of interesting artifacts: African masks, pots from Afghanistan, brasses from India, Nitsuki from Japan all of which totally disregarded any attempt at conformity or solidness of theme. They littered the corners, decorated the existing shelf space, giving the room the feel of an Oriental bazaar. The furniture was dusty, and newspapers and magazines were scattered everywhere.

They had met through a mutual friend. Julie and Bob were new in town, new in Canada for that matter. Liz had been born on the Prairies, as had her parents before her. She knew every inch of territory, she knew everyone who was worth knowing in town.

A mutual friend had informed them that the small publishing company David and Liz ran was financed by David whose father had died and left him a rather large sum of money, so large in fact that neither of them had to work unless they felt like it. Liz appeared to do so at her own leisure. When she talked about the business, she always made it appear more like a game than work. Certainly, the company kept a low profile, and from what Julie could gather, things hadn't changed very much.

She must have fallen asleep on the bed, for when she woke up David was standing over her. Julie was certain he hadn't knocked at the door.

"Had a rest?"

She nodded and sat up.

"I thought I should warn you, Liz has been drinking too much. She'll probably be fine but sometimes she gets through dinner and then passes right out. I didn't want you to be alarmed."

"I'm sorry. I didn't know it was that bad."

"Yes!" He hesitated for a moment and then left the room as silently as he'd come.

Later at dinner, his warning seemed absurd. The pre-dinner drink had been a mere one and Liz seemed more in command than usual. Never a good cook, what she lacked in inventiveness she made up for by knowing exactly where to go to buy exotic foods that gave the appearance of being home cooked: a dash of spice, or warming up, always disguised the fact the food had been made much earlier, perhaps even a day earlier, in some commercial kitchen.

David seemed tense and if anything *he* seemed to be the one drinking too much. What seemed gone now was the awkwardness of former years, the clumsiness that was inevitable when he performed chores to Liz's command. By now he seemed to know what was expected of him and circumnavigated orders. If anything, he was the one who was telling Liz what to do. It was an interesting switch of command and totally unexpected.

Liz wasn't really very good at generalities; she would ask about the kids without really wanting to know about them. Julie kept her answers short.

It was odd how totally self-conscious Julie felt in their company and to realize that it wasn't a new feeling, but certainly one not experienced since the old days. She couldn't make up her mind whether this acute awareness was in some way beneficial. Certainly nothing in the intervening years had caused her to feel this way — like some kind of electric current picking up too much static. She was suddenly and dangerously aware of heartbeats, of pulses, of silences, of looks. Her instinct was to run, but right now there was nowhere to run to. She was locked in.

David insisted on stacking the dishwasher and clearing everything away, and Liz offered no protest. Instead, she brought the wine bottle into the living room and filled both their glasses. Where normally Julie might have protested, and insisted on helping, she resisted the urge and followed Liz.

Liz barely made it to the sofa and had only just lit another cigarette when what David had said would happen, happened. One minute she was there and the next gone. She was slumped in the corner of the sofa, momentarily passed out; she had somehow managed to deposit her cigarette precariously on the edge of an ashtray, but hadn't managed to similarly arrange her limbs with any kind of symmetry; she looked dreadfully abandoned and sad.

Julie went into the kitchen. She didn't have to say a word to David — he might have been waiting for the call. She followed him into the living room.

Liz revived when he touched her and pulled away from him, only to sink again into whatever oblivion she'd been in before. Together they supported her, but she was surprisingly light. Julie was perfectly sure he could have slung her over his shoulder without any effort, but together they managed to get her upstairs to the bedroom.

He turned down the sheets and they undressed her until she was in her bra and panties and then he pulled the covers around her. She roused herself sufficiently to grasp Julie's wrist as she tried to leave.

"Don't go!"

"Have a sleep, Liz, you'll feel better!"

She refused to loosen her grasp on Julie's arm. Julie nodded for David to leave them. He moved reluctantly to the door.

Opening her eyes, she stared at Julie and blinked, "For God's sake ... go to bed with him!" Her voice was remarkably clear and momentarily in control.

She raised her other hand until she was grasping Julie's forearm with both hands now, her fingers digging into the flesh with all her might.

"I want it over ... Do you hear! ... I want it over." She loosened her grasp, and then suddenly her arms were around her and she was sobbing on Julie's shoulder.

"Please, please, for my sake."

"Hush!" Julie stroked her hair. "David can't do without you. You know that."

"I want it over." She faded away again, her grip on Julie's body loosened completely. She slid out of her arms and back against the pillows. She looked extraordinarily vulnerable. There was a high flush on her cheeks and all of a sudden she seemed terribly childlike. There were none of the ravages visible on her face that there should have been. Her skin was as clear as a baby's. Julie stood staring down at her for several more minutes, but she didn't stir. Julie pulled the covers up to her chin and turned off the light.

When they had first met, Julie had been pregnant. In her fifth month, Liz had announced she was pregnant too, and there had been much celebration. Liz had miscarried twice before and this time the doctor had announced she would have to stay in bed for most of the pregnancy if she was to carry the baby to term.

It was probably then that Julie began to hate the house for the first time. The disorder ceased to be quaint, it somehow represented something more pathological, more deliberately quirky. All the unpredictability in her own life came from Bob's transience. She created order in her own existence to balance that. However, not everything could be simple and neat. The marriage that she had considered almost perfect until only a short time before, was showing signs of strain. Bob was preoccupied with the Dallas office and the problems of keeping the business going in two places at once. She was preoccupied with being pregnant. Her best relationship was with the unborn child, monitoring every kick, every twinge, enjoying the novelty. Her second-best relationship was with Liz and David.

It was only much later that she began to realize how totally dependent she'd become on them. Nor had the lethargy of pregnancy encouraged new directions. She was content to let Liz order her life, even order it from her bed where she lay on satin sheets, surrounded by dirty dishes, old newspapers, candy wrappers and cigarette butts.

Liz was given to issuing commands to her friends. She had widened Julie's circle of friends for her but she kept firm control, organizing outings, parties, dinners, and through it all, Julie felt like a large contented cow. Julie allowed the interference, judging it most of the time as caring rather than manipulative.

How odd that pregnancy was. It was as though for nine months all judgemental abilities were suspended. She was a moveable womb, all moist and malleable; it had been the most utterly contented phase of her life. And yet with it all, the surprising sex drive that made her miss Bob so often and set her dreaming about a husband who at times looked disturbingly like David.

Liz phoned one night from bed to ask, or rather command, that Julie should accompany David to a fund-raising concert the following night. He had to be there, and she felt someone should go with him.

That Bob was out of town again made it easier to accept the invitation, but she would have preferred it if David had phoned himself. She remembered the vague feeling of contempt for him that he allowed himself to be used by Liz. But then, who was she to blame anyone? More and more of late she had felt drained of will. She usually managed to console herself with the idea that it was the child in the womb that had robbed her of her decisiveness, but privately at times she doubted she could remember what it was like to make her own decisions.

He came to pick her up the following evening. Alone, he seemed perfectly in charge; the feline grace returned effortlessly. The clumsiness had transferred to herself instead. She saw herself as a sort of animated pear. Even the smocked chiffon dress that Liz had loaned her for the evening she felt did little to give any grace to her form. He was quick to help her in and out of the car and solicitous of her every step. At one point he put his arm around her to steady her and held it there rather protectively for far longer than was necessary.

There was a pre-concert reception in the lobby of the concert hall. He faithfully introduced Julie as a friend of his wife's, until just before they were supposed to go in and sit down in readiness for the concert. Then a man came up and grasped Julie's hand, saying he was delighted to finally meet David's wife. She remembered smiling, waiting for David to correct the mistake, but he said nothing; instead, he looked at her and there was something so revealing in the look that any denial at that point would have made the situation even worse. He put his hand on her elbow and moved her slightly ahead of him, and any necessity for continuing the conversation with the man was gone.

She remembered only one thing the orchestra played that night: Debussy's *L'Après-midi d'un faune*. It was incandescent with a dreamy kind of emotion and yet shunned any kind of chromatic pattern. It seemed the most perfect accompaniment to the strange mood of the evening. Oddly enough, the child in her womb had gone absolutely quiet. She longed for a jabbing arm or sharp knee to fracture the mood, but there was nothing.

David put his hand over her arm.

"Are you all right?"

"Yes thanks, fine."

He held his hand there and she had allowed it, not moving it away.

Later when they were driving home it began to rain: large, heavy, padding drops, more like hail than rain. It fell noisily on the windshield, blurring their vision. He didn't turn on the windshield wipers, preferring to lean forward and peer shortsightedly into the night.

"Why didn't you say something when he thought I was your wife?" she asked finally when they were close to home.

"I don't really know," he said quietly. "I suppose I liked the idea."

The road ahead then became intensely interesting to both of them. They concentrated like mad on the shining wet pavement, on the centre line, on the oncoming headlights, on the narrowing gap between where they had been and where they were going. At the house, he got out of the car first and put up the umbrella, coming around to her side where she had already opened the door. She was conscious again of her size, almost as though her feelings had helped to swell the already existing girth. Elephantine with new emotions — all grace was gone.

She fumbled with the front-door key, aware of him so close. He shook off the umbrella and stepped inside behind her, closing the door, and there in the dark he wrapped his arms around her.

Then he put his hand on her stomach and held it there. The baby refused to respond. It lay stubbornly indolent under his hand. The heaviness that had filled every limb had been replaced by the most utterly sensuous sensation. She had the feeling that something quite frightening was happening, and in her debilitated state she was receptive to almost anything, open and ready, demented with a rare fever which she told herself for weeks afterwards had been purely symptomatic of her entire condition.

The phone began to ring and she broke away. He held onto her hand, "Don't answer it!"

"I have to." Even as she moved towards it she dreaded that it would be Bob. Her voice would be a total give-away. She knew somehow she couldn't deal with that.

"Hello, Julie? It's me, Liz. Has David gone?"

"No! He just left me at the door with the umbrella. I think he's still there."

"Do you have any bread to spare? There's not a crumb left in our house and I have this yen for a peanut butter sandwich."

"Yes, yes, I think we have some."

"Be a good girl, send it home with him. Tell him not to rush. If he wants to have a drink with you that's fine. He deserves a night off."

She hung up the phone feeling slightly ill. He was still standing in the doorway when she returned to the hall.

"That was Liz. She wants me to give you some bread, she wants a sandwich."

"Yes," was all he said.

Julie busied herself getting the bread for him out of the freezer and putting it in a bag. She couldn't bear looking at him. She knew exactly what she would see in his eyes. She knew now what had happened at the door was all that was to be and was sure she conveyed this in the briskness of her movements.

She followed him to the door. He turned when he'd opened the door and, leaning over briefly, he put his mouth to hers. Then, lifting her hand quickly, he kissed the palm.

She felt like some kind of murderess. No wonder the child was quiet: not only had she been ready to betray Bob but also that poor innocent. The only road to sanity in the following weeks was to put it all down to a rare form of dementia, a temporary sickness that would expel itself with the birth of the child, come away with the afterbirth. But it was never quite that easy.

She closed Liz's bedroom door. When she went back downstairs, David was in the kitchen, setting the dishwasher onto the wash cycle.

"I think it's maybe a good idea if I leave."

He spread the dish towel over the back of the chair and ran his hand along its dampness. He looked up at her.

"Let's go and sit down."

Julie followed him into the living room again. He took the seat that Liz had just vacated. Julie sat down opposite.

He lifted the glass that had been hers and filled it with wine, putting it to his mouth. He drank it in one gulp.

"Tomorrow she'll hate that it happened this way. She won't like it that you saw her in that state."

"I just feel so sorry."

"I know."

He set the wine glass down and turned it slowly by its stem, studying the circular motion.

"She wanted me to go to bed with you ... she said that's what you wanted," Julie blurted out suddenly.

He looked up at her.

"Based no doubt on the theory that once you jump off the high board you never want to do it again?"

He leant back, his hands relaxing on the wine glass, and stared across at her, his eyes making their usual slow perusal of her face, peering so intensely that she was forced to look away.

They finished the bottle of wine together and talked quietly about things that didn't really matter. Slightly intoxicated, like ineluctable planetary forces, they circled one another, conscious of the unbreachable distance between them, aware also that only some extraordinary circumstance would alter that.

She left him alone, still sitting on the sofa. He'd thrown more wood on the fire, so it still burnt brightly, too brightly to be left unattended. He raised his hand and grasped hers, holding onto it for a minute.

"Good night, David!"

"Good night!"

Julie found it almost impossible to sleep. She was certain David hadn't gone to his room to sleep. Towards morning, when she finally dozed off, she had a dream. She was standing in water and just in front of her was a raging flood with people floating by, or rather bodies floating by, all horribly bloated. Two figures came towards her, Liz and David, only a Liz and David she remembered from the old days. Both had their hands outstretched towards her. She was suddenly aware that she could chose only one hand and yet they kept smiling and urging her towards them as though there was no problem, she could rescue both. Then, behind them, she saw a wall of water and she knew that there was only a split second to decide. It was odd, though, because their clothes didn't seem to be wet and they didn't even seem to be standing in the water the way she was, and when the wall of water did reach them they went under, and almost immediately bobbed to the top again. The last thing she remembered was looking at them as they passed by, and they both looked like dolls now, perfectly intact, despite the battering of the water.

There was enormous relief when she realized she hadn't been the cause of their death and after that she woke up. She lay there for a while and for some reason she remembered vividly the morning Liz had phoned to say she'd lost the baby. She'd been home from hospital a week with Joanna when the call came. It had been a totally calm, totally controlled, dead-sounding Liz. A voice that would be forever imprinted in her mind.

❋

Liz was up making breakfast when Julie came downstairs, looking remarkably fresh for someone with a hangover. David was sitting at the table reading the morning paper. He looked up when she came in.

"Good morning!"

"Good morning!"

"Bacon and eggs?" Liz asked her.

"Toast's fine."

"I'm making some for David."

She looked at David and he gave her a kind of encouraging nod, as though to urge her to say yes. She wasn't sure why it was important for her to have the bacon and eggs but Liz was already putting more rashers on the pan and Julie offered no more protest.

It was odd — Liz had always claimed that the smell of food cooking first thing in the morning made her feel ill, and yet here she was, pushing a lot of grease around on the frying pan. In the old days it would have been David making his own breakfast and bringing her coffee to bed.

Julie remembered David telling her that Liz would feel badly about passing out, but she didn't notice anything apologetic about her bearing at all. She knew only one thing, she felt terribly uncomfortable with both of them. She had resolved during the night that she would somehow contrive a means to get out of there. She would speak with Bob on the phone and then pretend that he was arriving a day earlier than planned.

She ate the bacon and eggs, hating every minute of it, wondering why she'd even said she would have them. It wasn't difficult to fall back into the old pattern, the spineless one of the old days, and yet now she wasn't sure anymore who was the manipulator. She knew only one thing: she wasn't strong enough against the two of them. It was imperative to get out.

It wasn't difficult at all to lie. What was surprising was that Liz didn't put up more of a fight to keep her there. Nor did she even suggest that they should get together during the rest of the week. She had been prepared for a fight, for more lies, but none was necessary.

She drove Julie to the hotel before David got home from work that night, and after only one glass of wine together in the hotel bar, Liz made her move to leave. She drank the wine quickly, as though anxious for the niceties to be over, and yet there was no hint of malice in her attitude towards Julie, no sign that she knew her story of Bob's arrival had been invented. If anything, it was the other way around. Julie kept getting the feeling that she had performed some great service for her.

They kissed at the entrance to the hotel.

"By the way, thanks!" Liz squeezed her hand.

"For what? I should be thanking you." But she had turned and was already down the steps of the hotel, giving no indication she had heard what Julie had said.

She never looked back to wave or give any sign, and Julie watched her figure disappear around the corner towards the parking lot.

Julie had the oddest feeling: she'd been part of some stage play but had been focusing on something insignificant and somehow missed the real point. Her senses weren't allowing her to sort out what it had all been about. She stood inside the large plate-glass windows of the hotel and stared out at the street. She had a sudden empty feeling, the kind of feeling she often got when something long looked forward to was suddenly over and would never happen again.

Liz's little red sports car passed, moving far too fast as usual. Even though it wasn't nearly warm enough yet to have the hood back, she had it open and her hair streamed back from her face, lifted by the cool prairie wind.

# SNAKES

It was impossible to do anything at 31 Willington without being heard. Even Thelma, in the huge furry carpet slippers she always wore, could hear the floorboards squeak as she walked across the hallway carrying the tray with Eleanor McArthur's breakfast.

No carpets anywhere except small hand-hooked ones in front of the massive fireplace in the lounge, and the same in Eleanor's bedroom. Carpets were dust catchers and above all the McArthur's girl, Jane, was allergic to dust. Funny how she still always thought of Jane as a girl, a woman of forty-eight with all her supposed wits about her and that's what the neighbours all referred to her as, "the girl."

Thelma had been with the family since Jane was ten. Back then there had been no talk of allergies and illness. Back then she'd been a beautiful little thing, all pert and pretty, with a lithe, athletic body. Back then there'd been carpets, there had been everything in the house, everything that is except real happiness. Now the curtains were closed or partially closed all the time.

In Eleanor's bedroom, Jane straightened her mother's bedclothes. Odd, how with all that money, she refused a nurse and instead did all the deadening chores of washing and changing her, dishing out pills, feeding the old lady.

Thelma hated this room with its oppressive furniture. The old boy had inherited the bedstead from his father who had brought it from India. The bed was a huge four-poster with hideous carved water buffalo stomping all over the headboard. Thelma could never have slept on a monstrosity like that. She would have had nightmares about stampedes. Its companion piece was an even more enormous wardrobe that to Thelma's mind was out of place in a house that had all sorts of walk-in closets.

Thelma watched Jane as she straightened up. Her once shining blonde hair now had the lifeless tone of old, dried hay. Her skin was thin, the kind of skin that wrinkled early and was parchment in old age. She hadn't aged well. On top of it all, the ghastly clothes: the bell-bottom pants from the seventies; the back-combed pompadour with the great, heavy bun at the back; the shocking pink lipstick; the lacey knit suits that ended just above her knobbly knees. It was as though she was totally unaware of the outside world and how things had changed.

"Thank you Thelma, just put it by the bed. She isn't quite fixed up yet."

"Can I help?"

"Yes, hold her up and I'll put an extra pillow in behind her."

Thelma put an arm around the old woman, feeling the extreme fragility of the shoulder bones under her own arm, smelling the stale, sour smell of old age and ill health. The old woman registered very little. Immobilized by a stroke six months before, there had been only minimal progress.

*Pray to God I go quickly when the time comes,* the silent refrain repeated itself in Thelma's head. She had always found it difficult to like Eleanor McArthur, but now in her helplessness she seemed suddenly vulnerable and human.

It amazed her how dedicated Jane had become to her mother. Especially since there had never been anything but a kind of controlled anger between them over the last twenty years.

Thelma's eyes focused for an instant on the photograph that sat on the bureau, of Clymont McArthur, Eleanor and the two children. Eleanor with her double row of pearls and the dark silk dress, the smooth oval face blank. Clymont beside her, proud, not so much of her and the children, but of his possessions. Poor Frank, the mirror image of his father, with his hair all sleeked and those huge, dark, scared eyes that seemed to cry out for help. Jane, with an impish grin on her face and her hand firmly held by her big brother.

Happier times, surface happiness anyway. Frank McArthur hadn't taken a boat out on the lake and jumped overboard for no reason. Drinking, they'd said, lost his balance, but other people thought differently. She herself knew Frank had been well used to boats and had never been careless.

"I can cope now," Jane's hand moved to get the plate with the sliced-up mango from the tray. Her hand was steady. At one time her hands had been shaky, especially when the old girl had been on her feet and had her wits about her. Strange, now that her mother was ill, she seemed far more in control and sure of herself.

The old lady suddenly grasped Thelma's hand in a vice-like grip. It was the first sign of any movement since the stroke, and the strength of the grasp was amazing.

"Look!" Thelma said, staring down at the dry, speckled hand that held hers. The old woman's tendons stood out like whipcord as she held on for dear life.

"Good!" Jane said. "Good! It means she's coming back."

"There now, be a good girl and let Thelma go!" The hand felt rigid, and as Thelma tried to pry the fingers loose she felt for a moment that they might snap as easily as soda crackers.

Jane's face was suddenly grim as she felt the desperation of the old woman's hold.

"Let go!" she commanded and then the hand went limp and the old woman's eyes partially closed like a watchful salamander's.

"You can go!" Jane told Thelma. "I'll look after her."

Thelma backed out uncertainly. It had almost been as though the old lady wanted her there. Thelma hesitated reluctantly by the door.

"Go! It's all right. I'll feed her."

Thelma let herself out and stood for a moment outside the door listening.

Jane wrapped a large towel around her mother's neck, noticing as she had a hundred times the look that always came in her mother's eyes when they were alone. A look that balanced precariously between pleading and terror. A kind of warmth spread through Jane. "Now what was all that about? Don't you want breakfast? You like mango, don't you, Mother?"

There wasn't even a flicker in her mother's eye; the blank stare had come back, or maybe it was always there and she'd just imagined the other. She felt irritated now. Lifting the plate of mango, she stabbed a piece with the fork and put it in her own mouth.

"It tastes like you might think perfume would taste, Mother, wonderful, sweet and juicy. You would like this." She finished the rest of the mango slowly, making a production out of eating each mouthful.

"It might not be good for your bowels, give you the runs and we know how we can't have that."

Jane cut the poached egg and toast up into tiny pieces. "See how nicely I handle the knife and fork, Mother. No stabbing, held like a real lady. It's made a real difference in my life, Mother. Remember how you didn't like the way David Gorie held his knife and fork. You said he ate like an animal. He did other things like an animal too, I liked that. You didn't know what we did in the back of his car, Mother. Animal things like you and Daddy never did. Did you close your eyes when Daddy touched you? Did you part your legs, Mother, or did he have to force them apart?

"'Sit like a lady! Knees together. Never sprawl!'

"We sprawled, Mother. All over the back seat. I liked the things he did to me, Mother.

"There, now you're all dribbly, egg yolk on your chin. Never mind, we'll get that off." Jane put some jam on a slice of toast and bit into it. "This jam's good. Your favourite, rhubarb and ginger." It had never been *her* favourite jam. Just as everything her mother liked, she had hated. "Tangy, just right," she lied.

"I guess I wasn't a good girl, Mother. *'No lower than the neck, no higher than the knee.'* Remember what you used to say? How on earth did we ever get born, Mother? Poor Daddy, what a gyp!

"Remember when you found out David's family owned a couple of pulp and paper mills and suddenly his manners weren't so bad any more? Remember the talk? *'David, think of yourself as one of us!'* You were thinking you could teach him how to hold his knife and fork, teach him how to talk, teach him how to respond to people.

"Here we are." Jane pushed a piece of dry toast into her mother's mouth. "Chew!" she commanded. Her mother's jaws moved unenthusiastically.

"Remember how Frank ate his toast all in one piece, hated to cut it up and how you used to yell at him?

"Poor Frank, poor perfect Frank who never had and never would have been able to bring himself to touch a woman. *'My little man,'* that was what you always called him. None of it would have made any difference if we hadn't come home a day early from Florida and found Frank in bed with Bernie Edwards.

"*'Perverted! That creep Bernie Edwards! It's all his fault! Bring home your friends! Introduce Frank to some of your friends!'*

"*'Mother, Frank is only interested in men. It isn't some disease that he'll recover from.'*

"*'Wash your mouth out! Frank was perverted by that creep Bernie Edwards.'*" Jane laughed — an ugly sound in the stillness of the room.

"Bernie Edwards loves Frank. Frank loves Bernie Edwards. Frank would have gone on being single, hiding his behaviour from you if you hadn't made his life a nightmare. *You* needed the psychiatrist, Mother, not Frank. Poor Frank, months of Dr. Martin Knerer who only confirmed what everyone else but you already knew.

"University of Toronto for Frank when he wanted to get away from you. Never any hope. The only surprise, Mother, was that you didn't register with him. Every day the report of progress. Frank didn't go to classes that whole first year. He bought all the books, scattered them around his room, wrote notes, faked marks. Instead, he sat in the cafés on Queen Street and wrote poetry, mostly about you, Mother. Naming no names, but cries of help that talked about entrapment and failure. There was one, *'Moths, moths inside my mother,'* it began. It was too gentle. That was the problem with Frank, he wanted to make excuses for you. I would have written the poem differently, I would have written, *'Snakes, snakes inside my mother.'* In place of intestines you had snakes. Snakes that came out and struck whenever a person least expected them to.

" *'What did I do, Frank, to make you this way? Tell me what I've done wrong?'* What conceit. Trying even then to take credit for Frank's preferences.

"Me, you never cared about except what connection I would finally make, something you hoped that would do you credit. Jane loves David. David loves sex, but not commitment and definitely not family, not this family, not this sickness.

"All those stupid stories about the time Daddy and you met the Duke of who-knows-where, and how he related the story of watching a Canadian eating a piece of bacon with a fork. How funee-ee. How amusing wrestling the bacon like it was some kind of writhing reptile on the plate. David's blank face. How idiotic, Mother, David wouldn't have had a clue you were trying to reform his eating habits. David thought he was perfect anyway. What a waste of time. The problem is he thought you just plain boring, Mother, and you were. A name-dropping bore. Who cared about the Duke of what's it and his bankrupt estates.

"Know what this key is, Mother? I found out it was a key to a safe-deposit box in the bank. Daddy's safe-deposit box. Tut-tut. All these private lives that you never knew anything about. Here, have a sip of tea and listen.

"Daddy's girlfriend was a good writer. It was a proper love story. You would have been proud of him, though. She never mentioned you in the letters. Never mentioned any burden, never mentioned any unhappiness. Good old Clymont! After fucking him for five years, she moved away with her husband to Quebec City. They did it in the office, Mother. Remember the nice big sofa against the window? You took us in there once and we bounced around on it. Imagine, Daddy was bouncing around on it too with Joan.

"She was his little helper. His little corporate-law helper. Remember he said how he couldn't manage without her. He had to eventually, but they were still in love. From a distance of course.

"Good old Clymont. Nice Daddy. Funny, reading the letters was like reading about some character in fiction. Was that my daddy she talked about? Daddy with his three-piece suits and starched collars and colour-coded ties. You were so efficient for poor old colour-blind Daddy. What tie goes with what suit. Always correct.

" *'Yellow doesn't go with green!'* Remember? You were shocked when I went and bought my first skirt and blouse without you. *'Ghastly!'* That's what you said. *'No taste.'* I loved that skirt and blouse and people told me I looked pretty in the colours. *'All wrong for you. Yellow isn't your colour.'*

"Poor Mummy! Your control suddenly ran out when Frank drowned. But in a way it solved your problem for you. I wanted to kill myself too when

David left. He would never have left if he hadn't been terrified I would turn into you when I was old. I wanted to be dead too. Then I thought, no, that would be too easy for you. Instead I wondered what would be the worst thing that could possibly happen to you and suddenly I knew.

"Remember the Davidsons who had the little vegetable girl, her limbs all twisted, her spine all deformed? Nauseating, you said. You used to say she should be kept at home, not flaunted around the neighbourhood. I know you wished I would stay home. You would have liked it if I'd stayed in my bed-room and not come out. *Jane has such a mind of her own. Lord knows where she gets her taste from. Jane doesn't like change. Jane hates the consumer society. Jane wears her clothes until they fall off her back.* ' Who is Jane? Who is the little girl trained to be perfect, who never held her knife like a dagger, who waited for others to start eating before she did, who always put her knife and fork neatly side by side when she was finished eating? The brilliant little girl who was always top of the class?

"Sorry, Mother, now don't choke. Cough it up! There's a good girl. We don't want you to choke on toast. We want you all here, don't we? Tonight we start reading Joanie's letters and you want to be in condition for that, don't you?"

# DESCENDING

As Mrs. Mainwaring laboured up the four flights of stairs each morning, the sound of her heels was like some evil warning as they rat-a-tatted away, getting ever nearer and more menacing.

"God, mustn't those high heels of hers have been made by the same fella' who built the Gold Gate Bridge," Bridie would say with a giggle. "... Someone who knew all about stresses and strains."

By the time Stormwarning, for that was our nickname for her, finally reached the attic, her face was bright pink, and even in cold weather there would be little beads of sweat all over her forehead.

Always the same "Jesus, I'm done in!" and the whole attic floor would shudder as she flopped heavily into her seat to catch her breath.

Her desk was on a little raised platform facing the door. Like a judge waiting to pass sentence, she sat there for the rest of the day, barely budging. Anyone coming into the room could see straight up her skirt to where her suspenders hitched up her stockings. Surprisingly enough, her little legs seemed firm right to the top until everything above suddenly went totally wrong. She was proud of her legs and always wore stiletto-healed shoes and fine nylons. She wore lacy, pink drawers in winter that came mid-thigh and in the summer pink satin panties with scalloped edges.

It was hard to figure out her age. She had a young face underneath her wiggy-looking dead hair. Anywhere between forty and fifty, Ellen guessed. The Queen of Hearts on playing cards is what always came to Ellen's mind when she saw Stormwarning: the same smug, slightly bent head, falsely modest look; then the huge bosom which plateaued without any kind of indentation to the top of her legs.

She seemed to love it when the farmers tromped to the top of the Union building to see about missing editions of the *Farmers' Gazette*. Her legs would separate slightly and she would run her tongue around her lips to moisten her lipstick, presenting what she thought was her most beguiling smile.

The missing *Gazette* was inevitably either Ellen's or Bridie's fault.

"Isn't it terribly hard to get good girls these days?"

The girls would exchange knowing looks, recognizing as they did that nothing, but nothing, that went out of the office missed her eagle eye. If there was an oversight, it more often had to do with her ruthless deletion of the names of people who were a week late with their subscription.

Her nickname was well earned, for they both knew instantly each morning whether it was going to be a good day or a bad day. They'd decided that her moods were probably brought on by whatever was happening at home with her romantically named son Garth.

Her husband was dead, but she still went on about him all the time. It was always "My William" this and "My William" that. She seldom said anything about Garth. Neither Ellen or Bridie had ever caught sight of him. He might not have existed for all the proof they had. There were never any phone calls either from him or to him, but that might have been because she didn't approve of private calls during working hours. When boys phoned either of the girls, she gritted her teeth and made a funny face as though some bile was coming up in her throat.

It was Ellen's first experience of knowing that she was completely disliked. Being only seventeen and fresh out of school, she had no idea how to handle the knowledge. Nobody there had taught her about dealing with that kind of thing. Bridie seemed to cope with her better. She had the kind of happy-go-lucky view of life that made her see Stormwarning as nothing more than an unhappy woman.

The room they worked in was an airless attic. The only ventilation would have been through the skylight window, but that was right over Stormwarning's desk, and there was no way in a million years she would ever have allowed that window to be opened. She was a regular hothouse plant and constantly aware of imagined draughts.

There were days when things went well, but mostly she tried to make Ellen's life miserable. Ellen took her dictation, typed the letters meekly and presented them to her. More often than not, Stormwarning would find a comma missing or accuse her of not using a semi-colon where no self-respecting semi-colon would ever have allowed itself to be used. Then she would make Ellen retype the whole thing. She wasn't allowed to erase. Erasing was *verboten*.

Stormwarning's fat little fingers, all bobbled with rings, would move over the newly typed letters stabbing out where she thought there was an error. Ellen thought of an old film she'd seen of Charles Laughton as Henry VIII as she watched those fingers with all the rings. Stormwarning said her husband had given them to her, but Bridie had seen her at Woolworths on High Street buying a pile of cheap rings.

Ellen had dreams at night of her stumbling on the top step and dropping dead at her feet. Perhaps stumbling over her bag full of Penguin chocolate biscuits, crumbling them all under her immense weight. Stormwarning was addicted to Penguins. Ellen counted one day: she ate ten after her lunch. Surreptitiously slipping them out of their silver wrappers under the desk, hoping Bridie and Ellen wouldn't notice.

Ellen stood all her bullying for several months, sometimes standing up to her, sometimes defiantly refusing to retype a letter, but it was more than her life was worth. She would find more subtle ways to torture her. She watched Ellen one day as she walked back and forth across the room, sorting files.

"You remind me of a cousin." She smiled the sick smile that promised an insult.

"Do I? That's nice." Ellen said nervously.

"She had a good figure like you have, when she was your age."

"Thank you!"

"... but she turned to fat," Stormwarning said casually.

Bridie let out a snort of laughter.

"And what do you find so funny?" Stormwarning growled.

"She'll have to stop eatin' Penguins," Bridie said, her voice now breaking with laughter. Bridie knew perfectly well Ellen never ate Penguins. The sight of Stormwarning guzzling them down was lesson enough for both of them.

Stormwarning's face began to turn a familiar pink now as she realized the joke was on her. Ellen and Bridie waited for the eruption, but right at that moment, Mr. McCaughey came in to the room with Bert Garrett, the general secretary of the Union. Garrett paid them occasional visits, making vague promises each time about moving the *Gazette* to better quarters. Today, he'd brought a letter which had come from their office to Harry Edwards, who was the president of the Union. Stormwarning's face blushed scarlet as she read the letter that Bert Garrett put down in front of her. She got up swiftly, a smug look on her face, and went to the filing cabinet. She produced his card with a flourish.

"He was behind in his dues," she held out the card for Garrett to see.

"Mrs. Mainwaring," Mr. McCaughey started. "... being president of the Northern Ireland Farmers' Union automatically gives Mr. Edwards an honourary membership. You mean you sent him that letter?" Stormwarning's face was now puce. "One of the girls did," she looked towards Ellen and Bridie who pretended to be busy with what they were doing.

"You can't expect them to know something like that, but you should certainly have known."

She spluttered, defeated by the truth. So shattered was she it was almost possible to feel sorry for her.

As soon as Bert Garret was gone, Bridie said with an evil grin, "I'd send him *Gazettes* until the end of time if that's what he wanted. I think he's smashin'!"

To Bridie's mind, Harry Edwards was every girl's dream of what a man should be. He wasn't in the least weather-beaten or tongue-tied, as so many of the ones who came into the building were. He was dark and large and just brooding enough for everyone to think he was Heathcliff come to life. Bridie dreamed he would give her the eye one day, but it was a vain dream for he was all business when he was at the Union offices.

"That's all you ever think of," Stormwarning said scornfully. "Getting a man!"

"Not any man, that one in particular," said Bridie with her irrepressible grin.

Ellen saw, as she'd seen a hundred times before, that Stormwarning didn't really mind Bridie. If she'd uttered any of the things that Bridie came out with, she would have been crucified on the spot.

The combination of Stormwarning's moral indignation and her misplaced anger at having been told off by Bert Garrett made her relentless. Every single letter Ellen had typed that day had to be redone. Usually Ellen tore the old ones up and put them in the waste basket, but this time she quietly swept the first copy of all the letters into her desk drawer and put the cover on her typewriter for the day.

The letters never amounted to anything more than, "Dear Sir: We are sorry to say, because of unpaid Union dues, we cannot keep you on our subscribers' list." Or "Dear Sir: This is to notify you that because of unpaid Union fees your next issue of the *Farmers' Gazette* will not be delivered." Ellen always thought this one was really stupid. It sounded as though the *Farmers' Gazette* was going to be held in limbo somewhere by the postman.

Most of the variations of letters Ellen knew by heart. If she could have typed them up as form letters, it would have made more sense. Stormwarning could just have said, "Send out No.1 or No.3," as her fancy dictated. When Ellen pointed this out to her, she was furious and her whole face screwed up in anger.

One day an idea began to form in Ellen's mind. She would simply keep all the letters for a few weeks and then take them in to McCaughey, ask him if he found anything wrong with them, and then if he didn't, tell him what had been happening. It was no use complaining at home about Stormwarning; Ellen's father seemed to think that in everyone's life there was a

"Stormwarning," and it was somehow character-strengthening to learn how to deal with her. Ellen knew he wouldn't approve of her method. He was a firm believer in face-to-face confrontation, but then he hadn't met Stormwarning; hadn't stood before all five foot ten of her and stared at those ringed fingers which looked for all the world like knuckledusters.

They suffered on through the winter stifled by the heat from the electric heater that Stormwarning kept turned up full, and the smell of L'Aimant which emanated from Stormwarning's half-toasted body. Ellen wore short-sleeved blouses so that she wouldn't suffocate. The door was kept closed at all times, so that it was a mercy when somebody came to make a query or when Mr. McCaughey called them into his office which was modestly warm.

Mr. McCaughey moved like a man with a mission. He performed all tasks at a breakneck speed and was frequently bumping into things and people in his haste. He was tiny and compact with little hands and little feet, and sported a Charlie Chaplin moustache, only gingery in colour. Sometimes Ellen half expected to see him coming around the corner with a pair of boxing gloves on and his fists raised, like he was going to do battle. In his impatience to have things done quickly, he would occasionally give Ellen the gist of an idea and get her to write something out for him, and when that happened Stormwarning was furious. She would find all sorts of things for Ellen to do, things that would delay her, so that he would be upset. Sometimes he came to see what was holding Ellen up and she would explain that Stormwarning had given her work to do. The familiar flush would rise from Stormwarning's neck, even though all he said was, "*This is priority, Mrs. Mainwaring. My work first!*"

The pile of letters in Ellen's desk drawer grew quickly, and one morning after having spent a useless hour in retyping, she finally gathered the letters and stood up. Stormwarning watched her leave the room, her little eyes glittery with curiosity.

Ellen knocked on Mr. McCaughey's door.

"Come in!"

He looked up distractedly, only half-focused on Ellen standing there.

"Do you see anything wrong with these?" Ellen set the offending letters on his desk. He looked down at the letters and then up again at her.

"What are they?"

He began to leaf through them.

"Do you see anything wrong with the typing, or spelling, or punctuation?" Ellen pressed on.

He read the first one quickly, then went to the next and shook his head baffled.

"I've been spending the last six months retyping almost every letter Mrs. Mainwaring gives me. She always finds something wrong with them."

He put the letters down and frowned.

"I just think there are better things I could be doing with my time, that's all."

"I see." He was obviously embarrassed.

"You have some problems with her?"

Ellen shook her head. "I don't have any problems with her. I think she has problems with me."

"So what do you suggest?"

Ellen smiled nervously. "I don't know. I just don't think it's going to get any better."

He hesitated, his hand resting lightly on the letters.

"Leave it with me, I'll think about it."

Ellen paused, biting her lip.

"Don't worry." He tapped the letters. "I won't say anything."

"Thank you!"

The next morning he called her into his office. The speed of his response worried her. She imagined him saying, "*It's obviously not working out, perhaps you should go somewhere else.*" She thought with horror about being fired from her first job and what her mother and father would say.

"How would you feel about working for Miss Price?" he said with a smile. "... Moving down a couple of floors, and a bit more money than you get here, so in a sense you'd be moving up in the world."

She was staggered. It wasn't what she'd expected. Eveline Price was Bert Garrett's secretary and Ellen had only ever passed her in the mornings and evenings sometimes, coming and going from work. She had a benign round face, very pale with powder, not a sign of eyebrows and not a trace of lipstick to define her mouth. She had smiled one day when she caught Ellen running past Bill White's office. "*Good girl!*" was all she had said. There was scarcely a person in the building who didn't know about Bill White's reputation with young girls.

"What would I be doing?" Ellen asked.

"She needs someone to work on promotional material. I told her you were good at doing things on your own initiative."

He saw her hesitation. "I think you'd like Miss Price. She's a good sort, generous, they tell me. You don't have to decide right away, but let me know later."

"No, that's fine! I think I'd like that."

"Good! That's settled then."

"When would I be going?"

"You can go down right now if you want. Get your things, and I'll explain to Mrs. Mainwaring that you're needed downstairs."

Ellen's heart skipped a beat with relief.

"Thank you! Thank you so much!"

"No problem. I'm just glad we can sort things out for you."

Going back into the room, Ellen had trouble trying to keep her face expressionless. She felt her chest would explode with joy. She winked at Bridie and Bridie smiled back.

Stormwarning saw the exchange and frowned. Ellen went slowly to her desk and sat down. She began going through the drawers, taking things out that were hers and setting them on top of the desk.

"What are you doing?" Stormwarning asked.

"Clearing out my things."

"Why?"

"I'm not going to be working here any more."

Stormwarning looked suddenly brighter, obviously thinking she'd been fired. "What do you mean?"

"I got a promotion," Ellen savoured the words, allowing herself a smile. "Miss Price wants me to go and work for her."

"You?" Stormwarning's face began to turn beet, "... and nobody bothers asking me about anything ..." She was speechless now.

"Mr. McCaughey just told me, you could go and talk to him if you want."

Stormwarning rose from her throne and descended the platform heavily. Even the back of her neck was red. She lifted her handbag off the top of one of the electric heaters and a great wail of distress issued out of her mouth. There was a large patch of grey stuck to the heater. The bottom of her handbag had melted.

"Who put my bag there?" she demanded.

"It was lying over by the coats. I thought you might be looking for it." Ellen said, owning up.

"You stupid little *eejit!* This was my last present from William. It was genuine leather. How could you do something so thoughtless?" Ellen looked over at Bridie whose head was buried in a file as she tried to pretend she hadn't heard.

"It was the very last thing he ever gave me and now you've ruined it. Good riddance to you! That's all I say. Good riddance!" She slammed out the door.

Bridie turned. "Jesus, Mary, and Joseph! You've melted her genuine-leather handbag. That handbag came from a *plastic* cow, you understand, a very special *plastic* cow."

"Oh, Bridie. I feel rotten about that. I didn't mean to."

"Get sense, girl! The aul' bitch has done nothing but give you grief. She had it coming to her."

Bridie leant back on her chair. "So you're going to leave me alone with her?"

"Yes, I'm sorry about that."

"No, you're not. You're delighted and I don't blame you." Bridie began to giggle, "He does it with her right in the office!" Bridie said knowledgeably.

"Does what?" Ellen asked naively.

"Garrett and Miss Price. You know what," Bridie grinned.

Ellen felt her face flush. Remembering the pale, washed-out, puffy face that passed her on the stairs, it hardly seemed possible.

"His wife's an invalid. You know what they say," Bridie said with an evil grin. "... Any port in a storm."

"God, you're awful!" Ellen felt her flush deepen. At the same time feeling prim and judgemental, she turned her face away from Bridie.

"Everyone knows. You'll have to tell us all about it."

"I'm sure they'll invite me in to have a look," Ellen said trying to sound worldly, at the same time plumping her shoulder bag on top of a pile of books.

"You're a lucky *git* running away from this dump," Bridie said with a frown.

"You probably could too."

"What did you do?"

"I showed him all the letters she made me retype."

"God, maybe he'll sack her."

"I don't think so somehow."

"I'll miss you," Bridie said.

"I'm not exactly off to Timbuctoo. We can go an' have a cup of tea together whenever you want."

Ellen got her coat and carried her stuff to the door. "You're not going to say good-bye to our friend?" Bridie said with a grin.

"Tell her I'm sorry about the handbag."

"Jesus, you never learn," Bridie said following her friend to the door.

"I want the gossip, mind, keeps your eyes and ears open. I'll be waitin'."

Ellen felt such elation that she felt like climbing over the bannisters and whizzing down the two flights to Eveline Price's office, but instead she walked sedately and carefully until she was outside the second-floor offices. Pausing for a second, she stared at the plain frosted glass. For some odd reason she looked at her watch. It was 11:15 a.m. In her mind she recited the date, March 15th, 1956. She was quite prepared to wipe the last year out of her memory and begin again. *Oh, God. Wasn't the 15th March something to do with the Ides of March, and wasn't that somehow an unpleasant date?* She was rattled for a moment, but before she had time to think much more about it, the door opened and Bill White almost walked into her.

"Wee Ellen," he grinned at her — a big toothy, woolfish grin. His hand shot out and brushed her breast as he put an unnecessary arm on hers. "I hear tell you're going up in the world."

She nodded, and then saw with relief the face of Eveline Price behind his.

"Hands off her, White!" Eveline Price called out. "Come in, girlie ... and welcome to the second floor."

# EROSION

It was a lot steeper than it had looked from the top of the cliff, but then that was the story of her life. Everything always seemed possible at the start, before some malicious God, angry perhaps with her presumption, always chose to change the landscape of her intentions.

She should, of course, have left a note on the dashboard of the car, just in case. "Not suicide" would have sufficed, but not for a moment had she considered that what she was about to tackle was in the least dangerous. Now, as the rocks skidded from under her feet and went careening off the cliff face, she saw herself following. She would soundlessly thump against the jagged outcroppings, only to land like a limp sandbag on the tiny beach below. When they found her body, John would be only too happy to assume she had committed suicide. It was this one thought that kept her going on giving her feet purchase. Uselessly curling her toes in her running shoes, she imagined she was hooking herself tenaciously to the ground beneath.

The cove had been her goal, but now she knew that was impossible. She would settle instead for the rocky ledge that was only about twenty yards further down.

She grasped at the bracken that grew from the cliff face as her feet skidded uselessly, and she slid forward, temporarily out of control. Her heart pounded in her chest, but there was no going back now. In fact, even to think of the climb back up gave her a convulsive feeling of terror. No thoughts, just arms and legs moving onward. All she had to do was focus on actually being there, safe on the ledge.

The chosen ledge turned out to be accommodatingly flat, its smoothness only interrupted by occasional crevasses with mounds of moss softly scarring the shape. On top of the cliff the sound of the pounding waves had been more distant and muffled; here, with the wall of cliff at her back, they were no longer background music but demanded attention, almost echoing through her body. For an instant she allowed herself to feel frightened again. The reverberations seemed to destroy her very thought pattern.

It would be so easy to panic and yet even while she settled, placing her small knapsack beside her on the ledge, a marvellous feeling of oneness with her surroundings started to overtake all the other sensations. The waves were the actual pounding of the blood in her veins, and she could control even that.

She sat for a while, knees tucked up to her chin, smelling her knees the way she had done as a child, licking them, tasting the salt and faint sweet smell of grass. The wind whispered around the curves of her body, intermittent gusts grabbing at the edges, even producing the occasional quick rash of gooseflesh that she could trace with a fingernail while she wondered idly about the body mechanisms that produced such a phenomenon. No, she wouldn't wonder about anything. She'd be as mindless as a mollusc attached to the rock.

This was the coming-back-to-life stage, it was something that shouldn't be rushed. The trip was a step forward. The descent down the cliff was another kind of risk she was becoming adept at handling.

The beauty of the surroundings pressed in on her, demanding some kind of equation, but nothing had to be hurried. She would allow everything to seep into her bones, nourish the very marrow, and not for a moment would any of the old self-pity be allowed to enter with it. There was herself, then there was John. The shock and numbness of his betrayal had reduced her to an automaton with no other function than to feed and bathe herself at suitable life-sustaining intervals. But that was past, over and done with.

She took a deep breath. It was easy enough to believe that she was entirely alone in the world. She might indeed linger for an eternity on the surface of the rock, allowing erosion to take its toll, let the tides and seasons diminish the last traces of pain from her body.

She took her clothes off and using them as padding stretched out lazily on the rock.

The sky was an unusual one for the coast, monochromatic, almost blending with the sea, only the textures so different. She closed her eyes and visualized an unending pattern of smooth and ruffled blueness, and her mind drifted off, contented with the simplicity of the pattern.

Perhaps she was five miles from Halifax, perhaps twenty, it didn't really make any difference. There were no deadlines anymore, no imposed patterns.

Her entire life had been one of intense order and planning and never more so than in the past ten years with John. She had been stop-watched constantly: *"It will take forty-five minutes to here, twenty-five to there."* Was he doing that now with darling Valerie?

She had lost all sense of time when suddenly she woke with a start, staring straight upwards, aware of something else. Even when she saw him, she shut her eyes quickly, refusing to believe that it was anything but a dream. She opened them again, convinced that this lewd interjection was a trick her mind was playing. It was after all a mind that had become almost twisted of late, imagining John's Thousand and One Nights of passion with the eager Valerie. But the figure was still there, starkly white against the blue of the sky, absolutely naked and distinctly proud of his erection. Proud enough to wave at her with no sense of shame. She could feel the blush start around her feet and cover her body like a blanket. She could only think of those Greek urns with the cavorting satyrs.

He cupped his hands around his mouth and shouted down to her, "Can I join you?"

*Did she have an option, where was she going? Certainly not down.*

"I was just leaving," she shouted feebly, as though it was some cocktail party she was quitting early. He paid no attention and began to nimbly hop over rocks. She stood mesmerized at the speed of his descent. Any chance of getting away was impossible, her haste would surely kill her if she tried.

He was almost upon her when she remembered her own total nakedness. She grabbed for her shorts and had one leg in when he was suddenly beside her. She managed to untangle the shorts and get them on, but by this time he was sitting comfortably on her shirt and bra, and at the same time blocking any possible means for her to escape. He didn't look at her face at all. His eyes focused on her breasts. Absurdly, now that she had her shorts on, she felt far more conspicuous than if she had been totally naked.

"I'd like my shirt, please."

"You would?" he smiled an easy smile but made no move to give it to her.

"Look, I don't know what you have in mind, but it won't work."

"I din' say I had anything in mind." He shook his head, adopting the baffled look of a little boy.

He was big of frame, rather powerful in the chest and thin in the legs. He reminded her of some of the Third World children with largish torsos and thin extremities, and for some reason that worried her.

"What you doin' here?"

"Sunbathing."

"You don' look like no sun goddess."

"I don't get out too often." *Was she actually apologizing for her whiteness?*

"You should take the pants off and let the sun get at your parts."

"I feel more comfortable with them on. Look, I have to go. Could I have my stuff?"

"But I just got here."

"I know ..." *How was it possible to bustle when there was nothing to bustle with?* She fumbled awkwardly with the belt on her shorts.

"You got great tits."

She turned her back.

"Good bum too."

She felt her knees giving out and the shake in her body was rapidly moving upward.

"You scared?"

It was important to control it, she knew it was important to control it.

"No, why should I be scared?"

"'Cause you're shakin'."

"Look, maybe you get your kicks this way, but it's sick."

He frowned, "I ain't forcin' you to do anything, am I?"

"You won't let me leave."

"Come and get your things, I ain't stopping you."

"You're sitting on them."

He moved slightly and smiled. She was suddenly terrified. Her body refused to move in his direction. She felt like an observer of her own terror. She wasn't inside her body actually experiencing it. The sweating palms belonged to the person on the rock who was "dealing with the situation." "Dealing with situations" was John's forté, never hers. She had always been the victim caught like a twig in a cross-current. But not to deal with this one was certain death, of that she was sure.

"Well, what's stopping you?"

"Look, what do you want?"

"To talk, jus' to talk."

"What do you want to talk about?"

"Whatever." He squinted up at her, his eyes focusing around her nipples again. "What do you do, for instance?" He patted the ground beside him. "I hate talkin' to someone standing. It's like they don' want to stay."

She crouched uncertainly and then slid her bottom onto the ground. Sliding sideways, she supported herself on one arm.

"That's better." He smiled, "What do you do?"

How did one engage in casual conversation with someone whose eyes never lifted above breast level?

"Physio."

"What's that?"

"When people have problems with their body, I work on them." The minute it was said, she knew it had been disastrously worded.

"I'm all yours," he grinned and opened his arms.

"I gotta pain right here," he pointed at his penis which thankfully had subsided. She found herself swallowing hard, her mouth was absolutely dry.

"Could you pass my knapsack?" She pointed to the khaki bag.

"What do you want?"

"Something to drink, that's all."

He opened the bag and looked in. "Heh! A san'wich. I could do with that."

"Have it!"

"We can share it."

"I'm not hungry."

He handed her the flask and tearing the paper off the egg sandwich, he bit into it hungrily. "Not bad!" He held it out towards her, "Go on, have a bite!"

She could smell the sulphurous odour of the egg. It made her want to throw up. "I'm not hungry."

He shrugged. She poured herself some water from the flask. It was like drinking in hot air, the tepid quality left her mouth as dry as ever.

"I could do with some of that."

She nodded, but he made no move towards her. She edged over, perambulating with one leg, holding out the bottle, but he refused to reach for it. She set it down on the ground.

"Give it to me!" He commanded.

"Look ..."

"Quit arguing, jus' do it!"

Tentatively she moved to the bottle again and put out her hand. With a quick movement he grabbed her wrist and with his other hand cupped her breast.

"Nice! Very nice!"

"Look, I don't know what you plan, but it won't work. You'll feel rotten afterwards. You always feel rotten afterwards, don't you?"

He shoved her away.

This wasn't "dealing with it," this was screwing it up completely. Her "observer" was noticing a certain crumpling of facial muscles, then the tight spasm of anger. Vulnerability perhaps?

"You think you know it all. I've never done nothin' before."

The roughness had disappeared again; in its place a certain amount of pain was registered. Perhaps he was telling the truth. He didn't look that old, nor did he have the face of someone truly violent. Not that she could comfort herself with that thought. Psychotics, she knew, were notoriously mild-looking people.

"There's always a first time, isn't there? Wouldn't you like to make it with me?" His dialogue was curiously dated.

"No!"

His face darkened perceptibly.

"Not that I've anything against you, but this isn't the way to go about it." This was John's voice speaking, a voice of reason which once she might have detested, but today embraced.

"Do you have a girl?" It was worth trying a new tack.

He shook his head.

"Ever had a girl?" *Careful. This was challenging his manhood.*

"Plenty." His chin went up.

"Then why this?"

"It gets boring, that's why."

"You want to hurt someone?"

"Who said anything about that?"

"Isn't that what this is all about?" She folded her arms across her chest in an effort to break his focus and tried desperately to think of reasonable arguments, but panic was scrambling her thoughts.

"Just think about your knees, for one thing."

"You some kind of comedian, or somethin'?"

She shook her head.

"You're gonna go down on me, lady, you heard of that?"

Her mind rummaged in panic for those essential arguments that would surely stop all this. Then she remembered the last time she'd been with John sexually. Even at the moment of consummation she had been desperately aware of the betrayal of self. Furious and angry with him, half-guessing about Valerie, but still not really sure, she'd been engaged in some final battle for supremacy. She remembered the moment of total power when her teeth had begun to sink into the flesh and his nails had dug into her back, still in ecstasy, and then lockjaw had taken over.

She raised an eyebrow towards her tormentor. "You would risk that?"

He stared at her face for the first time, and then it seemed to dawn on him what she was talking about.

"There's nothing to stop me pitchin' you right over." He waved a hand at the rocks below.

"Would that be a turn-on too?"

"You think I'm gonna let you go runnin' off to blab?"

The small traces of composure that had been coming back to her were instantly wiped out. She could feel the arm she was leaning on begin to tremble.

"What would I say? Some guy came and joined me on a rock naked? I'm naked too, don't forget."

"I'm not forgettin'."

"Look, you don't want to screw up your whole life just because you're feeling horny. My husband just did that." *It was a ridiculous statement to make, when what had really happened was that John had ruined hers. And if she allowed it, this total stranger was about to make her experience that total humiliation yet again.*

"He threw you over, huh?"

She nodded.

"He gave up a great body like yours for someone else?" His eyes had realigned themselves once more.

*Was the common denominator after all just a body? Perhaps this was part of her madness. She was sitting on a rock facing the Atlantic, her body the only commodity to be traded, and traded for what, her life? Something that until now she hadn't even been sure she wanted.*

"You mean he's off screwin' someone else and you're lying on a rock thinking about it?"

"Something like that."

"Fuck that! That's all you're going to do?"

She nodded. Why had she even mentioned John, it somehow made the proceedings more intimate. Now the question was how to back off the topic of sex.

"What do you do for a living?" It sounded like a typical singles-bar question, but it had slipped out before she could think properly.

"I'm a fireman."

She laughed nervously. *Was it possible, a fireman who said 'ain't' and dropped his g's? But one didn't put out fires with words or rescue people with syntax. And whether or not the fire department had some basic educational requirements was the least of her worries at this point.*

"What's so funny?"

What was so funny was that her mind could follow such inane patterns of thought under this kind of duress. Perhaps she really was cracking up.

"Nothing!"

"You laughed."

Did condemned people even smile, let alone laugh?

"I don't know."

"I'd like to know, lady." His voice was tight and she started to feel chills again.

"You just don't think of public servants running around trying to rape people."

"I haven't done nothing to you, yet."

"No, that's true." There wasn't enough pride in his voice to give her any comfort, the "yet" was too tentative.

"Haven't you got a nice girlfriend? I mean you're a nice-looking guy ... there are all kinds of girls out there."

"I told you, I've had plenty ... just none special."

"That's not true either, is it?"

"What's with you? You into people's minds too?"

*Into people's minds. That was a joke. If she had been she would have known sooner about John and Valerie.*

"Is that what physios do too?"

She stared at him, noticing how little hair there was anywhere on his body, unlike John, whose body was perfectly bisected down the middle of his chest with a furrow of fine hair.

"How old are you?"

"Twenty-seven."

"Twenty-seven and there hasn't been anyone?" This was asking for swift death and she hadn't meant to let it slip out.

There was silence for several minutes, his only movement the grinding of his knuckles into the rock beside him. He then straightened out his hand and she could see there was blood where he'd scraped off the skin.

This was the point where she made the decision that she wanted to live. It should have taken more time, considering how often in the past month she had seriously contemplated death.

There was nothing to stop him throwing her over as he'd promised and she would be gone without a trace. There was no one expecting her arrival in Halifax. It had been her decision to surprise her cousin Audrey. John didn't know where she was and probably couldn't care less.

Her voice came out surprisingly firm.

"Lie down!" she commanded.

"He looked up quickly, his eyes brightening.

"You gonna do it?"

She shook her head. "No! I'm going to do something better, give you a massage. Lie face down!"

His eyes narrowed, "You think I'm stupid or something?"

She held up her hand, "I'm not going anywhere. Besides, if I tried, you could catch me quickly enough. Right?"

"You're goddam right!"

Lying on her shirt, he positioned himself on his stomach.

"Look, I'm the one who has to use my knees. Can I at least have my shirt to kneel on?"

He lifted his body slightly and she removed her shirt. Folding it several times, she tried to make as much of a pad for herself as she could.

"I don't understand why you're doin' this?" He peered at her sideways from his prone position.

"Neither do I. Now just shut up. If it's to do any good, you're not supposed to talk."

"Can't I lie on my back?"

"No! Now shut up!"

It was a form of relief to be working on his body, it stilled the shake in her hands and somewhere there was the belief that through the magic of her fingers she could transfer some tranquillity into his body. Satisfy him by the mere pleasure of her touch. She had done this often for John, easing the tension out of his muscles after his jogging; massaged him literally to sleep. There were times when it had worked the other way too, when it was a prelude to making love, but she didn't want to think about that now. Surely, thinking about it would transfer itself into her fingertips.

She tried to persuade herself that everything was normal, but she knew so much depended on the ability of her hands to quiet his body.

Starting on the back of his neck she worked around the spinal cord, feeling the tension underneath her palms. Even though flat on the ground, his entire rib cage was puffed out. She felt certain that with enough push on her part, she would be able to crack him open like a walnut. She heard him expel air as she pushed down and knew, like always, that the process was beginning.

His body had no excess flesh, but it wasn't particularly well proportioned; the torso was too long, the hips too narrow. She could imagine him a few years down the line, with a sagging belly and poor posture. She concentrated on the vertebrae and every few minutes he gave small ecstatic cries. Only when she touched his legs, did she feel his body stiffen again.

"Relax!" she ordered. "You're spoiling it all." His legs which had looked so unmuscled were harder to the touch than she had imagined they would be. Moving down to his feet and toes, she began to work on them. The occasional contented groans were less frequent now but were curiously comforting to her. *Poor bugger!* In his prone position he suddenly seemed impotent and very sad.

Turning to his arms and hands, she worked individually on each finger, but holding his hand she felt a ridge of hard skin on the palm. She turned it over and looked at it. There was heavy scarring that ran well up to the first knuckle of each finger. She lifted his other hand and examined it too. It was the same.

He had suddenly come to life again and was turning, now facing her, lying on his back.

"From a fire?"

His eyes were closed, but he shook his head.

"What then?"

There was silence and then he finally opened his eyes and stared at her. She could have sworn there were tears in them.

"I've never had anyone touch me that way in my whole life. It's beautiful."

"How did you get the scars?"

He closed his eyes again, "My old lady used to put my hands on the burner when I was a kid."

She shivered involuntarily.

"What for?"

He opened his eyes and looked at her.

"Please! Please! Couldn't you?"

He obviously had no intention of answering the question. She looked at him, at his entire body, at the penis lying insignificantly curled against the pubic hair and she knew that whatever her decision, she had nothing more to fear. Something else too: after weeks of feeling subhuman and directionless, she felt oddly important again. The thought of John and Valerie had been pushed away by the more pressing problem of lifesaving. There seemed to be some debt to pay, but for whom or what she wasn't certain.

"What difference would it make?" he pleaded.

Later, he sat up, hands around his knees and stared morosely down at the rock.

"I feel rotten."

She nodded, "Would you do something for me now?"

"What?" He looked up eagerly.

"Leave me! I need to be alone."

He looked disappointed, but he nodded and got up slowly, almost painfully. "Couldn't we ..."

"No!"

"I don't know what to say."

"Please, just leave quickly."

He hesitated and then moved off, beginning his ascent. Pausing somewhere above her, he looked down.

"Good-bye and thanks!"

"Good-bye!"

She didn't bother to follow his entire retreat, she knew he was gone. She took up her yoga position on the rock. The air was cooler now, the wind fresh against her face. She was whole, untouched, all trembling and uncertainty gone. She was now part of the rock she was sitting on, but under the fossilized, hard shell she had visualized earlier, life was stirring once more. There was substance enough to endure for at least a decent lifetime.

# IN THE DRIVER'S SEAT

It was the first funeral in ten years that Emma had been to without Fran. But in a way Fran was there, even if she was laid out in the other room with rosy cheeks like one of those alabaster Virgin Marys sold in religious shops. How they'd done it was a mystery because in real life Fran had skin more like wax paper that had been done to a turn in the oven.

All you heard were people sayin', "Now isn't she a picture?" *or* "Doesn't she look fine in death?" Jesus sake! Dead was dead. You weren't supposed to look like you was goin' to open your eyes an' go "Boo!"

If Emma hadn't been feeling so mad about it all, she would surely have fallen apart. For it was Fran lying there. Beloved Fran. Since their husbands had died some twenty years before, both men taken within a month of each other, there had been no sitting around for Emma or Fran. There had been bus tours of Europe and the British Isles, and right until Fran had her heart attack, neither of them had missed a single funeral, christening or tea in the Carlisle district and that was through wind, sleet or snow.

Emma did the driving and Fran sat back and enjoyed the scenery. The nice thing about Fran was that she never bitched or whined about a damned thing. In and out of ditches they'd been together, and once Fran had even been pinned when the car did a turn in Simmond's field, but Fran hadn't even complained then, just brushed herself off and laughed about the bruises.

*"I see us goin' real quick!"* she'd said once to Emma. *"Sort of flying, like on one of our trips, and we won't know what hit us."*

*"Reckless!"* Emma's Bob had always called her driving. But she didn't care. She'd gotten them places for years and they'd survived. Only Fran had been wrong about them goin' together. She'd opted out early. She'd have been glad of that. They'd often talked about death and they'd made each other a solemn promise, no tubes and bottles an' things. *"Pull the plug real quick!"* Well someone had sure pulled Fran's quick enough, but who was going to pull hers now that Fran was gone?

She looked across the room at her daughter-in-law, Sharon. She'd be the last person. Sharon, strictly because of her principles of course, would keep her hooked up for an eternity like a spent battery waiting for a charge that wouldn't take.

Sharon in that same damned green pant suit, stuffing a piece of carrot cake into her mouth, licking off her fingers the way she always did: a fat rock lizard, the little red tongue flicking out greedily, making sure not to miss a crumb.

Sharon had started off pretty enough, but time hadn't been good to her. She'd been one of those soft-lookin' blondes with five-year-old voices, but the face was big and round now an' the voice had hardened in pitch so that it grated on the ears.

It was no use pretending about Sharon, they'd never liked each other from the word go. Sharon had thought by marrying Will she was entering some kind of competition, only there was none. Will, unlike Donald, her oldest, had always been a slow youngster: slow at everything, a week late bringing in the crops and then it would rain and they would lie soggy in the fields. Like all slow people the harder you push them the slower they go. Sharon had been too dumb to know that. Later, when she'd realized she was wasting her time nagging, her frustration had turned into bitterness.

Sharon came across the room to her. "Well, Mother-in-law, you'll have to put the car on blocks now." Her little eyes glittered with enjoyment.

"Not a darned thing wrong with the car that I know of," Emma smiled.

"Won't be the same on your own, will it?"

Marge Jedzinsky joined them and put a hand under Emma's elbow. "You'll miss her?" Marge said with sympathy.

"I was just sayin' that," Sharon said, pushing more cake into her mouth. "I sometimes think Mother-in-law shouldn't be on the roads. Some people just don't know when to quit."

"Oh, I don't know," Marge said with a grin. "She couldn't drive worth a darn forty years ago, nuthin' much has changed."

"It wouldn't do her no harm to stay home for a while." Sharon wiped a wrist across her mouth. What she'd wanted to say was, *"Stay home and clean up,"* Emma guessed but she didn't have the nerve to say it. You couldn't set a foot in Sharon and Will's house without having to take off your shoes. The whole house was covered in plastic from top to bottom. What in God's name she was saving it all for was a mystery to Emma.

Sharon exchanged a look with Marge, but Emma didn't give a hoot. She'd never been one for housekeeping, but it hadn't bothered Bob, her husband, one bit. What she had done was cook good meals and raise the boys as best she could.

Donald was a professor in the city now an' she was proud of that. There was no denying that she had a lot more in common with Donald. They could talk about anything together, but there was also a special feeling there for Will because he'd been so helpless in so many ways. Donald, she knew, would always manage by himself; it would be Will who would have the struggle, and God help him, with Sharon he wouldn't get much comfort.

Will came over to her house a lot these days and lay around the living room with his legs stretched out, leafing morosely through old magazines. Emma reckoned he came for peace and quiet because the T.V. was on over at his place from morning to night. He probably came too to put his bum down on some honest-to-God fabric for a change. Lord knows it must be horrible to have to sit on plastic all the time.

Emma closed out the buzz of voices in the other room. *"Hey! Remember the time we went to New York?"* She heard the familiar voice distinctly, but she didn't open her eyes, she just smiled.

*"Them cab drivers drove just like you, Emma. I felt right at home. Remember you could see them eyeballin' us in the mirror to see if we was gonna pass out from fright and there we was sittin' up tall and havin' a good smile?"*

"What you doin' in here talkin' to yourself?" A green shadow by Emma's elbow asked.

"I wasn't talkin' to myself. I was having a talk with Fran." Emma said defiantly.

"It isn't healthy talkin' to the dead."

"Who said I was talkin' to the dead?"

*Gone off her rocker! Definitely gone off her rocker!* There'd be the voices whisperin'.

Will jogged her elbow. "You'd better come in the other room, Mother. Have some more tea," he said.

"I've had all the tea I'm gonna have. An' I'd appreciate it if you'd leave me to pay my last respects."

"It's no use being morbid, Mother."

"Who's bein' morbid?"

"Sharon says you've been talkin' away to yourself."

"I wasn't talkin' to myself, Son, I was talkin' to Fran."

"That's even worse." Will said. Sharon nodded in agreement.

Emma sighed. "I've been talkin' to Fran for forty-five years, Son, old habits die hard. Now if you don't mind I'd like to be alone."

The next couple of weeks were horrible. Emma got some kind of chest infection and had to stay in bed. The worst thing of all was having to be beholden to Sharon who came and went with trays of food: steak turned into shoe leather, swimming around in a morass of red-clay gravy; or meat loaf that turned to sawdust in the mouth.

The only good thing was that Fran kept coming and they went over all the good times they'd had together. She tried to keep Fran away when Sharon was there, but sometimes Sharon came sneaking in on them. She came in on them when she an' Fran were having a good gas about the Picasso exhibit they'd seen in Montreal.

"At it again, Mother-in-law?"

Sharon shoved the tray down on the side table, knocking a book onto the floor. Yanking out a tea towel she'd brought with her, she tied it like a bib around Emma's neck.

"I don't need this thing." Emma tried to take off the bib.

"Yes, you do, you'll drop all over yourself."

"I wish you'd stop treatin' me as if I'm demented."

"Maybe when you stop talkin' to yourself."

"Just because you can't see no one doesn't mean no one's there," Emma said.

"You think there's someone there?"

"Not someone! Fran."

Sharon sat back with a piece of chicken impaled on a fork and stared at her mother-in-law. Emma could see she'd gone too far. It was shortly after that they brought in the nurse, a female with a breath worse than Reggie, the farm dog's.

Emma's cough wouldn't go away, it wore her out when she got into one of the spasms. She knew she was a lot worse when Will came and sat with her for about an hour every day. She wasn't sure why he sat because they didn't have much to say to each other, but she liked him there and he did hold her hand.

Days had a way of folding into one another, dawn rolling into dusk, lights on and lights off, voices coming and going. Vaguely she heard, "Mother, there's going to be a storm an' we're scared we'll get locked in down here an' you not gettin' any better. Dr. Bell thinks we should take you into the hospital."

"I'm not goin' anywhere!"

"Donald's on his way."

"That's nice, but he's wasting his time. I'm not going to no hospital."

"Mother we can't look after you here if you get any worse." An' she knew he wasn't talking about her cough, she knew he was goin' on about her conversations with Fran, although God knows why he should have been worried about those. They didn't harm anyone and they kept her from being lonely.

Donald came finally, trying his best to hide his worry, but that would be because of Sharon's lies. He gave her a hug and sat down beside her.

"Hello, Mother!"

"Hello, Donald!"

"Will says you're being difficult."

"He's the one being difficult."

"We're all worried about you."

"About what?"

"Your cough."

"An'?"

"And nothing ... your cough."

She knew it was no use to argue. They would use any trick to get her out, and she didn't feel she had enough energy for the battle. The nurse helped her dress, breathing her awful dog breath in Emma's face. At least they would have young ones in the hospital with fresh breath.

The awful thing was that as they left the farm she had a sudden, terrible feeling she was leaving Fran behind. When Donald had settled her into the car and gone to say his good-byes to Will and Sharon, Emma asked,

*"Are you still there, Fran?"*

*"Darned tootin' I am. You don't think I'd leave you now?"*

*"I wasn't so sure."*

*"You're makin' a mistake, you know."*

Emma frowned, *"You don't have to tell me, but I couldn't fight 'em all."*

*"Don't see why not. This way it's the last time you'll see the place. They turf you out and then Sharon will come in with a scrubbing brush."*

At that point Donald climbed into the car beside her and patted her blanket-covered knee. "Are you O.K., Mother?"

Emma nodded, she was feeling anything but all right. It had already begun to snow outside, those big heavy cotton balls of snow that promise snowdrifts. Donald drove cautiously out of the driveway. It was already getting greasy the way it always did with the first layer.

"Looks like we just started in time."

"In time for what?"

"Before the storm comes in full force."

Donald drove just the way his father had, ten miles an hour, as if he expected to meet the worst around every corner. They were silent. She could see Donald needed his concentration, but there were things on her mind.

"I don't want them to put no paint on my face," she said finally.

"Paint on your face? What do you mean?" Donald didn't take his eyes off the road and had his "humour her" voice in place, although it wasn't as casual as usual.

"When I go, I don't want them makin' me up like I was some sort of china doll."

"Mother, you're not going anywhere but to hospital."

"No paint, mind!"

She was content she'd said what she had to, and she knew he'd paid attention even if he'd pretended it wasn't worth thinking about.

Sometime later, they turned into a service station for some gas. The attendant came out and he and Donald commiserated about the weather. She heard them only vaguely, because she wasn't feeling too good, like there was a big band tightening around her chest. Donald mumbled something about new wiper blades for the windshield and was gone somewhere. Suddenly she heard Fran's voice clear as a bell.

*"So you're just gonna sit there an' let him take you to hospital? Just like that?"*

Thank God it was Fran. Emma smiled, she knew that Fran would never abandon her.

*"What else can I do?"*

*"You gotta car, get goin', hightail it back before the witch gets her shovel in to clear out your place."*

*"It don't seem right."*

*"It's not, but what they're doing isn't either. Come on, girl! Get a move on!"*

Then she was in the driver's seat without even knowing where she'd found the energy to move and somehow the car was going.

*"Way to go, girl!"*

*"You know I reckon all those years you've been eggin' me on, Fran?"*

*"Never needed too much urgin', that's for sure."*

There was a lot of buzzing going on in her head.

*"You're sure gettin' cautious in your old age. Remember how we talked about flyin'? You still have a chance, you know. Perfect time to do it, nothing but soft landings."*

*"Fran, you old rascal."*

But she was right about soft landings. Even now she felt as if she were inside a vast ball of wool, cushioned from any kind of hurt or danger. Where she was didn't really matter. She was conscious of the windshield wiper moving uselessly back and forth. Donald had been right, it was no earthly good, it cleared things for only a second, long enough for her to see someone's face peering at her, maybe Donald's, maybe not. No, it couldn't be Donald, she was on the highway, she could feel the car moving beneath her.

*"Atta girl! I knew you could do it!"* Fran's voice said.

She could see big white tracks in front of her just like the snow plough made when it came in up the lane to the farm, and what sounded like Reggie's barking when he always ran out to greet her when she got back from one of her trips. Then it was like she was on a runway and everything around her was flying past and she was soaring, soaring and in the background Fran was laughing and urging her on ... An' the weirdest thing, somehow Reggie was hangin' over her an' she was trying to avoid his breath.

*"Atta girl! Atta girl!"*

Thank God for Fran!

# FRANGIPANI

Marg Seibert peered at the coloured pictures in her tropical-flower book, trying to identify some of the plants and shrubs she had seen in the last few days.

Behind her Frank's complaining and curses rang out with less clarity than usual. The waves that exultantly united the waters of the Atlantic with the Caribbean on this south-west tip of the island had enough rhythm and sound as they surfed against the rocks to muffle his humping bad humour.

She breathed deeply, inhaling the faint iodiney smell of the sea mingled with the humid odour of lushness and growth, and made a vain wish that the foreign air could renew her, fill her with joy, or even a tinge of hope.

"Where the hell is it?" Frank shouted from the bedroom. She turned to the next page. Her back thickened and hunched, waiting for the next round.

"Shit, woman! What did you do with it?"

She looked down at the photo of the frangipani tree and tried to concentrate. Her eyes traced the monkey-puzzle type contrariness of the tree's shape — the early-spring nakedness of its branches and then the exquisite bloom right at the end of the branch. Life was like that tree, she mused, long stretches of barren absurdity and then the small rewards for endurance. She read on, "... *when trimmed, the plant exudes a milky sap which was used by Indians to cauterize wounds.*"

Marg hunched tighter in the chair, her arms cross-braced. The ever-present feeling of unfamiliarity with her own body alarmed her: the loose flipper of flesh on the upper arms, the bunching of excess flesh on her waist, and the white doughy roundness of her stomach were an insult to her sensibilities. There were days when she could dream them away or else see herself as Rubenesque and proud of her dimensions.

*"You're out of touch with reality!"* Frank snarled when she complained that there didn't seem to be enough room on the planes any longer. *"... fat asses need two seats."* She'd arrived at the airport crying. The tour guide thought she was homesick.

It was his illness that made him even more difficult. He'd never had a moment's sickness until the heart attack. He'd been bewildered at first and then angry, railing out at everyone around him but most of all at her.

The sky was deepening into wine red shadings, and the water was now oil-slick dark. Up above, a pinpoint of light moved towards the island, yet another load of tourists for paradise. She closed the book and stood up. Unless she made a move to sort out his pills and medication, they would eat late and the pain would come. It came frequently now, just under her breast bone.

He was anxiously taking his pulse again. Since his triple bypass, he took his pulse ten times a day.

Sitting on the edge of her bed she could just see her face over the array of bottles: three different kinds of panacea for ageing bodies; Metamucil, Agarol, Pepto-Bismol, plus the smaller bottles, multiple varieties of pills to keep the blood pulsing through tired arteries. The face that stared back at her was the fat plastic-doll face from her childhood: puffy and artificial-looking against the pale peach colour of her cotton caftan. Somewhere in the fluff of blonde hair and the hopeless moon of that face had been a beautiful young girl.

"Three damned weeks here!" He stood up, fastening his shirt.

From the dresser she picked up the frangipani blossom she had rescued from the ground of the courtyard earlier in the day. Its waxen paleness was still perfection as though it needed only the air to survive. She walked to the balcony to throw it over but set it instead on the table.

Holidays were always his idea. There hadn't been one since the triple bypass two years before, and it wasn't something she had missed.

They ate out every night and seldom was he happy. The food was too expensive, too cold, too tasteless, the service too slow, the place too noisy, and through it all they sat, strangers, trying to remember how it was they were where they were, and with one another.

She went downstairs ahead of him and sat down on the couch in the lobby to wait yet again while he searched for a sweater. She would like to have taken the flower book, it made her feel peaceful, but he wouldn't have wanted that. He would want full attention for his silence.

One of the women she'd seen on the patio that afternoon came along the hallway.

"Good evening! My, don't you look lovely."

Marg smiled back and for an instant blushed. She wasn't fooled. She knew condescension when she heard it. The woman and her friend had looked at her with pity when Frank had cursed loudly as his legs had touched the burning pad of the chaise that afternoon on the patio.

They had made up their minds about her and Frank right then and there and this one, so liberal with her compliments, was ready to offer pity. Only, she wasn't ready to receive.

There had been lots of times when she had remembered why she married him; remembered his body when it had been strong, his face when he had smiled and felt good; remembered the rewarding times, how there were always flowers when the children were born: six red roses for the girls and twelve for the boys. He would have given her the world for giving him sons and she'd been happy, briefly, but memorably happy, carefully snipping the ends from the roses each day and refilling the water, but his goodness which more often than not seemed conditional, had faded not long after the roses had died. There were times in between the six children when she had wanted to run away, or merely die, but both these possibilities needed planning and somehow the years had slipped by.

A bronzed and gleaming young couple passed them on the narrow street that led towards the restaurants, slipping by on a carillon of laughter and happiness. The girl was almost bosomless and proud of it, the way all the young girls were nowadays. No more padding, no more pretending, postage-stamp bras on postage-stamp breasts. Marg envied their verve.

In the restaurant Marg ordered a double scotch. She drank it down quickly like it was medicine and defiantly caught the waiter's arm when he passed and indicated she wanted another one. Across the table Frank frowned briefly and returned to taking his pulse, squinting at the minute hand on his oversized watch.

She got up from the table. The room revolved around her, she felt as though she were at sea. Her caftan caught on the bamboo arm of an empty chair and she carried it with her for a moment, like a ship proud of its wake. Frank would be shaking his head in disgust but she refused to turn.

In a bathroom pungent with the odour of disinfectant and urine, she groped under her tentlike dress and removed her bra, stuffing it quickly into her handbag. She did a quick step dance, feeling the breasts swing weightless and free.

He didn't notice when she came back to the table, his only comment was about her clumsiness.

"Why did you order another drink?" Frank glared with anger at the Scotch.

Wordlessly she downed the Scotch in one gulp.

"What the hell are you saying?"

"I didn't say anything."

"Have you made up your mind what you're having?"

"Yes, I made it up ages ago. Broiled kingfish!"

"The steak will be shoe-leather no doubt."

"Don't have it then, have fish!"

"I hate fish."

"Suit yourself!"

He looked at her, puzzled. "You're drunk!" he accused.

"Possibly."

She slept that night with her head on a book. Frank, in the neighboring bed, looked at her in astonishment.

"What the hell are you doing?"

"Old sea-captain's remedy for a revolving room."

Frank smiled. "Sometimes you're a silly old woman," he said with the slightest hint of affection before turning to down a handful of pills.

Frank always swam first thing in the morning. She usually stood on the balcony and watched him descend down the wooden steps that led from the patio into the water.

"It looks rough this morning," she warned as he came to join her for a moment on the balcony.

"It's rough every morning, but it's only hip deep."

"Be careful, anyway," she warned.

"I'm always careful."

Taking her *Flowers of the Tropics* to the balcony along with her coffee, she sat down and waited for him to appear on the patio.

He walked carefully, the familiar slightly bandy-legged gait, his shoulders hunched anxiously as though he expected to encounter land mines. The green swim-trunks sagged around his shrunken thighs, the towel draped casually around his neck to hide the huge scar from the chest surgery. He looked up briefly and she waved. He gave a grudging answering nod.

She couldn't see all the steps, they were obscured by the overhang of the patio.

She waited impatiently to see his flailing strokes out into the ocean. He'd always been a good swimmer and he had never been bothered by a rough sea. Today it wasn't exactly rough, but close to the small cliffy overhang of the hotel the waves were powerful enough. Suddenly she saw him, but instead of doing his usual attacking crawl, he was on his back and floating. Something about the angle of his arms and legs seemed strange. From where she sat he looked like a green water lily pad, almost passive and limply stuck to the water.

What if he had slipped on the steps and was drowning? She lifted her coffee cup and took a sip of the coffee. She opened the flower book and peered with desperate concentration at the pages. *"Nymphaea Alba,"* as the water lily was called, *"... requires still water with a temperature of 20 degrees to 25 degrees."*

She looked down again and saw him lifted by a wave and disappear from view. Her sightless eyes returned to the book and she tried reciting *"nymphaea alba"* over and over again. She could feel the pounding of her heart and the dryness in her mouth and she tried to read on, to block out all thoughts.

Barefooted, with her housecoat flapping around her, she stumbled to the bedroom door. Grabbing the excess cloth that hampered her movement, she ran as hard as she could.

The startled receptionist looked up as she passed. There was no one else on the patio. She saw him now being carried by a wave towards the small stretch of beach that ran to the west of their hotel. The steps were glutinous with algae and seaweed towards the bottom and she nearly slipped and lost her balance. Her robe ballooned out in the water, almost enveloping her head. She stooped and pulled it through between her legs and knotted it with the front. At the same time a wave washed over her and carried her out. The water was colder than tropical water had any right to be. Panic and salt water choked her as she fought to find her feet, momentarily aware that there was no sand beneath them.

She had always used the pool at the hotel because she was frightened of the sea. Now she felt sure she was going to drown. Great drafts of sea water caught her nose and made her choke. Then, mercifully, she felt solid sand underneath her, but her eyes stung with the salt water, and the landscape had become blurred and incandescent. She couldn't see him anymore.

"What the hell are you doing?" She heard his familiar voice. He was standing now and staring at her as though she'd gone stark raving mad.

"I thought you'd fallen and hit your head and were drowning."

"I was floating."

"But you never float."

"Jesus, but you're a foolish old woman!" He reached out and pulled her towards him. "You have no bra on," he said grinning and looking down at her chest.

She struggled within his grasp. One of his large hands held one of her breasts. "What is this, you trying to seduce me?"

"Oh, Jesus! I thought you were gone."

"You can't even swim and you came in to save me?" He looked at her with a certain amount of disbelief.

Then she felt the anger mounting in her chest. She pounded on the scars on his chest, realizing that there was no strength in her anger and not even knowing anymore whether she was mad with herself or him.

"Come on, old lady, let's get out of here." He drew her towards the slimy steps and pushed her ahead of him. She knew she must look a sight with her robe clinging Turkish-style between her legs and her hair soaked and hanging around her face, but she didn't much care. She stumbled ahead of him, blinded by tears.

Upstairs he set her on the bed and helped pull the wet housecoat from her shoulders. He dried her with a towel and then fumbled around in the cupboard for something dry for her to wear. She sat limp and exhausted with her own impotence, allowing his administrations.

"Come on! You sit on the balcony and I'll make you a cup of coffee!" He led her like a child to a seat on the balcony and helped her into it. She sat immobile, conscious only of the waves which sounded for all the world like the static from an old radio.

Her eyes strayed to the frangipani blossom on the table where it still lay from the night before. It was perfection, defiantly plastic and unreal. She was sorry now she hadn't thrown it over the balcony.

Frank came back with a steaming cup of coffee and handed it to her. "Here, darlin', here you are!"

# THE WAY TO A MAN'S HEART

Gina stood half-paralysed by shock at the telephone. There was no recollection of how she had finished the conversation with Gerry Hiller. What had started as a simple call to make an appointment for a massage had turned into something else altogether.

"We've all been worried about you. How are you managing?"

*Managing? What was he talking about?*

"Everyone at the Club ..." There was a slight pause. "... Our sympathies are with you. Hang in there! Men are such damned bastards!" The fact that Gerry didn't quite fit himself into the male category allowed him to be vituperative.

A wave of nausea overwhelmed her. What she'd always dreaded had obviously happened. So far Bernie had always been discreet, keeping his liaisons outside their life, outside Toronto in fact, sometimes Montreal, sometimes Vancouver, but right in his own backyard, this was the final humiliation.

At that moment she detested Gerry Hiller, detested his false sympathy. The fact was that Gerry was the worst gossip at the Club. It was amazing what people told him when they were slack and comfortable under his soothing hands.

How long she sat by the phone staring into space she didn't know. She felt mortally ill, unable to move.

The phone rang again, Margie's voice at the other end.

"Two o'clock, Gina."

She didn't answer.

"I've got a court for two, Gina, is that all right?"

The last thing she needed was a game of squash. The very idea of walking into the lobby of the Club filled her with nausea. Right then and there she felt like going to bed, diving in and covering herself and hoping she wouldn't wake up.

*"Poor Gina! Poor dumb Gina! Poor stupid Gina who was getting a little fat and didn't know how to keep a man."* They would look at her walking past and, safe in their own little domestic igloos, would feel nothing but sympathy. But much as she didn't care about playing squash, she had to see Margie. Margie would know, Margie would fill her in on who it was.

Later, much later, as she sat sweating on the locker-room bench, feeling drained and empty but peculiarly focused on the subject she had to broach, she asked quietly, "Who is it, Margie?"

"You were a demon today," Margie said, stripping off her whites and ignoring the question.

"Who is it?" she repeated.

"Who is what?"

"Who is it that Bernie's laying?"

Margie stared at her for a moment and sat down beside her. She dried her pink forehead with a towel and looked miserably at the towel as though she expected to see blood.

"You really want to know?"

"Why not, everyone else does."

"Patti Rhys," she said and looked up at Gina.

"Patti Rhys?" Margie nodded. It was rumoured that most of the single men at the Club knew Patti intimately and that she wasn't averse to the married ones either. But Patti Rhys was tall, blonde and gorgeous, at least a half head taller than Bernie, and athletic, which is something you could never say about Bernie.

"Patti and Bernie, I don't get it." She stared at Margie, looking for an answer.

"Power! Patti's into men who have power, and Bernie kind of fits into that category. She likes his profile, you might say." Margie wrapped herself in a towel.

"Didn't you know about Bernie?" Margie asked, looking pityingly at Gina.

"I suppose I did, but it was never on the doorstep before."

"You think not?" Margie managed to look embarrassed.

Gina felt the blood slowly ebbing out of her extremities. One minute she had been scalding hot, now she felt a shiver of intense cold all over.

"Heh, you all right?" Margie leant over.

"Who else?"

"God, I don't know, people like to talk. All I know is rumours, all rumours." Margie touched her arm, "Throw the bastard out!"

"Then what?"

"Then get on with your life."

"Bernie sort of is my life." She stood looking at herself in the long mirror in the locker-room. What she saw was still reasonable looking, if a bit over-weight, but nothing that was irreversible.

"Funny," she smiled at Margie. "Things seemed to be so great, Bernie had been so loving lately, so appreciative. He's in love with this gourmet cooking course I'm taking. Thought it was cute that I should do this now for him."

Later in the coffee shop, Gina asked, "How did the word get out?"

"Patti's been going around telling everyone Bernie's leaving you."

"She has?"

Margie nodded. "Gerry probably assumed it had already happened."

Patti was a fool. She might not be any judge of behaviour, but Bernie was deep in his gift-giving phase, one that told her he was dealing with a lot of guilt. Their lovemaking had taken on a new fervour, another sign of deep regret. She knew all the signals. Bernie wasn't about to leave. Bernie would deny to the death that he was having an affair. They'd been through it all before.

None of this Margie would understand. Nor would it do any good to describe Bernie the loving husband, the good son-in-law, the all-around good guy. She wasn't sure she could even rationalize it all to herself, or why she'd always forgiven him.

Bernie was home for dinner that night. She served up bollito misto that had been simmering since morning at a low, low heat, and topped it off with suet dumplings. Cooking was a way of temporarily forgetting about the pain. He'd brought her home a bouquet of roses and arrived early for dinner, kissing her neck and telling her that he'd thought all day about the food.

Bernie loved his food. On her bad days she told herself that she had cooked her way into Bernie's heart. Now, as she watched his heaped plate dis-appearing and saw the small layer of fat that ran around from Bernie's chin and bulged over his collar, she knew that if Bernie had to pick between sex and food, food would win out every time.

She had made double chocolate-mousse cake for dessert. He barely noticed that she didn't eat. Bernie was an absorbed eater, a concentrator on food. He didn't talk much when he ate and never had. He wouldn't notice that she was quiet or that her face was white with the strain of what she'd learned that day. Over his cappuccino he would begin to talk, talk about the deals he'd made, proud of the fact that, even in a bad economy, he had a knack for making money.

She put another helping of mousse cake on his plate and calculated in her head how many calories Bernie had consumed in that one meal. Probably around 3,000, not to mention the pancakes he'd had for breakfast and the lunch he would have had with one of his clients. Bernie didn't skimp on lunch ever.

It wasn't easy to get through the evening without mentioning what she'd found out that day. The problem was the memory of all the other times. The accusations, shouts, screams, yells, the petulant, affronted Bernie who swore always on his mother's grave that he was totally innocent, and next, inevitably, the lovemaking which for her started slowly and stiffly, then his incredible ability to make her feel that she was the only one in the entire world who mattered. She couldn't face that tonight.

As she dried the large butcher knife she'd used to slice the meat with, she looked at Bernie's back as he spoke on the telephone. She saw the soft handles of flesh hanging over his pants.

He was talking to Vancouver and was yelling as though trying to cover the distance without a phone. A moment of intense dislike for him overwhelmed her. It would be so easy to insert the knife cleanly between his ribs. Argument over. No fight, no right or wrong.

She heard him belch as he hung up the phone. He would have to take something for his indigestion later; it was always the same. Bernie simply didn't know when to stop eating. He didn't even seem to be aware that he was putting on weight. How would darling Patti feel about him if he were fat and sluggish? She smiled to herself.

For breakfast she cooked savory crepes, filled with sour cream and Brie. Bernie was ecstatic. "Honey, you outdid yourself!" He helped himself to the last crepe in the dish. "Aren't you having any?"

"I don't seem to have an appetite."

"You've been awfully quiet. Are you feeling okay?"

"Fine, a bit tired."

"All that squash playing. Take a break! Have a rest today, stop pushing yourself!"

She tried to smile, but nausea filled her empty stomach and for an instant she felt like retching. Bernie's idea of what she should want to do with her life had to do with her lying around all day on the couch and eating chocolates.

The more she thought about Bernie and his knowledge of her, the more she came to the realization that her likes and dislikes were completely unknown to him. The things he did for her were things he would like to have done for him. He assumed, somehow, that she was part of him and should cultivate his tastes.

"Too bad you can't come home for lunch. I'm trying out the quenelles," she said casually.

He frowned, "I have to go to Brampton, maybe I can have some when I come home?"

"Sure." She knew by noon his stomach would be growling and there'd be a phone call. She was a little generous in her estimate, the phone rang mid-morning.

"Hi, honey. Gonna take a detour and try out those quenelles."

She smiled to herself. "Great!"

She made some Lady Curzon soup and checked the refrigerator to make sure she had plenty of cream. By twelve it was simmering on the light. She stirred in the egg yolks and whipped cream and added the Madeira.

Bernie was early, but luckily it was all ready. His eyes were shining. She noticed that the buttons on his shirt were beginning to pop slightly. It would take some tact to suggest larger sizes, but perhaps she could buy them, similar to his old ones, wash them and slip them into the closet and he might not notice.

Six months later, the once slightly overweight Bernie Ravens was unrecognizable to anyone who had known his 165-pound frame. He had gained seventy-five pounds and everything had stopped except his enthusiasm for Gina's cooking. As Bernie got fatter, Gina got thinner, fed by her consuming energy to produce something new and interesting for Bernie to eat. She saw it all as a crusade to keep Bernie.

When Gina looked at herself in the mirror, she was astounded by the face that was reappearing. She had dropped to a size ten in dresses, and a kind of light seemed to have come back in her face, a light she remembered from long, long ago.

She thanked heaven that all attempts on Bernie's part at lovemaking had ceased. He had tried only a few weeks back to heave his great whale of a body onto hers, and all that the encounter had produced was lashings of sweat as his body poured with the disappointment of unsatisfied desire. It had been a revolting experience and looking at the rolls of neck fat with the tiny protruding hairs coming out of humped pores, made her shiver in disgust.

She knew without having to be told that Patti was a thing of the past. There were no more apologies for absences. Instead, Bernie was there all the time, out-of-town trips postponed as he hovered near her in the kitchen, attentive and loving as he waited for her latest culinary efforts.

But it was odd; now that he was there, all hers, she felt nothing for him. It didn't have much to do with his size, but everything to do with his *neediness* and greed. Oddly enough, in her efforts to get Bernie back she had inadvertently discovered two things: her own talent for cooking, and the fact she no longer loved Bernie.

A couple of weeks later, on Monday morning, she produced a list for Bernie and set it in front of his breakfast of pecan cinnamon toast and bacon. It neatly listed the week's menu.

"What's this?" he said with his mouth full.

"Dinner tonight: Gruyère soup, cassoulet and apple pie. Tuesday night: squash and corn soup, osso buco, cassis ice cream," she recited, enjoying the sound of the dishes that she'd devised. Bernie's eyes were shining, but not with their former clarity. She'd noticed of late that the whites of his eyes had become even more yellow.

She might have been able to feel pity for him if there hadn't been a trickle of corn syrup on the side of his mouth wending its way down on its sideways track to his chin.

"Why are you telling me, hon?" he smiled lovingly at her.

"Because I won't be here and it's all in the fridge labelled."

He stopped with his fork halfway to his mouth.

"Where will you be?"

She didn't say anything for a moment and then she opened the kitchen drawer and slapped down an envelope in front of him.

"This time to-morrow I'll be sliding out of Miami, bound for the Virgin Islands — Assistant Chef on the *Viking Princess*, deluxe liner."

Bernie's knife fell from his hand. "You're joking?"

"You've been a great tester, Bernie. Thank you!"

"What about me?"

"What about you?"

"You can't go off like this, without another thought."

"I'm not, Bernie. I thought a week of food in the fridge would get you used to the idea, and then you can have time to plan your menus and the rest of your life."

Instead of putting the letter back in its envelope, she attached it to the refrigerator with one of the little magnetic bananas. She had its content memorized anyhow, but it made it all official and final for poor Bernie.

She congratulated herself for having been more than humane; attached to the last container in the refrigerator, along with the vichyssoise, the pesto linguini and the pots de crème à la vanille, she had attached a brochure from Weight Watchers and had heavily underlined the number of the local branch.

# THE GATE

The garden gate had six black iron spikes on top, ugly spikes. The distance between each railing was exactly the width of Meg's forehead, so that after leaning her head against its magic coolness and peering out at the world, there were two large pink stripes on either side of her ears.

The railings framed all there was to see, just as the frames on picture books did. The gate kept Meg safe from the rest of the world and at the same time kept her mother prisoner. Nobody could ever escape past that gate without being heard: it was heavy and creaked, it would announce anyone leaving.

"*I've had enough! There has to be more to life than this?*" When her mother said this, Meg longed to point to all the lovely things around that she thought maybe her mother couldn't see.

Her mother never told Meg she loved her, but at times Meg thought it might be possible. At other times she didn't believe it for a moment.

When Meg tried to help in the kitchen, her mother would yell and wave her arms impatiently, "*Get out of my hair!*" That's when Meg collected her stool and went to the bottom of the garden to set up her lonely post guarding the gate so that her mother couldn't run away.

It was nice by the gate. It was a window to watch the world go by: a world bounded beyond the gate by the row of tall red-brick houses that soared upward, blocking out the sun until midday.

There were things and people to watch on the street: the man across the road with the funny collar and bow tie and his bundle of books, the odd skinny lady two doors away whom her mother always called "the lady with the two left legs." It was true, she had a funny lopsided look as though her knees could bend both ways.

Then there was the dancer lady who on summer nights, when it was daylight for so long, waved from her window to Meg and brought out a puppet doll to make it dance on the ledge. The sun caught the third-storey windowsill at that time of night, lighting it up like a stage. It was magical.

When the lady saw Meg in the daytime behind the gate she would wave but she never came over to speak, and Meg was glad. They shared a secret, and to speak about it would spoil everything.

Meg was in love with the dancer. She was tall and dark with her hair drawn back from her face. She walked turning her feet out and sort of glided along, exactly like her puppet. Meg practiced walking that way, imagining she was getting it just right.

Then, in the afternoons, the other children came home from school and played ball on the street. Sometimes they asked Meg to come out from behind the gate and play with them, but she wouldn't come. They started calling her "Monkeyface." Her father heard them one day and he began calling her that too, but when he said it, it was different and Meg was happy.

One day something dreadful happened, men came and took the gate away and all the railings, leaving only the hedge. Her father said it was for the war effort. Meg was baffled. How could the war effort need their gate and railings? Meg decided maybe it was to build a fence around the country to keep the enemy out.

She didn't go out of the house for days after that and her mother got angrier and angrier, complaining to Meg's father.

"Do something about her! She's tripping on my heels morning, noon and night."

Her father took her on his knee and stroked her hair.

"What is it, Monkeyface? Can't you leave Mummy alone?"

Meg began to cry.

"Stop mewling!" her mother yelled. "Thank God she'll be gone to school soon."

Meg had trouble getting to sleep at nights just thinking about the day school would start. She was certain when that day came her mother would run away. But there were other things to worry about — different things all happening suddenly. First, it was the gate; then her sisters and brother left home, went away to the country where they would be safe in boarding school, and there was just Meg and her mother and father left.

A huge iron dining table arrived with mesh sides that hooked on and off. Her father said it was a shelter against air raids. Then he made them practice going under the table.

It was lovely underneath the table. There were candles, a mattress and blankets, and it was cozy. When the sides were on, it was just like being in the garden again with the railings and gate — safe, where nothing could touch you. And when they actually went under the table her mother hugged Meg and cried. Her father was out driving an ambulance down at the dock and her mother cried and rocked her and it was warm and lovely in her arms even though her mother was crying.

Then things changed again. Her father's office was evacuated to the country, and he wanted to take them with him, but her mother wouldn't leave Granny Dunne.

Her mother and father fought about that for days, shouting and yelling, until finally her father didn't say anything more.

When he came home at the weekends her mother said he was lucky to be able to run away each week, and Meg looked at her father and wondered if that was what he wanted. She hadn't ever thought of her father as wanting to run away.

He hugged Meg a lot when he was home and in the summer took her places. Once she even went to the country with him and stayed in a long room with other people where she had to sleep on a funny iron bed.

She liked it there because everyone seemed gay and carefree. There were no air raid sirens and there was one lady, her father's secretary, with a powdered face and a strawberry red mouth who kept giving her things and putting her arms around her. She liked the presents but didn't really like the lady, although she wasn't quite sure why. The lady smelled of perfume, and long after she had hugged her, Meg still smelled the perfume. She was sure her father didn't really like her either because he was funny when she was around making a fuss of Meg and speaking in a funny voice.

Back in town there were the endless walks to her grandmother's each day. Granny Dunne was lame and always sat in a wheelchair, but apart from that she didn't seem to need much looking after. She had a maid called Rose and a budgie called Sammy.

Meg didn't really love her grandmother, she was scared of her. But then everyone seemed scared of her, even Rose — everyone but her mother. She had a big deep voice for someone so tiny.

"Run away and play!" The same words as her mother's, the same frown. "Go look for chickweed for Sammy!"

But it was all right because it was safe in the garden. For some reason the garden still had a gate. Perhaps Granny Dunne had scared off the men who came to take it away.

Each day her mother stayed a long time at Granny Dunne's. It was lovely in the garden, picking out the chickweed from between the flagstones to feed to Sammy, then roaming by the flowerbeds, feeling the stickiness of the snapdragons, getting the orange dye from the big lilies all over her fingers; and then when she was bored with the garden, she went to the garage where the door was always open and stroked the flanks of the big shining car that only ever came out for weddings and funerals. She pretended the car was a great gentle horse and that someday she would be able to climb on, and lead the horse wherever she pleased.

Then it was the end of summer and things changed again. She went to school — that awful first day of school when she cried all day and her mother came to pick her up. She called her a baby for crying, but Meg didn't care because she was there scolding her and she hadn't run away and that was the important thing. All the time she complained, she held Meg's hand tightly and Meg smiled even though she was being scolded.

Her father came home at the weekend and talked to Meg about growing up, and about how big girls didn't cry, and so she stopped crying at school, but she was glad each day when she could run home quickly to make sure her mother was still there.

In the winter her mother didn't complain so much anymore and at week-ends, when her father was home, men from America came to the house, men wearing uniforms. They brought chocolate bars and nylons and Lucky Strike cigarettes and they had names like animals and gnats: Buck, Midge and Bill. When they came, her mother was nice to her, nicer than she'd ever been, and Meg was glad the men with funny names were around.

The house was always filled with smoke and the smell of food cooking, and Buck and Midge taught Meg how to play card games. Her mother laughed a lot and called Meg "darling." The men said her mother was too young-looking to have such a big daughter, and Meg said "You should see Evelyn," indicating with her hand how tall her sister was, and then her mother was mad and told Meg to run along and play.

One day the soldier came during the week when her father was away. Meg didn't like him as much as she liked the other soldiers. He was always giving her money and telling her to go and buy herself some candies. Her mother said candies were sweets. But he was stupid because there were no sweets to buy; he didn't seem to remember about rationing and shortages.

One day when she came home from school she found the soldier standing close to her mother with his hand on her arm and she knew for sure she really didn't like him. He pounced on her and swung her up in the air and she could smell a sort of sweet familiar smell as her face passed his, a sort of "mother" smell and she wanted to cry. He set her down again.

"Hey, hon, run down to the store and get me some matches!" He pulled some change from his pocket.

"We have matches!" Meg went into the kitchen and brought the box that was always kept by the stove. Then she sat on the piano bench and swung her legs. The soldier and her mother sat and looked at each other and the room felt funny, all hot and clammy. But her mother suddenly wasn't mad anymore. She came over and put her arm around Meg.

"Want to hear her sing?" her mother asked the soldier. "She sings like an angel."

Meg looked up at her mother and saw how pink her face was and how pretty she looked, prettier than any other mother on the street.

"Sure!"

Meg knew he didn't really want to hear her sing.

Her mother made her get up from the piano bench and she sat down and then turned the pages of the song book to the one with "Beautiful Dreamer." Meg liked "Beautiful Dreamer" and knew she could sing it well.

"Beautiful dreamer, hark unto me ..."

He stood over the piano and stared at her mother. She made her sit down beside her and instead of looking at the soldier, she looked at her, and Meg saw that her mother loved her at that moment.

The soldier was there some days when she came home from school, but when he tried to get her to go out to buy him things or even bribed her with the money, her mother gave her a look that said, "Don't go!" And it was as though they were playing a game together.

One day when she came home from school there was nobody there in the house except her mother, and her eyes were red and she was walking around the kitchen as though she wasn't sure where she really wanted to be.

"Isn't he coming?" Meg asked.

"No!" She grabbed Meg by the shoulders, "I don't want you mentioning his name. He's not ever coming again."

That night there was a terrible air raid and the floor shook underneath them. Her mother unhooked the side of the table and ran to the window. When she lifted the blind, Meg could see the entire street lit up, lights flaring and dying, just like at Halloween.

Her mother came back under the table. Large tears were trickling down her face but no sound was coming from her. Instead of fussing and talking as she usually did, she said nothing. Rather than hugging Meg, she held her arms across her own body and rocked back and forward, shivering. Meg tucked the blanket around her mother, but she didn't notice and kept on rocking. Meg felt her own tears flowing, and because she hadn't brought a hankie under the table with her, she had to rub her nose on her school jersey.

"Are we going to die then?" Meg asked finally. Her mother stopped rocking and stared at her. She smiled suddenly and put an arm around her, pulling her close.

"No, darling! We're not going to die. We're going to the country, to Daddy."

"To the country? What about Granny?"

She kissed Meg 's forehead. "Granny will be all right."

"What if Granny sleeps on and doesn't hear the air raid siren?"

"Nobody would bomb Granny, darling. Nobody would dare, would they?"

Meg stared at her mother. "We could take her to the country too, couldn't we?" But she saw her mother wasn't thinking about Granny Dunne anymore.

And then it was over: the long shrill scream of the "all clear" sirens told them the bombers had gone home, and her mother was unhooking the sides of the table. Meg wished suddenly that, like Sammy, the budgie in his cage, they could stay forever under the table, safe and sound.

Her mother held her hand as she walked her upstairs to bed.

"Anyway, Granny has a gate. She'll be all right behind the gate," Meg said brightly, looking up at her mother. But her mother had a faraway look on her face and didn't answer.

# A BLIGHT ON THE ROSES

"Now you can take your cities. Look at that! Nuthin' in the world to beat a grain elevator against a prairie sky."

The car did one of those gravel skids that Jane was famous for. She was proud of the fact that she had been in a ditch at least once a year since she'd first started driving. Barbara tried to unclench her fingers.

"Pretty! Really pretty!"

"Pretty?" Jane snorted and blew at a hank of straight white hair that kept shading her eyes. "It's darned right majestic, none of yer 'pretties.'"

Her mother-in-law had never been given to understatement. She was an unashamed dealer in hyperbole.

Rivulets of sweat inched and pricked down Barbara's back like so many sluggish insects. Damn it! Jane could afford an air-conditioned car, could have afforded one years ago, but was too damned stubborn to give in. Rust had eaten its way through the floorboards of this old monster, and great swirls of prairie dust were fogging up the car's innards, covering them in a film of grit. Barbara visualized them arriving at their destination, dusty and aged, looking as though they had stepped out of an old sepia print.

"Look at it!" Jane waved an arm again and the car skittered dangerously close to the side of the road. Barbara directed Jane's hand back to the wheel.

"I'm looking."

It was beautiful in its odd, two-dimensional way. Surely nowhere else in the country were there two distinct and uncompromising landscapes — summer and winter. She knew Jane wouldn't agree with that, she would insist there was spring and fall, but if it were so, they were so brief as to make no real impression. Spring came late, very late, and volcanoed overnight into sweltering summer, and fall was a mere suspicion, starting as a wind over the prairie and ending in a blizzard.

"They're all anxious to see you," Jane said, making the curious blowing gesture with her bottom lip again, wafting stray strands of hair away from her eyes.

Was it likely that the Stoney Creek Women's Institute were anxious to see her? She seriously doubted it but it was important in Jane's mind that they would be. No doubt the groundwork had been laid. The casual events she had faithfully recounted in her letters from Toronto, would, by this time, have assumed mythic proportions. Yes, she was an editor from down East, but her magazine had no real circulation, only an imaginary one devised by the promotions department to ensure that advertisers wouldn't drop away. But she would be the "big editor" from down East if it were required. Don, one of the many vice-presidents of his company, was "president" to his mother, and no matter how often he corrected her, it made no difference. In her mind it was the next logical step. This was one of their reasons for sharing the duty of going back to Treager each year. Age, rather than blunting Jane's enthusiasm for myth-making, had sharpened and honed it, so that it was an intensely embarrassing experience to be bounced around from farm to farm, representing everything that Jane imagined Treager needed.

She would have dearly loved to have stayed at home on the farm and fallen off to sleep on the big soft double bed that Jane always kept in readiness for their visits, lulled to sleep by soft sounds so different from the sounds of the city: a dog barking, a tractor off in the distance, an unhurried voice calling across the yard, the long insistent trill of crickets making their telegraphic territorial calls across the wild grass.

"Of course you'll hear about her blessed rosebush," Jane said as she swung recklessly off the road and into the long driveway to the Krumins house.

The house where the meeting was being held could have been a dozen other prairie bungalows. The only change Barbara could see, or rather feel, was the air-conditioning, a curious phenomenon afflicting most of the farms in the district now. Air-conditioning seemed all wrong amid the comfortable tweed sofas and faded velour armchairs; an uneasy presage of other possible changes to come. Ten years before, it had been gazebos. As a matter of fact it had been her own father-in-law, Will McKinley, who had started that fad. He'd built the gazebo out from his living room, pushing it onto the front lawn like a kind of ugly blister attachment. It hadn't weathered at all well over the years. In no time at all the entire district was building gazebos of every possible shape and design and in the most unlikely places. Some were so far away from the farmhouses that in walking to them every mosquito in the province had time to take aim and attack. Now the gazebos had been made redundant by the air-conditioners.

Five years later it had been swimming pools, and now anybody who was anybody had a swimming pool. Usually those who could afford them least had the best, or so Jane informed them. Perhaps that was mere justification for Will's stubborn determination that he wasn't building "no fool hole in the ground for a fad that would pass." In consequence, they had a metal-plastic contraption with a stepladder that looked for all the world like one of those ancient tanks that stunt artists dived into at local fairs.

Jane had difficulty forgiving Will for his determination not to have a real pool, since the one sporting thing she excelled at was swimming. But her mortification hadn't lasted long. It had taken her no time at all to organize the entire district, and she'd taken at least fifteen of the farmwives through from tadpole stage to bronze medal before they'd eventually tired of her zeal. Since few of them ever went to a lake or the sea, there was a certain irony about having fifteen women in one district, a district with one dried-up watering hole, all qualified to save drowning bodies.

It was difficult to get the meeting started because Jane was always talking. With Barbara firmly in tow, she reminded each and every one of them of Barbara's imaginary fame. Barbara saw the women exchanging looks. She knew Jane was loved in the district, but there was always a faint scorn there too. Right from the beginning she'd never been a typical farmer's wife. Liberated long before anyone in Manitoba had even thought much about women's lot, she'd always been a kind of leader — not the kind who won all the prizes for buttermilk rolls. There was very little Jane didn't know or couldn't find out. When encyclopedias weren't handy, a phone call to Jane could straighten things out. She'd always "just heard" or "just read" or "just seen" something and it didn't do not to pay attention because Jane was usually right.

Someone had supplied Molly with a small gavel, and as president of the Women's Institute she raised it and tapped gently on the table. Some people stopped talking, but Jane's tongue and head were still wagging.

"Can we get this thing going?" Molly pleaded.

"Now what about the Baseball Tea? Are we going to do it or are we not?"

"When are we going to get to see your rosebush?" Myrna Berthold piped up from the back of the room.

"Later! Now about the tea ..."

"Did we make money from the last one?" Edna Bell asked. Barbara noticed that Jane's attention was still not on the meeting; she was talking earnestly with Inga Bolger.

"Seems to me," Myrna said slowly, "... we always done the tea. Why should we stop now?"

"Did we make money?" Edna persisted. Edna was the wife of the owner of the local hardware store. Like most hardware-store owners she looked miserable. Perhaps it had something to do with the impossibility of stocking grummets and widgets for every type of machinery and equipment imaginable. Barbara's father-in-law had always complained that they never had anything in the store when he needed it.

"So what if we don't make money," Myrna snorted. "We make money for charity, sure, but sometimes charity begins at home. We always done the tea. Everyone expects we cater the baseball game an' that's what we should do."

"Can we have a show of hands on this one?" Molly pleaded. The show of hands was in favour of doing the tea and Edna looked more unhappy than ever.

The meeting went on by fits and starts. Molly, an inexpert president, failed to use her gavel often enough. Finally it seemed they'd run out of business.

"So now we get to see the rosebush," Inga said brightly.

"No, we have the great Canadians, remember?" Molly reminded her.

"The what?" Liz Summers asked.

"We had to think about one great Canadian and say what he'd done ..."

"Or she ..." Jane interrupted quickly.

Edna Bell was staring across the room at Barbara, an unhappy twist to her lips. She was a big woman with snow white hair and startlingly black eyebrows. When Barbara smiled at her, she only rearranged her mouth slightly in reply, the very immobility of her face showing that she disapproved of Barbara in some way. Possibly it was her clothes, maybe her fuzzed-up hairstyle. Jane had selected the dress she should wear and Barbara had felt it wrong, too brash and too city. Edna's glance told her she'd been right.

"I forgot all about that," Myrna Berthold said.

"Make one up then," Edna said in disgust.

"I'd rather see the rosebush," Myrna said. "I'm near frozen in here." She was one of the few in the district who had no air-conditioning and was always quick to express her disapproval of overly cool houses.

"Come on!" Molly tapped her hammer sharply on the table, obviously losing patience. "Who has one?"

"Harold Fulton Carruthers!" Edna offered, looking smug.

"Hells bells, who was he?" somebody giggled.

"Harold Fulton Carruthers, for those who're ignorant, was one of the prime movers behind the marketing boards. His father was an evangelist and his wife was the first person in the Egmont district to teach French in school."

"Wrong!" Jane stood up, eyes blazing.

"My mother started French in the school and she sure as hell never married no Harold Fulton Carruthers."

There was a burst of laughter.

"Well, that's what it said in the book I read." Edna looked chagrined.

"Well, they were wrong." Jane's jaw stuck out stubbornly and no one would have dared to argue. They all knew better than to challenge her on such a thing.

"What about your choice, Jane?" Molly asked.

Jane delivered her choice with authority. She knew every detail of the life she'd chosen, and most of the room had tired of hearing those details long before she had finished.

Barbara observed her mother-in-law with a mixture of frustration and love, realizing suddenly how old she'd grown. The voice wasn't as sure anymore; the slight tremor of speech and the odd little headshake that had seemed a mere affectation, were more than that now.

Where the others had travelled to the meeting with their muffins and pies, Jane had armed herself with research, and while it was respected, Barbara was sure that a failed apple-pie would have been more appreciated.

Jane sat down eventually and shot a look at Barbara, a sort of "aren't you proud of me" look, and she realized suddenly that she *was* proud of her. Never mind all the frustrations; this woman's mind was razor sharp and would stay that way until the day she died. It had probably been Jane who had organized the famous Canadians thing, because certainly none of the others, with the exception of Edna, had spent much time thinking up a candidate.

"Well, I picked Pierre Berton," Marian Kelsey said. "I reckon he's done as much for this country as anyone ... what with his histories an' things."

"Landsakes, Pierre Berton! ..." Edna said in disgust. "Everyone knows him ... You were supposed to pick someone we din' know and tell us something about him."

"No, she wasn't!" Molly was into the fray with both feet. "She could chose who she liked."

"What about your daughter-in-law?" Inga asked Jane. "Would she like to mention someone?"

Barbara felt her face flush as they all looked at her. Her mind was a total blank.

"Never mind!" Molly said kindly. "'Tisn't that easy."

Barbara could see the disappointment in Jane's face. She'd let her down yet again.

Business over, they served tea and coffee — a feast of muffins and cakes: orange muffins by Inga Bolger, pineapple ones courtesy of Marian, gingerbread of Myrna's, Liz Summers' banana bread, and on and on. Most of which Barbara had to sample for fear of offending someone.

"So, you meet a lot of famous people in Toronto?" Liz Summers descended on her with her banana bread. What had Jane told them now?

"Ever met Pierre Berton?"

She shook her head. She saw a faint smile on Edna's lips now. It wasn't precisely true. She had met him. In fact she'd mentioned it briefly in one of the letters to Jane, but it had been a fleeting confrontation and certainly one he would never remember.

Jane came quickly to her side.

"Course she met him." She pinned Barbara's arm to her side and pressed on it hard. "She hates to drop names."

Barbara smiled in embarrassment. "Well briefly ... just briefly."

She had a wild urge to play up to Jane's wishes and make up what she knew Jane wanted to hear, but common sense told her it wasn't the thing to do. If she failed to live up to the picture that had been painted, they would forgive Jane, perhaps even feel a little bit protective of her after she had gone; and somehow it was essential, as it had never been before, that they should see what a truly terrific woman Jane was. They could laugh a little at her extreme pride in family but forgive her, remembering that they had kids around them, taking over their farms and giving them grandchildren, and Jane had only one chick, born late and left home too soon, and no grandchildren.

"Now can we see the rosebush?" Inga asked again.

"Such a fuss about a rosebush," Molly said modestly, but not without pride, "... it's only got a few roses, nothing special."

There was a general exodus towards the back door. Jane held back and managed a smile at Barbara, but it wasn't a warm smile.

"I heard nothin' but that rosebush all week. Beginnin' to think it's a myth," Liz Summers said.

For a moment, Jane and Barbara were excluded from the circle that surrounded the rosebush until someone realized that they were standing on the periphery.

"Let Barbara have a peek!" Marian said, pushing aside to leave an opening.

"Isn't that something?" Myrna said in awe.

Fourteen years of living down East had made Barbara forget about rosebushes in Manitoba — it certainly hadn't prepared her for the fragile thing she now saw. It grew unconvincingly out of the prairie soil, its petals shell pink and fragile; half of them had already begun to fall on the ground.

"I don't know how you did it," Myrna shook her head. "I just can't get hardly nuthin' on mine."

"How many blooms are there anyway?" Inga asked.

"Can't remember the last time I saw a decent one like that. Eight ... no seven ... that's pretty darned good."

"First year I've had a decent display," Molly said proudly. "Can't keep the danged dog out of the flower beds neither. You just get the flowers goin' good and he's in there diggin' holes and buryin' bones."

"You should see the roses Barbara has down East," Jane piped up from her new position in the circle. Barbara was sure she heard a groan coming from somewhere.

"Makes this look like nuthin'." Jane looked pleased with herself.

They all looked at Barbara. She shook her head. "No, I've had a blight on my roses the last three years. They've been terrible."

"Nonsense!" Jane interjected. "I saw them with my own eyes last year."

"You've forgotten," Barbara smiled equably. "Time flies. Last time I had a half-decent rose was four years ago."

The women looked back and forth between Jane and Barbara, uncertain of who was going to win.

"Nice to know we have somethin' better than down East," Edna said dryly.

Barbara's clothes felt sticky on her, but not from the intensity of the sun that beat down on her head as they stood clustered next to the rose bush. She plunged on, trying not to see Jane's disappointment.

Some time later when they'd moved inside, she heard herself saying, "Thank goodness for the air-conditioning here, that's what we could do with in our house."

"You spend all day in air-conditioned offices," Jane protested almost in desperation. "No call for air-conditioning at night too."

"My niece down East has an air-conditioned home," Molly offered ingenuously, but with no hint of malicious intent.

"Probably lives in one of those suburbs," Jane came in quickly. "Barbara lives downtown in those smart older homes ... high ceilings." Some of the women looked amused now. "No need for air-conditioning in those houses."

Barbara moved off to the edge of the group; she sensed the tone of despair in Jane's voice and she would have done anything to save her from further humiliation. At the same time she felt a great surge of anger, not directed at any particular city or country, individual or group, just anger towards the position she had been forced to choose.

The rest of the afternoon became a blur of polite, nonsensical dialogue and all the time she focused on Jane, wanting to go to her and put her arms around her and give her a hug.

The drive home was a quiet one. The usually hyperactive Jane had somehow shrunken and settled. She fixed her eyes steadily on the road ahead and didn't bother to blow the hair out of her eyes.

"I'm sorry about the rosebush," Barbara said finally. "... but I had to tell the truth." Jane's face remained immobile, her eyes squinting straight ahead of her.

"I think it's maybe better not to talk so much about us ... Don and me ... I know you're proud of everything we do, but they don't seem to like it, do they?"

There was silence for a minute or two, and the only sign she gave of having heard was a slight tilt to her head and a narrowing of her eyes as she focused on the road.

"Don't make no mind about the rosebush anyhow," she said, finally giving a sudden laugh. "I showed them pictures of your roses from last time I was there."

"Not the last time, Jane."

"No matter ... time before ... They sure seen those roses." She snorted with laughter again. "They make that puny bush of Molly's look sick."

She put her foot flat down on the gas pedal and the car made a frightening leap forward and a sideways skid began. For one awful moment Barbara saw them headed for the ditch, but then the car righted itself and lurched on precariously. From having hit the soft shoulder, the inside of the car was now a cloud of dust. They could have been driving through fog.

"Makes it look sick all right ... They remember for sure." She turned to Barbara with a grin, at the same time waving with one arm to dispel the dust.

"Notice how long it took for her to show the rosebush? You can bet your last dollar she remembered the photos of your roses. No sir, couldn't forget the sight of that no matter how hard you tried."

# PAULINE

The first thing we did on the train was solemnly remove our socks and stuff them into our suitcases. Then we sat for long stretches of the trip with our bare feet on the floor of the carriage, feeling the grains of dust and grit under our soles and imagining that we were already walking on the sand. During the four weeks of blissful rock climbing, cave exploring and swimming, our pure white feet and legs would first turn pink and then gradually modulate to a deeper shade, the best that the Irish summer could do for us. By the time we made the return journey to civilization the white socks, back on, would glisten against the modest tan of our legs.

I calculated that it had been around ten times we had taken the train together, or twenty times if you counted there and back: Pauline, her younger sister Laura and myself. I was seven when I was first allowed to go that August and sixteen the last summer. Her father always dropped us off at the train station in Belfast and her aunt met us in Whitehead.

This time the entire journey was something that had to be done alone, alone that is except for the tin box. It was a gold box, shaped like a tea tin, but spare of decoration. Holding it in my hands I felt awkward, "butter-fingered," my father's old term for my curious lack of hand dexterity. I imagined someone sitting beside me in the railway carriage, asking me where I was going and for what purpose. They would wonder about the tin box and lack of suitcases. The memory of those long-past joyous summers would crowd in on me ... destroy me before I reached my destination. I would have to be urged, cajoled, along with my numerous ghosts, to leave the train.

It was exactly one month since I'd sat on the bed opposite Pauline in the London flat, exactly one month since I'd recognized what was actually happening. I would be able to click the camera in my mind forever and see the moment over and over again: everything grey and white and totally still. Only the opaque quality of the light, slanting in from the prison-high window, capturing the glint of moving things in the air, gave any feeling of continuity or motion.

They had given me their room and were planning to sleep in the living room on the fold-out sofa bed. There was a tiny unbalanced dresser in the nook under the window and, for a bedside table, a glass-topped garden table. The bed was a white-enamelled maid's bed that took up almost the entire room. The only splash of colour was provided by the posy of spring flowers that Pauline had arranged on the table, tulips and daffodils. Everything else was white or dove grey. Herself, almost a nun in the simple tailored pinstripe dress, with the Chinese-style collar high against her throat, drawing even more attention to the stark whiteness of her face.

I can still feel the tufts of cotton from the bedspread between my fingers and recall the dark patch of grease on the front of my skirt. First, the inspection of the bedspread, textures momentarily absorbing, blotting out certainties and recognition, then attention on the stain. All the time her eyes watching the movements of my hands. The moment filled with a thousand unsaid things.

"It was perfectly clean when I left home." I rubbed the spot on my skirt again.

"You've come a long way," she smiled.

I lifted the suitcase from against the wall and heaved it onto the bed. Half of its weight came from the huge Eskimo carving that I had lugged from Canada as a wedding gift for her. I'd brought a piece of my world to her, but it should have been something more persuasive, something that would tell her how I felt about her. Instead, I'd chosen this god-awful rock that had been mercilessly expensive and was ice cold to the touch. We both sat silently contemplating the Eskimo bent on kill, his arm raised over the seal. She put out her hand and allowed it to curve along the back of the figure, exploring the marble cool surface of the carving. I couldn't remember anymore why I'd chosen it, but vaguely I knew it had struck some chord deep inside. The hopelessness of the animal caught at random on the ice floe with nowhere to go as the blows descended, had touched something.

"Thank you!" was all she said.

"It's not much use, but I didn't know what you might have in the way of useful things."

I wanted to go to her, put my arms around her and tell her that everything would be all right and hope that perhaps saying it might make it so.

"What was it like?" I asked instead.

"Not bad!" She smiled a falsely cheerful smile and hunched herself defensively, her hands clasped around her knees.

"I'm getting on when it comes to having kids, anyway ... they might not have been born right."

It wasn't true of course, thirty-two wasn't considered old anymore for having children.

"Is everything all right then?"

"Fine!" Her eyes flickered and she looked down at her hands. "Rotten for Trevor. I feel as if I pulled a dirty trick on him."

"Don't be silly, how could you possibly have known? Don't they say that once five years are up you're not supposed to worry?"

"They say that," she said grimly.

As children we had registered each instant of each other's growth: graduation from training bra to size thirty-two, the moment of first bleeding, the time of the first proper open-mouthed kiss, the first love, the first disappointment, and yet that moment six years before when she had learned she had to have a breast removed, I was only able to read about it on a flimsy airmail letter and know that by the time she had put pen to paper, she had battled the worst horror and uncertainty alone, and anything I might write would sound empty and help her not one whit with whatever still had to come.

"Just the womb," she said, her eyes sliding away and concentrating on a corner of the room.

*Just a breast, just a womb.* I wanted suddenly to blubber and cry, but it wasn't possible. Instead of tears there was a weird feeling in the roof of my mouth as though some kind of iron clamp had been inserted that would inevitably hinder any kind of outpouring.

The room suddenly began to make sense: the pristine quality of the space, no clutter, no mess, no dark corners for the mind to squirrel into and lose itself. It was the hospital room at home. There was no real part of Pauline anywhere in the small flat. There were boxes in the living room still unpacked and a temporary quality to all the furnishings. She excused the make-shift style of things because, she insisted, they were still considering Canada, once Trevor's studies were finished. But somehow Trevor wouldn't transplant, even I could tell that. There was no rationale though for the tentativeness of the way she and Trevor approached one another. I longed to have them on a series of long strings and, like a puppeteer, move them towards each other into each other's arms, to make the most of what they had, but there were no threads from either of them. They invited no interference.

He taught at the London Tech and was working on his doctorate. He spent long hours in the tiny room that had once been a pantry and was now set up as his study. The room was cold as all pantries usually are and its chill had already begun to set on him. When he emerged he seemed blue at the edges. He was always upset about small things and bitched constantly about his work, both his studying and his teaching. He yapped around her heels like a terrier that needed to be soothed. It was easy to see why he had been attracted to her. She wasn't a complainer, never had been. Her quiet courage would have definite appeal, and in the end her tragedy would give him further shape; perhaps even make him interesting.

He was slightly smaller than Pauline in stature. I remember how she had always sworn that she didn't care about her height and whether or not a man was smaller than she, she would keep on wearing her high-heeled shoes. I noticed she now wore flats.

It seemed Trevor only made his appearances to complain about things: a missing pen, someone vacuuming on the floor above. Perhaps these were the diversions that kept the hours passing safely, each minor crisis a small anchor of certainty: problem, discussion, resolution; problem, discussion, resolution. The pen found, the neighbour quieted, he took his pale body back once more and all was silent again.

He appeared only long enough to show me the remembered side to Pauline, the instant of vulnerability to his anger. Pauline had never been scared of things, only of people and their anger. As children together I remember being jealous of her almost uncanny lack of physical fear. I had deliberately ignored the slight heave of her chest before she tackled things. My mother always told me that people without cowardice were also without imagination. My envy of her fearlessness wanted it to be true. Her intake of breath told me otherwise, but I preferred not to think about that. It helped justify my own miserable fear of drowning, of great heights and a multitude of other things, both tangible and intangible: death, birth, insects with wings, insects of all kinds. Once Pauline had planted a huge earthworm on a leaf in my purse and laughed heartily when I threw purse and all into the bushes. It hadn't been a deliberately cruel act as much as a challenge to my stupidity.

Later we were able to recognize each other's weaknesses, but happily, we were a team. I had courage with people and she had physical courage that made her daring. When we stole apples from a neighbour's garden, I was the one who defended us when we were caught. We would throw our ball into the neighbour's yard and then climb the fence to get it and line our knickers with apples collected from the lower branches and the ground. Overly ambitious one day, our navy elasticized knickers crammed to the point where they began to sag beneath our skirts, we were caught and anchored by our burden.

"And what do you two think you are up to?" the neighbour, Mr. McDowell asked, taking a firm grasp on Pauline's arm.

"Well, we saw them rotting on the ground," I invented.

"Rotting my foot!" His eyes narrowed, "They were picked yesterday." His gaze fixed on Pauline, "I'm surprised at you, Pauline Jamison. Wouldn't your father whip your backside if he knew what you were up to?"

Pauline began to cry. "The next time you get the urge for an apple, try the front door and don't do it like sneak thieves."

Pauline stood still, mute to the reprieve.

"Off with you then!"

I twanged the elastic on my knickers and the last of the apples fell around my ankles.

"You can keep them now you've picked them," he offered magnanimously.

"No thanks. They're a bit overripe," I lied.

At this he threw back his head and began to laugh. I tugged Pauline's arm. "Come on, let's go!"

We could still hear him laughing as we made our way back over the fence, scrambling with unladylike abandon over the dividing wall.

Pauline was quiet and sulky. To this point she had been remarkably free of adult disapproval. Her mother had died when she was too young to have any proper memory of her. Her father was only vaguely interested in Laura and Pauline. He kept them clothed, fed and well housed, but they roamed, rather like two young wild animals with nobody ever to tell them what was right or wrong, scold or chastise them. They had a housekeeper who picked up after them but made no attempt to behave like a mother. I was over-mothered and fathered and had continually tested my wits against adults. I was usually beaten back, if ever so gently, and would recover to wait for the next time. Neither Pauline nor Laura knew that it was possible to fight with someone and then shake hands. Each confrontation must have seemed rather horrid and irrevocable.

There was the time when her father took us for a drive to Bangor one Saturday afternoon. We were given sixpence each for fish and chips while he went into Dogherty's pub. The routine was always the same. It was his occasional day of contact with the girls, which he softened by spending the afternoon in the pub drinking. We were given a time to meet him at the car, but he was seldom back when he promised.

This particular day we were all anxious for him to come as we badly needed to go to the bathroom. It would never have occurred to us to go into one of the cafes and ask for a bathroom; we were sure you had to eat something in order to use the toilet, and we had no money left to buy anything. We had a single penny, so we decided to go to the public toilet close to the beach.

It was a place we had always considered sinister. It was painted a dark green and even from a distance it smelt of rust and urine. There was a huge woman sitting on a tiny stool in the corner. She was tearing bits of newspaper into small bits, no doubt to be used as toilet paper. Beside her there was a pail of muddy grey water and a large filthy wet mop.

I went in first and then held the door open for Pauline. The woman roused herself.

"Shut the door!" she commanded.

"We don't have another penny."

"It's the rules."

"Go in Pauline!" I urged. Pauline hesitated. "Go on, stupid, hurry up!" Pauline scuttled in and slammed the door.

"You can't stop people from peeing." I stood tall. "She has to go an' that's all there is to it."

"I'll wallop yer arses for disobeyin' me," she threatened.

"You try and I'll put my father on you. He's a policeman," I lied.

It was Laura's turn while the woman and I were still exchanging insults. Pauline quietly cried and the woman directed her stream of invective towards her.

Laura seemed to take for ever, and then, when she finally came out, the woman grabbed her by the arm and pulled her in to the toilet while she inspected the seat and floor.

"Yez peed on the seats too."

I was quite sure it was possible. We had all been trained never to let our bums come in contact with strange lavatory seats and I knew I, at least, had stood tall over this particular one. I pulled Laura by the other arm and the woman lost her grasp.

"Run!"

"Youse come back here an' clean this place up," she hollered after our retreating backs.

"She'll report us," Pauline sobbed.

"They don't put you in jail for peeing on a lavatory seat," I argued logically.

They weren't convinced; Laura's teeth were chattering and not from the familiar chilly sea breezes that were blowing in from the Irish Sea, but from straight fear. I was delighted to talk about what might happen and momentarily enjoyed my superiority, pretending I hadn't been in the least scared by the woman's enormous bulk or her venom. Nevertheless, we huddled on the back seat of the car and kept below window level in case she had followed. Never had Pauline's father's alcoholic breath and presence been so welcome when he finally arrived back at the car.

The roles were now fixed, it was Pauline's to be the physical adventurer and mine to defend her from people and anger. On our summer holidays together it was she who explored deepest into the caves and climbed the steepest cliffs, while I hung back issuing warnings. In school too, it was Pauline who was fearless on the parallel bars. Her tall, lithe body could twist itself into any shape. She could scale to the top of the rafters like a monkey while the rest of us stood watching. She did everything without effort, only the tiny give-away intake of air and then she was off, no real stopping to reconsider.

Then came the morning she perched on the parallel ladder which was about twenty feet off the ground and decided to do a Tarzan act. She made someone swing the rope towards her as a test several times to make sure that she could catch it and then, while the rest of us stood petrified, she swung herself off into the air, first one hand on the rope, then two. She sailed across the room to our cheers. No one else made an effort to compete, it was her triumph and we were content to let it be so.

On the second try, something happened: first one hand then somehow she was flying without the rope, spread-eagled above us like a large graceful bird, defying gravity itself. There was no look of horror on her face, only a faint hint of surprise as she hung suspended above us for an instant. Then she crashed to the ground with an enormous thud. And somebody had laughed, though it was nothing to do with the fact that she had missed the rope, but because, for one exhilarating moment, she had flown. This magnificent human creature had, for a moment in time, floated above us.

We viewed the crumpled body in front of our feet the way we viewed a bird that had temporarily stunned itself against a pane of glass. We knew there was nothing fatal about her crash. It took seconds before we realized what an enormous distance she had actually fallen and that she was deadly still on the floor. We stood mesmerized by the unexpectedness of it all. Our teacher rushed out of the room, presumably to phone for a doctor, and Pauline began to move, slowly and gingerly, her hand clutched to her breast. She pulled herself to a sitting position. She smiled a crooked grin and we knew we had been right not to worry.

What small bright avenues of adventure were open to her now, I wondered? Her days were monotonously the same, bounded by medical check-ups at the hospital and worry about whether or not Trevor was getting enough peace and quiet to study.

There seemed to be nothing else but peace and quiet. Neither appeared to have confronted the idea that their time together might be limited. It was life as normal, and more horribly normal than one could possibly have wished for anyone. Some awful premature peace seemed to have descended and settled.

Because she had always been a tall well-built girl with a sturdy frame, she managed somehow to hide the fact that her flesh was gradually disappearing off her bones. The wedding ring, which once must have fitted, moved from knuckle to the base of her finger with ease.

They had friends who came from time to time, Trevor's fellow teachers, economists and mathematicians, some with wives, some without. The men wore argyle socks and smelled depressingly of deep dark closets; the women discussed the shocking price of bacon and the quality of Marks & Spencers' kippers.

In the sixties the same types would have been Marxist and raved on about the privileged hegemony. Now most were staunchly anti-Union. Some of their views made Margaret Thatcher's seem liberal. In their presence Pauline kept reverently silent. She seemed almost scared of them and their curious contradictory passions. I didn't blame her, they were queer fish, passionate with words, yet cold to each other.

Privately, I christened them the "pantry boys." They were all working on theses or dissertations of some sort and in my mind's eye I saw them, like Trevor, sequestered in icy rooms like so many individual barrels of chilled lard.

I had already overstayed my time with them, and my planned visit to relatives in Belfast was long overdue, but I was reluctant to leave her. However, I was running out of excuses to stay. She assured me that she was fine and that nothing had changed, but everything about her told me otherwise. Her face was a ghastly yellow grey and her clothes hung far too loose on her body. She could sit for long periods of time with her hands in her lap, one curved around the other, thumbs clasped, her feet close together, and stare off into space. Her terrible inertia was almost frightening. At times I had the strongest urge to spirit her away from the flat and Trevor, and smuggle her on a plane back to Canada. I would fly her into the bush and drop her somewhere with a survival kit. I was overwhelmed with the idea that, away from the damp and chill of the flat and from Trevor and his group of friends, she would somehow forget she was waiting for something to happen. The outdoor challenge would wake up the sleeping cells, and they in turn, would drive back the enemy.

At other times I wanted to charge into the pantry and shake Trevor, shout at him to open his eyes and look at her, but perhaps he saw too much already and this was his way of hiding from what he saw.

I eventually left and went to Belfast. Three weeks later Trevor phoned, Pauline had just died in hospital. Instead of being happy that at least she hadn't suffered longer than was necessary, I was enraged that it should have happened so quickly and when I wasn't with her. I had trouble pulling myself together to hear what he had to say. He wanted to read her last letter which was addressed to me and concerned the funeral arrangements.

He began:

*"Dear Roz, dear, dear Roz, I write soon after you leave and I feel somehow that you will still be in Belfast when you get this.*

*Don't cry, because I feel I've done all I wanted to do. The time was only a bit short, that's all.*

*Probably what I'm going to ask is the hardest thing you might ever have to do, but I feel I can't ask anyone else. I would like to be cremated and I want you to take my ashes and scatter them off the cliff above the caves at Whitehead. I'd like that. Do it please on a sunny day when the waves are big and the breezes strong and remember the good times we had, but not with tears. I know we'll meet again. Pauline."*

To Trevor's credit, he came over personally with her ashes. He even accompanied me to the railway station and saw me off in the train, his eyes not looking at mine but fixed on the metal box. For an instant I thought he was going to spring into the carriage beside me, but instead he firmly slammed the door and with a quick wave was gone. For a moment I had actually liked him.

Nobody came to sit in the carriage with me, nor did anyone get in during the other short stops along the way, I needed it to be that way.

My mind had played tricks on me about the size of Whitehead. Childhood memories had expanded the geography in my head. I had remembered the distances from one place to another to be greater.

On the walk to the headland, the bag with the tin box in it banged against my knee, like a reminder of the ordeal ahead. I needed the distance to be greater or even for the elements to be out of kilter with Pauline's last wish, but the weather was perfect, as though specially ordered: the sky blue, the breezes strong, and the waves rolling in their familiar wide swathe as though some giant hand unfurled them from a bisecting line in the middle of Belfast Lough. They broke hard on the shoreline, churning white and frothing out again in a paler spume.

Dandelion seeds flew in the air, clinging to my arms and chest in temporary respite from the urgency that battled around them.

I welcomed the effort of the climb to the headland and the push of wind in my face. I occupied myself by thinking how difficult it would be to scatter the ashes so that they wouldn't be blown back to the land behind me in the direction of Belfast. The wind always blew in hard and strong from the Irish Sea.

The gorse was at its most vivid bloom and in places matted the purple rock, rooting itself in the clefts and clinging thickly, yellow as flax. At the top of the cliff that old remembered feeling came back as strong as ever. The sensation of being poised on the arm of a catapult. At any moment the ground under my feet would contract and then spring back and hurl me out, out far into the ocean. It was the wonder of this particular spot. The sister arm of land across the Lough, which was County Down, didn't have half the magic. As children we had stood here, Pauline and I together, and fantasized that we could shoot out from this very spot and land almost anywhere in the world.

Ironically, I was the one who had been out and back again. Yet nothing had quite matched that first exhilaration of standing here and dreaming; dreaming that the roots and tentacles of Belfast couldn't reach this far and that we could spring free at any moment, nothing hooking our ankles or hampering our journey over expanses of water and sky.

I delayed the moment of opening the box and then, when I did, I was surprised by the small handful of ashes, so very little after all. I was filled too with the awful feeling that I would somehow fail her. My timing would be off. Just as my arm flew out, the wind would die.

I might have stood for ever contemplating my possible failure if I hadn't taken a step to position myself more carefully and stumbled slightly. My arm flew up and the box flew out of my hands. The ashes scattered and then were suddenly caught in a kind of vortex that drew them upwards and out toward sea, forming a sort of V, almost like the shape of a gull. The tin box pinged somewhere in the distance as it hit the rocks.

I felt an odd choke of joyous laughter and heard it like an echo all around me. There was none of the sadness and dread that I had imagined would accompany the moment. It was like Pauline had stretched out her arm, given me a shove and said, "You goose, don't be afraid!"

# FULL CIRCLE

The rain was that fine stuff that always fell in Belfast, that made you feel dishraggy and dirty, bringing with it particles of soot and grime. He could feel it from his shoes up and especially on the inside of his leg.

"Open the umbrella, Jean! The damned umbrella. Open it! I'm wet."

His wife Jean was carrying a tightly rolled, striped golf umbrella. He noticed she seemed bone dry while water puddled around his own ankles.

"You are wet, you naughty boy. Your hose has come off."

He opened his eyes slowly and it was a minute before he recognized where he was. He had been dreaming a lot about rain lately, and always when he awoke he'd wet himself like a baby piddling in its diapers. Only there were no diapers because he hadn't allowed them to put diapers on him.

"Now if you had a bit more in this department, we wouldn't be having all this trouble." Nurse Meffe yanked at his penis. He'd never once had a complaint about its size when he was running around using it for other things besides peeing. He remembered when he was seventeen and in the army illegally and over in Paris, a woman there telling him she liked the small ones, they always "doing better" was how she had put it in her pigeon English. Jean hadn't complained either. Said he used it too much maybe, but never a word about it not being enough.

Nurse Meffe was all right, but there was no respect for the part she was trying to connect. She might have been tugging at his little finger. He'd come into the world attached to his mother's umbilical cord and was about to go with a nurse yanking on his penis. Not a bad thought if there had been any pleasure involved, but she had a heavy hand.

You'll pull it off if you go on like that," he complained bitterly.

"I reckon it's been tugged before," she teased.

She was always good about the wet bed, and he knew if only he didn't have the dream about Belfast and the damned rain it wouldn't keep happening.

"It's the dreams I'm having that do it."

"Wet dreams at your age, Mr. Hamilton?"

"About rain, not sex, Nurse."

He liked Meffe; she was no prude. If he were about thirty years younger, she was the type of woman he would go for, no nonsense and sort of solid all over, no sylph, but with the kind of meat on her bones that wouldn't sag with age. "Borderline peasant" he called the type, good mothers, good wives, and all around good sports.

"Are you getting up?"

"Not yet."

He could see she thought him an old nuisance. She rolled him over unceremoniously and tugged the soggy sheets out from underneath him. How many similar beds would she have to do? Rows of dirty old men and women who had dreamt of dignified old age and instead lay in their own mess.

Once she'd settled him and put the head of the bed up to a position where he could see, he tried not to think about what his dreams had been, but stared out of the window.

"*We could see the writing on the wall*" had been the phrase he'd used over the last twenty years to describe why he and Jean had left Belfast. The real reason was that the children had come to Canada. The "Troubles" in Belfast had started for real after they'd left home, but he could have lived with that. The last time he'd gone home it was like all his friends had found a new lease on life. They loved the excitement of the conflict. They liked the reporters coming from all over the world and all they ever talked about was Paisley or Bernadette Devlin. They hadn't given a good goddam what life was like in Canada or what he and Jean did in Winnipeg. But that had been all right for they didn't do a hell of a lot anyway except watch the telly and discuss what the high and low temperatures were for the day. It fitted in nicely with the Canadian obsession about weather.

The senior citizens' home was built right across the street from a sewage treatment plant, a sort of nondescript red-brick box. Fitting in a way to be across the road from that. On the other corner was a boarded-up Freeze Queen, and beside that there were a row of stucco bungalows all painted white with different-coloured trims. Those bungalows couldn't belong to any other city in Canada. He thought of them as Winnipeg bungalows. Most of them pre-war with little stucco projections that substituted for front porches and small windows that wouldn't let in too many drafts in the chill of winter.

Bert watched those bungalows, and the odd time he saw people coming and going, but for long stretches in January and February they might have been empty. The only sign of life was after a snow storm when miraculously in the morning a deep trench had been dug up the pathway for the mailman.

There was a dog in the house with the red trim. It came out some days by itself and roamed and sniffed at lamp posts, lifting its leg every minute or two as though badly affected by below zero temperatures. He could sympathize with that. An ex-neighbour, Marjorie Corbett, came once to take him out for the day and he'd done exactly the same thing, only not against a lamp post but against the back wheel of her car. It was that, or wet his pants. He'd had no choice, but it had been an embarrassing experience.

Now, when people wanted to take him out, he mostly refused. The doctors said his problem was a prostate gone wonky, but then doctors always looked for the wrong causes for illness. It was like Jean. They said she had died from heart trouble, when what she had really died from was Winnipeg. She hated the long winters and hot summers but hadn't wanted to go back to Ireland either. Jean was no good at admitting she'd made a mistake; so in the end she'd opted out altogether.

He felt tired again, mostly from the monotony of the view: the snow-banks of unwanted ploughed snow, the rutted roads, the eternal whiteness of the landscape sliced and bisected by hydro lines and telephone poles. The skies were the only good thing about winter in the prairie. They were tantalizingly blue, but then again, even that was a fraud. In fact, the fiercer the tint of blue, the colder it usually was outside.

There was a loud rap at the door and in a split second Gord Telfer was in the room. The first time Bert had met Gord, he'd been delighted. Someone living on the same floor actually on his feet and still full of piss and vinegar. He'd soon come to change his mind as Gord was constantly after him for some of his preciously guarded Scotch.

"Just ran out, old man! Wondered if I could have a couple of nips from your bottle?" After fifty years in Canada Gord's limey accent was as strong as ever.

"Sorry, Gord, ran out myself last night," Bert lied. He knew Gord well. If he saw a bottle he'd be off with it and there would never be any replacement.

It was amazing how Gord managed to keep himself together despite the intake of booze. Here it was eight in the morning and he was already shaved, and dressed nattily with a clean white shirt, cravat and blazer. He might have been on his way to an audition, although those requests came only rarely now.

For years Gord had been Winnipeg's resident "grand old man" of theatre and telly. For the last thirty years it seemed he had been playing old men and was still at it. Bert suspected that he had a good five years on him, but he never talked about his age. He was like a woman as far as that was concerned.

Bert hated anyone to be in his room first thing in the morning, he was sure it still smelt of urine. He liked time for the room to air, but there was never any keeping Gord out. Thank God, this time he hadn't brought his scrapbooks. That in itself was a mercy.

Wildmere was an ideal setting for Gord. He could carry his scrapbooks from room to room and, nine times out of ten, the inmates didn't remember he'd been to visit the day before, and he could rehash his memories again. It was like being on stage every day, only here the audience were captive and grateful "first nighters."

He wasn't sure when Gord left. Perhaps when the breakfast trays came he edged out, perhaps before. It didn't matter anymore. It was no good being rude to Gord; it was best just to pretend he wasn't there, and then he would slide away.

"Aren't you getting up then?" Nurse Gillick asked. Gillick was no Meffe, she wouldn't stand for any nonsense.

"No! Bloody tube comes off when I move."

"When I've finished putting these around, I'll come back and help." She set the tray down just out of his reach. He knew she'd done it deliberately to force him to get up himself. If he didn't, the food would be stone cold by the time she got back. It was bad enough already, almost always tepid. In a way it was a mercy Jean didn't have to suffer this. Jean could never stand her food anything but piping hot. She would have been miserable.

He got out of bed with difficulty, clutching his attachments, and managed to reach the tray. He pulled up his trolley and sat on the edge of the bed. He lifted the metal lid that covered the breakfast and condensation dripped onto his lap. There was a plastic-looking poached egg sitting on a bit of seaweed spinach which in turn rested on a soggy bun. He knew exactly what it would taste like. The most solid thing in his mouth would be the egg. He slapped the metal lid back over the obscenity. He would let them take their bloody breakfast back where it came from: the plastics factory.

He could hear someone's television set blaring away through the wall. Then came a long wailing sound. That would be Mrs. Dykstra who rolled her wheelchair into the walls and clawed at them every time she was let loose in the corridors.

He put his headphones on, the ones his daughter had given him, and started the tiny cassette machine with one of the tapes in it. It was ironic in a way — here they had come halfway across the world for family and there was no one in Winnipeg any longer. Bruce had been transferred to Montreal about five years back. He visited once a year and apart from that they spoke on the phone on Sundays, managing to talk for ten minutes, mostly about the weather, vying pointlessly with one another for the largest amount of snowfall in the winter and the highest degree of humidity in the summer.

Margaret was a travel writer, divorced now, and happy to spend most of her time on the road. While she was away she always took her tape machine with her and talked into it, so that he could follow along no matter where she was. Of course she didn't do it for him but for the newspaper, but he loved getting the tapes. All he had to do was close his eyes and he was with her in Venezuela, Peru, places he'd only ever read about. He closed his eyes. She was standing in Red Square in Moscow. It was too bad it was there, he could have done with warmer climes, but still he was there with her, standing staring up at the minarets, awed by the space and feel of time.

"Where are you now?" Gord was back in the room, pestering him again.

Bert sighed and took the earphones off. "I've told you, Gord, the bottle's empty."

He'd obviously managed to get some booze from somewhere, his breath was fruity with rum.

"I've been thinking: with Easter coming up we should do a little entertainment."

"Thinking of a 'Resurrection,' were you?" Bert said sarcastically.

"You and me, that is."

"Count me out!"

"Come on, Bert. You're the only one here with any spirit left. I need you."

"Go rent yourself a dummy!"

"I don't know what's the matter with you lately. You might as well be dead."

Bert put his headphones on again.

"*Fortunately, the sun is shining today,*" Margaret spoke into the machine. "*I can't imagine what it would be like here on a dull day, dreadfully depressing I should think.*"

Tell me about it, Bert thought.

Gord went out of the room without a backward glance. Bert had a feeling he hadn't seen the last of him that morning, and sure enough, just as Margaret was about to go into Gorky Square, he was back.

"For Christ's sake, Gord! I said no. I'm just at the interesting part."

"Where you've been a hundred times before."

Gord had his scrapbook with him this time. He sat down on the bed and opened it up. Excitedly he jabbed his finger at a photograph showing a much younger Gord wearing a straw boater and a striped shirt.

"Look! Remember Norbert and Tell?" He pointed a finger at another figure in the picture. "The old vaudeville act? This is Willy Johnston and me doing a take-off. We did it for the Ad and Sales Club back in the forties, brought the house down. You and I could do it for this lot."

"Sure, we could work my hose and bag into the act."

Gord ignored him. "You're the straight man. You'd hardly have to do a thing. I think I can remember most of it. I can write it all down for you."

"Count me out!" Bert shook his head.

"You'd enjoy yourself. I guarantee it."

"Look, I was on stage once in my life, that was enough."

Actually he'd never quite made it on stage. His mother had sent him to Miss Pringle's dancing class when he'd been eight years of age. God knows what it was she was trying to do for him — give him grace, take some of the lout out of him — but whatever, it hadn't worked too well. He'd completely spoiled Miss Pringle's Christmas concert.

He'd flatly refused to go on stage until Miss Pringle had given him a costume with bells all over it. He'd fancied that costume from the start, and when he put it on, it jingled like crazy.

The night of the concert he had to stand backstage, waiting for his cue; he was supposed to leap on stage and run around from person to person, shaking himself so that the bells rang out. This was supposed to provide comic relief, but backstage he'd been having a lot of fun running around chasing everyone who came offstage, especially Milly Foster, one of the wood fairies. Halfway through the performance an enraged Miss Pringle charged backstage and cuffed Bert on both ears, not just once, but what seemed like a hundred times.

"Those bells have been ringing since the concert started. What have you been up to, you bad little boy? Go immediately!" She pointed a quivering finger towards the dressing rooms.

"But my part?" Bert protested, knowing his mother and father were eagerly anticipating his appearance.

"You have more than done your bit, thank you very much," she said icily.

He'd been expelled from dancing school — if there was such a thing as expulsion. At any rate, his mother had been asked politely to find some other sport for her youngest, something better suited to his temperament. Like Miss Pringle, his mother had boxed his ears until they were purple and swollen.

"So you're just going to sit around holding your hose and feeling sorry for yourself?" Gord sneered. "God forbid you might enjoy yourself for a minute." He got up from the bed shaking his head, "There's more life in a rotten egg."

Bert felt his resolve weakening. What, after all, had he to lose? As long as he didn't have to do too much, it might even break the monotony of the day.

"What do you want me to do?"

"That's more like it." Gord turned cheerfully and slapped Bert on the shoulder. "I'll write it all out, you haven't got a thing to worry about."

"I'm not worried, just bored by the whole idea."

He put his headphones back on and went into Gorky Square with

Margaret. She got critical here, so Bert fast-forwarded the tape a bit to skip over that.

Gord didn't bother him for two days and he managed to go through several of the tapes. He went on a tour of the Middle East and one of the vineyards of France and he was almost word perfect on both trips. He could have recited it along with Margaret. He'd noticed of late she wasn't as chipper as she used to be, a bit blasé about everthing she saw, and he didn't like that. He'd learned to fast-forward through those bits.

Bert hoped Gord would forget the whole idea, or that someone would put a kibosh on his plans, but unfortunately the nurses were as enthusiastic as Gord and even began helping him to organize the concert.

As the day of the performance drew closer, Bert's dreams of rain intensified. True, he didn't have much to do, he was to be a "yes, no" man sitting at a bus stop waiting for a bus. He wouldn't even have to walk, but still he was terrified.

A few days before the performance he woke up feeling sick. When Meffe brought him his breakfast, he refused to eat.

"Cold feet, have we?" Meffe inquired with a grin.

"I don't feel well." Bert snarled.

"Scared of the rain?" she asked sympathetically and patted his hand. "I could solve it for you."

Bert looked up at her round, cheerful face. He knew she was going to suggest a diaper before she even spoke.

"No!" Bert turned away from her morosely. "Never!" he said emphatically.

"You're chickening out," she accused him.

"I'm sick."

"Sick my foot! You should be ashamed of yourself." She squared in on him, "You have your vision, your hearing, your legs, your heart, and your head, although sometimes I'm not sure about the last part. You have one small problem and you're ready to give up."

One small problem indeed! Let her try going through life with wet knickers. For a moment he detested her round, good face. He fumbled for his headphones and recorder and retreated to Peking, where he'd left off the night before. It wasn't the best of places to be, Margaret was snarky about the food because she'd seen a rat somewhere near the kitchen of the hotel where she was staying. He fast-forwarded, aware that Meffe was still talking and gesticulating. He caught a snatch of something that sounded like "opting out" and immediately pressed the play button and landed in Bangkok, Thailand. Again, not the best place to be. Someone had tried to con Margaret in Bangkok, and she went on a lot about a lack of ethics.

In no time at all Gord was in his room. Not wanting to be called a coward, Bert stopped Margaret just as she was registering at the Oriental.

"Well, I didn't think you'd do it." Gord shook his head sadly. "All that time wasted. Go on! Back to your eternal tapes. I doubt you've ever done much else but live through other people anyway." He turned on his heel and left the room.

Bert felt genuinely sick now. Margaret was describing the hotel with its glorious marble floors and old-world elegance, and then she came to the balconies that overlooked a cesspool of a waterway and spoiled the whole picture. A note of weariness was definitely tainting Margaret's latest tapes. Five years ago the waterway would have been a colourful part of Bangkok's magnificent diversity. Now she saw everything as being plain dirty. He clicked off the tape and lay there despondently. The daughter he relied on to take him out of his dull world was letting him down.

The next day, when he expected Nurse Meffe, a new nurse came instead.

"Where's Meffe?"

"Nurse Meffe's busy. Can I help?"

"No, you can't. Send me Meffe!"

He could tell she didn't like his tone. She flushed slightly. "I'm sure she'll come when she's finished."

Twenty years ago he would have worried about hurting this new little one's feelings, now he didn't think much about apologies or things like that. Trouble was life was so damned short, you had to be brief about what you wanted.

He waited but Meffe didn't come. Suddenly everything was confusing; he saw himself lying on the bed and yet he was actually in the bed, and Brigid Kinstry who ran the sweetie shop on the corner of the Lisburn Road was leaning over him and her rosary was clunking on his chest, heavy as a great anchor. She was sort of running it over his chest, bumping it off his nipples, and all the time he felt himself sink deeper and deeper into the mattress as Brigid's big, sloppy camel mouth, with the breath to match, was closing in on him.

"I'm going! I'm going!" he heard himself saying over and over again and Brigid, who clutched his shoulders, kept calling out, "You're going nowhere! You're going nowhere, do you hear?" And he couldn't make out whether or not she meant he wasn't going to die or that he was going to die and was actually headed for purgatory. Purgatory was big with the Catholics, he knew that for sure. He wasn't even sure why this bothered him. He had never believed in purgatory.

"She's right, Daddy!" Margaret was there with her tape recorder, trying to jam it on his chest.

"Fuck off, the lot of you!" he managed, but nothing happened. Now the rosary was in competition with Margaret's little portable tape recorder for a place on his chest and was tangling up with his chest hair.

"Fuck off!" he yelled again, and suddenly he was sitting up in bed, his hands tugging at his chest, and the new nurse was there with her lips pursed.

"Really, Mr. Hamilton, there's no need for such language."

He remembered now what he'd been yelling. It hadn't been at her, but he let her think what she liked. Meffe would have just laughed it off. She left abruptly, her face still all puckered with disapproval.

Fancy dreaming about Brigid Kinstry, he hadn't thought of her for years. The breath had been real enough, so had all the little dark hairs that outlined the long rubbery upper lip. He would gladly have taken a stab at purgatory to avoid smelling that breath again.

He lay thinking about Brigid Kinstry and the rows and rows of boiled sweets in clear bottles: humbugs, peppermint stripes, chocolate éclairs, fruit bonbons, toffees, licorice twists, peppermint creams, anise chews, cream centres.

Poor old Brigid had almost died during the war when the bottles had all been empty, except for the few pink-and-white-coated almonds that came in occasionally and were responsible for more than one person breaking a tooth.

Even though she disapproved of smoking, Brigid had taken to selling cigarettes. At about the time the cigarettes had appeared, a big dark crucifix showed up on the back wall of the shop. It was the same crucifix he'd seen in his dreams, a kind of jagged thing with spiky edges.

He smiled to himself as he remembered the nurse's face. He dragged himself off the bed, carrying his tube and bag. Putting on his dressing gown carefully, so as to cover all the attachments, he headed down the corridor to Gord's room.

Gord was sitting staring out the window; he barely turned when Bert came in. Gord's room was like a theatre dressing room with flowers everywhere and pictures of Gord stuck on the mirrors and hanging on the walls — only the greasepaint and disorder of costumes was missing.

"I'm feeling better," Bert said in a grudging tone of voice.

He had Gord's attention now. "You'll do it then?"

Bert nodded.

Gord stood up grinning, "Good man, I knew you'd change your mind. How about another practice then?"

Bert held up his hand. "No, no more practices, I'll do the performance, that's it."

"O.K! O.K! No problem. I can go through things on my own."

The next thing to do was to find Meffe and make sure she was going to be around when he needed her. He walked down the corridor, passing Mrs. Dykstra doing her usual wall-bashing routine. He turned her chair out for her and she looked up blankly. Her face looked as though it had been squashed under a truck; one eye was semi-closed, her hair a pointed, tangled mess that nobody had combed. A trail of spittle from her mouth attached itself like a sloppy spider weaving to the front of her matted pink shawl.

Meffe was at the nursing station writing in some kind of notebook. They were always writing, this lot. Logbooks for everything, it was worse than being in the armed forces. He wondered who really cared.

"Well, are you feeling better?"

"Yes. I'll need that diaper then, but just for the night."

"Oh, I see." She quickly glanced down at the book she'd been writing in and then up again at him.

"Sensible decision," she smiled at him.

*Sensible decision* indeed! Nothing was sensible about the whole dumb idea of the concert.

It was odd seeing them later all piled into the dining room. The tables had been pushed to one side and a couple of risers had been brought in to serve as a platform. There was a piano on the platform. Somebody had made a half-hearted attempt to decorate the room, and there were several pots of Easter lilies posted in various corners. Bert hated Easter lilies, they looked too plastic and their odour was the odour of cemeteries and death.

Most of the women were decked out in their best clothes. Bert felt ridiculous, diapered up like a piece of supermarket meat, but at the same time he felt more secure than he had in months. At least this way there would be no pools on the floor. Even if there had been, Gord would no doubt have found a way to work that into the routine.

He noticed Mrs. Dykstra had already manoeuvered her chair so that her back was to the stage, probably anticipating an escape route.

The nurses had organized a whole programme. Wally Pederson had some kind of magic act that suffered severely because of his shakes, but no one seemed too critical when things went wrong. Geneva Frith sang a song. She'd dressed up in a sequinned dress that sagged over her hollow chest, but she got a cheer for the dress alone, never mind the song. She sang "Jealousy" and swayed off the high notes like a demented banshee, but nobody seemed to care.

He could almost hear Margaret's voice on the recorder putting them into perspective: "Inmates in an asylum," and he was one of them. There he was eighty years of age, in a diaper. He knew he had already wet himself because he felt all hot down there, and it seemed to be sort of cooking on him. It was a bit like being encased in a damp heating pad.

Gord was turned on by the audience. He did a routine by himself that wasn't really very funny and then he introduced Bert. Bert had a sudden wild desire to get up and run, or scream at them that he didn't belong, that he wasn't part of the whole travesty. He caught Meffe's eye and she shook her head as though she might have been mind reading.

He stood up, feeling momentarily dizzy. He was positive he was going to forget everything that Gord had coached him on and, sure enough, he did forget his first response. Gord stayed perfectly calm and just repeated his question, and then it all began to come back.

Mrs. Dykstra had turned her chair to face them and was kind of bleating like a sheep caught in a ditch. The rest of the audience seemed to think she was laughing and, before long, everyone was rolling with mirth.

"What the hell!" Life was ridiculous anyhow. Perhaps this lot, all staring up with expectant faces, some of them with their lives like blank tapes, were in an odd sense beginning again, perhaps even practicing for some higher level where you didn't have to be encumbered with memory and a past. Surprisingly, he began to enjoy himself, so that it was almost a disappointment when it was over.

They were the hit of the evening and Gord's cheeks were gleaming with genuine joy, not from the flush of too much booze, but the glow that comes from a momentary, small triumph.

Rose Shymka planted a kiss on Gord's cheek and then, turning to Bert, kissed him too. "Best concert we ever had!" she said emphatically.

Gord winked at Bert. "You were great, man!" He pumped Bert's hand. "A natural."

"You were pretty good yourself."

"Thanks! We could do a regular for them," Gord enthused.

Bert laughed, "Why not?"

Nurse Meffe came over, her arms crossed and a big grin on her face.

"Hiding your light under a bushel, Mr. Hamilton?"

"Gord was the star."

She smacked Gord's shoulder, "I always knew he was a ham."

Later in bed that night, when Nurse Meffe came, he still had the diaper on. "Want me to attach the tube, Mr. Hamilton?" she asked.

"No, Nurse Meffe. I reckon I should have another one of these," he indicated the diaper.

"Are you sure?"

"It's not good enough you should have to change the sheets every morning, is it?"

"Not every morning, Mr. Hamilton."

"Most mornings, Nurse Meffe, most mornings."

"Would you like your cassette player?" she lifted it off the dresser and held it out.

"No thanks! Not tonight."

Tonight he didn't want to fall asleep listening to Margaret's new, querulous tone of voice. The next tape in order was Jamaica, and Margaret was definitely anti-Jamaica.

Surprisingly, he didn't dream of rain, and for the first time in months when he woke up in the morning he was dry, the diaper was perfectly, spotlessly dry. He remembered thinking of his mother, almost expecting to see her at the end of the bed, but instead it was Meffe who came. She didn't enthuse over his dryness. In fact she didn't even mention it, which was a disappointment. That was the bloody thing about women, you never could please them.

# SATURDAY LADY

Wearing the purple winter coat, Rosa sat down tentatively at the table, like a visitor in her own house. She poured herself tea from the china pot that one of her ladies, Mrs. Nora, had given her. It was a lovely pot with red roses all over and "Canada Centennial 1967" written in large gold letters across its middle. She added milk to her tea, milk from the cut-glass jug she'd brought all the way from Lisbon, and then she treated herself to a chocolate marshmallow from the package she kept for Albie's friend Rui. She ate it carefully over the bread plate so that she wouldn't drop any crumbs on the embroidered tablecloth — the cloth that had been a wedding present from her mother.

The birds twittered behind her in their cage, reminding her that she had forgotten one tiny thing, their ritual Saturday-afternoon moment of freedom when she let them out of their cage to fly around the small apartment. It was the little red bird she liked best. He always came and settled on her shoulder and tweaked gently at her ear.

They were Albie's birds and yet she was the one who fed them every day and cleaned the cage out on Saturdays. Albie didn't like them out of the cage. The best he could ever do was lift them out for a brief moment and hold them in his calloused, rough hand, rubbing a thumb down their back with an abrasive stroke that made the poor creatures shiver and shake.

Albie had built the cage right against the window, so that the birds had mesh on three sides and constantly battered their bodies against what must have seemed to them the free side, in their endless attempts to fly off. When

Rosa had suggested it was cruel, Albie had smacked her hard. She still remembered the sting from his hand.

She and Albie and their son Manuel had been in Canada for a year now. "Land of opportunity" they always called it in Lisbon. Opportunity it certainly was, opportunity for work and more work. From Monday lady to Friday lady: on and off buses and subways, up and down stairs, in and out of houses, different vacuum cleaners, dusters, mops, polishes, and brooms. Then home again each day to do the same in her own place. Even though Albie was often in before she was, he expected her to run when she did get home for he liked to eat on time.

Saturday there was shopping to do, carrying all the bags of groceries home and then cleaning the apartment. There wasn't even Manuel to help because he'd become a proper Canadian: hockey practices in the winter, baseball in the summer. Besides, Albie didn't like Manuel to help. Housework was not men's work, he always said.

But she would put thoughts of housework out of her mind. This was her brief moment of pleasure, the only time in the entire week when she could imagine things.

There was a sudden knock at the door. For an instant Rosa was startled. Who on earth could it be?

Albie had cleaned himself up, put on his best clothes, his extra gold chain, and gone out for the rest of the day the way he always did. Manuel was probably playing street hockey somewhere; besides, neither of them would ever knock.

She went to the door and tentatively unlocked it, opening it a crack. It was Mr. Sam, the owner of the garage.

"Sorry to bother you, Mrs. Dos Santos ... Would Albie be home?"

"No, never ... he go out on his day off."

"I thought I saw him go ... but I had to try anyway. Somebody needs some work done in a hurry. I thought he might do it if he was in."

Rosa shook her head.

"Sorry to bother you then!"

She closed the door. Her legs were trembling. What if it had been Albie? What a scene there would have been then. What would have made it all even worse was the fact he had never seen the purple coat that Mrs. Nora, her Tuesday lady, had given her, nor any of the other clothes she kept hidden under the bed. If he had, he would have insisted she take them to a secondhand shop and sell them, for they were good, barely worn, the kind of clothes that never in a million years she, Rosa Dos Santos, would ever be able to buy. Saturdays, when Manuel and Albie were both out, was the time to play with the clothes — the day when she pretended she wasn't in her own house but visiting some fine lady in a big house, a house like some of the ones where she worked, where there were microwave ovens and dishwashers. Or best of all, that she was sitting out on the street, back on the Avenue da Liberdade, watching the world go by and listening to the birds; dressed exactly like some of the grand ladies she had seen there, having people look at her, admire her clothes, admire her face.

She was fairly sure she suited the purple coat, the mirror told her so, but then she couldn't be sure of anything anymore — certainly Albie never gave her any compliments. However, when Albie brought home his friend Rui, a fat, swarthy little man with built-up shoes and hair that stood up in alarming peaks on the thinning areas of his scalp, he looked at her in a certain way.

*"Ah, you keep her well hidden away,"* he said to Albie. *"If I had such a Rose, I would do the same."* Albie had paid no attention, just grunted and gone immediately for a beer for both of them, and together they played cards at the kitchen table. Albie ignored her while Rui winked at her behind Albie's back and once even made a funny gesture that Rosa hadn't liked.

She prayed sometimes that Albie would say something, would even look at her the way he looked at some of the women who came in with their cars. She could watch him from the window, for they had rented the apartment above where Albie worked, and she could see how he put on a performance for them, strutting and puffing out his chest the way he had once done for her.

There, in the garage, was Albie's real kingdom. He could oil and lubricate, make their cars purr back into life. She didn't like the way he wore his overalls open halfway down his chest, displaying the curls of black hair and the gold chains that waited for someone's fingers to untangle. She sometimes saw the way the women looked at him, high-class women too. They could smell something off him that they couldn't smell from their own husbands, and they liked that smell. She didn't hate them for feeling what they did, but at times she hated Albie.

Rosa sat down again at the table and lifted the tea cup. She waited for the little red bird to come back, but they had scattered and he didn't come. She looked around the room, she could see the others, but the red bird was nowhere to be seen. She rose in panic. Was it possible that when Mr. Sam had come to the door, the bird had flown out? She couldn't imagine it happening, for everything the birds ever did, they did in a great flurry of wings. But he was nowhere to be seen.

A feeling of dread was building in her. What on earth was she going to do? She went to the window and looked out, hoping absurdly that she might see him, but of course there was nothing.

She put the others back in their cage and, taking only her key, she raced out, forgetting to be cautious. She almost fell on the broken bottom step. She didn't quite know where she was going, but perhaps somewhere on the back street, in the little park where the railway land formed a slight ravine, she might find the red bird.

She became aware all of a sudden that it was actually a beautiful day. How rarely did she notice her surroundings or feel anything lately. It was one of those lovely autumn days, all soft and shimmering, almost magical. The leaves had lost their vivid hues and were milky pink as though someone had drawn a softening brush across them. They seemed to hang on the branches by a mere thread. She remembered her first winter and shivered. Her little bird could flirt with the leaves today, but later, against the ice blue skies and naked branches, he would be a mere flash and then he too would drop, like a leaf to the ground.

She had to find him and bring him home. She moved on, hope fading by the minute, and then suddenly he was there, sitting on a large mound of construction gravel that had obviously been dumped for some maintenance work, happily pecking at the ground. Behind him, at a suitable distance, there was a group of respectful sparrows, all hopping when he hopped and observing every move, so that they could fly in unison with him. It was a most amazing sight, thought Rosa, a bit like a king with his courtiers.

She sat down on one of the benches that ringed the flower beds and watched. He perched on a telephone wire. The sparrows followed, but again gave him room, forming a long deferential line. Like a row of humans waiting for a bus, they waited patiently for some further sign from him.

Rosa heard a sudden laugh beside her. She turned and saw that a man had seated himself beside her and was watching the bird too.

"Somebody's pet," the man said.

"He mine," Rosa said, "... or my husban's ... I let him fly away."

"Quite a show-off," the man said. Rosa looked at him and smiled. Never in her life had she struck up a conversation with a total stranger, but he seemed like a nice man. He carried a newspaper, was respectably dressed, and had one of those kind faces, probably someone's husband, a good family man.

"My husban' she will be very mad." Rosa frowned as she stared upward again at the truant bird.

"It's too nice a day for anyone to be mad. Birds shouldn't be in cages anyway, don't you think?"

"Yes, yes I do," Rosa agreed eagerly.

"You let him out deliberately?"

"Yes, I mean no ... well, I let them fly on Saturdays when Albie, she go out and today, the door ... it knocked ... no one comes to door on Saturdays and I got ... how you say ... excitable ..."

"Excited," the man helped out.

"Excited and the bird, she slip out. My husban' ... she will be mad."

"'He' will be mad," the man corrected. "'Husband' is male, so it is 'he.'"

"Thank you, no one ever help me ... I like."

Perhaps she shouldn't have said that, it was too forward. She focused on the bird and wished that she could learn to accept things without always saying too much.

"How long have you been in Canada?"

"One year."

"You are doing very well then ... with English."

"I try, but not so good, yes?"

"Very good. At least you try."

Rosa looked shyly at him and he smiled encouragingly.

"I came from Poland many years ago and it took me much longer."

"Yes?"

"Yes, I was too scared to try."

"An' now you speak so good ... Is good you speak so good. Maybe one day I will speak good too."

The bird landed now at Rosa's feet. The other sparrows had become wary; they settled a little further off, watching, surprised perhaps at this strange, brightly coloured creature's bravado.

"I could bend down and pick him up," the man said, but made no move to do so.

The bird rose from the walk in front of her and perched on her knee, looking cheekily up into her face as though daring her to try and catch him.

The man stared at her. "It makes a very nice picture ... two pretty creatures together."

Rosa felt her face flush. She enclosed the bird gently between her hands, concentrating like mad. The bird fluttered feebly between her palms. For an instant she felt not a bit like herself, almost as if she were holding her own veins, her own blood. A harder caress than her present one and they both would die. Then there was the option of opening up her hands and letting the creature go. She had the sudden image of blood spurting from her. Perhaps with that one gesture, she would bleed to death too.

She knew the man was watching her, and there was another strange feeling, something from way back in the past when she had first met Albie, a feeling of power, but almost as quickly as it came it was gone again. She opened her hands suddenly and, perhaps sensing her uncertainty, the bird rose swiftly into the air and distanced himself as quickly as possible.

"You think it fly south to warm?" she asked the man.

"I'm sure it will."

"If no ... she might get dead ... is possible?"

The little bird was on the move again, flying further and further afield. The sparrows had narrowed the gap between the bird and themselves; they were still attracted to it like moths to a firefly.

The man didn't answer her question, he was staring at her intently. He leant over and patted her hand.

"You did the right thing."

She smiled, "Yes?" She looked at him questioningly and he nodded his head.

She stood up, "You kind man ... I must go now."

He rose and stood beside her, "Good-bye!" They shook hands solemnly.

"Someday when you fly, don't worry about the winter."

"Thank you!" Rosa said pointlessly because she couldn't think of anything else to say. She was sure he meant something nice but she hadn't time to brood about it, she had to get home. It was unlikely Albie would be home, but she had to go back quickly and put everything carefully away: wash the cup and saucer, fold the tablecloth, and pack the purple coat away under the bed. She hadn't thought yet what to say about the missing bird. She could feel her own heart thumping in her chest, exactly as she'd felt the bird's, the beat quickening as her feet pounded on the pavement in her rush for home.